PLAY DEAD

PLAY DEAD

RYAN BROWN

GALLERY BOOKS

New York   London   Toronto   Sydney

Gallery Books
A Division of Simon & Schuster, Inc.
1230 Avenue of the Americas
New York, NY 10020

First Gallery Books hardcover edition May 2010

GALLERY and colophon are registered trademarks of Simon & Schuster, Inc.

For information about special discounts for bulk purchases, please contact Simon & Schuster Special Sales at 1-866-506-1949 or business@simonandschuster.com.

The Simon & Schuster Speakers Bureau can bring authors to your live event. For more information or to book an event contact the Simon & Schuster Speakers Bureau at 1-866-248-3049 or visit our website at www.simonspeakers.com.

Manufactured in the United States of America

10   9   8   7   6   5   4   3   2   1

Library of Congress Cataloging-in-Publication Data is available.

ISBN 978-1-4391-7130-1
ISBN 978-1-4391-7161-5 (ebook)

For Victoria and Raff, with all my love.

PROLOGUE

THE drums outside beat hard enough to form ripples in the water.

He knelt with his face only inches above the surface and watched the small concentric rings expand with each percussive thump.

He watched until his nausea subsided, then came up off his knees. The toilet was clean, but he kicked the flush handle anyway. He stepped out of the stall and struggled against shaky hands to thread the laces at the fly of his pants.

He felt worse for having *not* been sick. He had hoped that in getting sick he might purge himself of . . . everything.

The nerves. The fear. The regret.

Now he would carry all of it onto the field.

Hell, maybe it was better that way. Maybe it was the only way he could get through this.

His cleats tapped over slick tile as he moved past shower stalls, towel bins, Gatorade coolers, and a chalkboard on which remained the pale ghosts of innumerable X's and O's.

Back at his locker he continued to dress. Over the past four years the routine had become mindless, something he did as quickly as possible to get it over with. But now he was happy to stall. He approached the work methodically, taking special care with every detail. Shoelaces were double knotted, tucked in, and taped over. Ankles were wrapped as stiffly as plaster casts. His jersey—crisply pressed and wrapped snugly over his shoulder pads—went on last.

He reached above the locker and took down his helmet. Its appearance was in contrast to the immaculate jersey. Every well-earned scrape and nick had gone untouched. They were too precious, worn too proudly to be cleaned or buffed. He ran trembling fingers over the scars and the curling stickers and the screws filled with grit.

He pulled the helmet down over his ears. There was comfort in its tightness and weight. He sat and closed his eyes.

A peculiar silence hovered over the room.

In fact, there were sounds all around: cleats pecked at the floor, tape ripped, pads clacked, lockers slammed. And still the drums pounded outside. They came heavier now, each thump matched by the stomp of countless feet on wooden bleachers.

It was the absence of voices that made the room seem silent.

His eyes opened and he watched his teammates dress around him. Their movement was slow and labored, their eyes haunted. He wondered if the others felt any of the fear that gripped him. He had no doubt they carried the same fury that he did, but as he studied their hollow expressions, he saw no *feeling* at all, just a cold awareness of what had to be done in the next sixty minutes by the scoreboard clock.

From across the room the coach's whistle blew and his stomach coiled.

Game time.

He stood and closed the locker.

He knew that tonight there would be no coach's speech, no unifying chants or pregame rallying cries. And it was a night far too godless for a prayer.

Because this wasn't a game about victory or defeat.

It wasn't even a game about life or death.

After what he'd done, it had become a game about salvation or damnation.

CHAPTER 1

Three Days Earlier

GAME day.

Cole Logan had awoken and begun working long before the alarm went off. He considered it work even though it was something he did while lying in bed, his eyes closed. It usually took him a good half hour to run through the entire offensive playbook, watching the X's and O's shift around his mind like Scrabble tiles. Years of practice had enabled him to visualize with vivid clarity the pass routes of his primary and secondary receivers, to read shifting defenses and assess the balance of the field. He was about to start in on the no-huddle offensive series when the clock radio sounded.

"*. . . was brought to you by Hardware Dan's on Jenkins and Mason. Find it all at Hardware Dan's. The time is now six thirty.*"

The local announcer went on to wish everyone a "cracking good morning and a happy Halloween."

Halloween?

So it was. He had forgotten about it until that moment. The holiday was just another thing that had faded into the background over the past few months, when he'd had little time to think about anything *other* than the X's and O's.

"*. . . can expect more clouds, with temperatures much cooler than yesterday's. Highs in the upper forties with late-afternoon thunderstorms likely to hang around through the evening. Gonna be a sloppy night for football folks, so remember to bring . . .*"

Cole clicked off the radio, flung away the sheet, and came up off the mattress on the floor. His knees and ankles creaked as he rose onto his toes and stretched his arms toward the ceiling. He rotated his throwing arm until blood flowed into the gravelly joint.

Stepping over strewn gym clothes, he moved to the door and peered across the trailer's narrow hallway. Two sets of feet poked out from beneath a twisted sheet on his mother's bed. A tattoo wrapped around one of the man's ankles. It looked like either a mermaid or a dragon. Something with scales. It might have been familiar, but he couldn't be sure. They had all started to look alike lately.

Cole hadn't bothered to check the time when his mother and the man had come stumbling in last night. He'd heard the front door swing open, some laughter, beers being cracked open. Then came two or three minutes of creaking springs before, finally, snoring.

He shut the door, slipped Guns N' Roses into the CD player, and put on his headphones. He did fifty quick push-ups as "Paradise City" rang through his head, then he lit a Marlboro and smoked slowly as Axl Rose wailed through "Sweet Child O' Mine." When the song ended and the cigarette was finished, he stopped the CD and threw on the nearest T-shirt and Levi's from the floor. At the dresser, he slipped a silver hoop into his earlobe, then ran gel through his matted black hair.

His little visitor came calling right on schedule, scratching at the window beside the dresser. Black Mona's cats never slept in. The old woman in the next trailer over had to have three dozen of them now; they seemed to breed like a virus. There were times Cole wanted to shoot the damn things, especially when they appeared early on weekends. He'd have done it, too—shot them dead without remorse.

If the cats had belonged to anyone but Black Mona.

If even half the rumors he'd heard about the old woman were true, he wasn't prepared to take any chances. In fact, to stay in her good graces, he had even made a habit of feeding her cats a little something when they came around.

He slid the window open a few inches. A gray tabby stood on the cooling unit below the sill. It cocked its head and gazed at him through sleepy eyes. He noticed the eyes were mismatched. One was coal black, the other crystalline blue. A plaid collar hung from its neck with a tarnished copper name tag that read COODLES. That was just one of the things he hated about cats—they always had stupid names.

Coodles blinked, stretched, yawned, and purred expectantly. Cole took mercy. Knowing he would surely come to regret the dependence that would follow, he tossed out what remained of last night's bologna fold-over from the paper plate beside his mattress. The cat tucked in without so much as a sniff of inspection.

Cole slid the window closed and checked himself in the mirror. He'd take shit for it from school faculty, but he decided shaving could wait one more day. For fear of waking the sleeping couple across the hall, he decided that brushing his teeth could wait too. He smeared toothpaste over his teeth with an index finger, then grabbed his boots and leather jacket. He tiptoed through the trailer, took a pint carton of milk and a Pop-Tart from the kitchenette, and crept out the front door.

The rain-soaked *Killington Daily* was puffed like a sponge on the front step. He looked at his picture on the front page, taken at a press conference on the practice field the previous afternoon. Ink bled down his face, making him look like a young Alice Cooper in shoulder pads. JACKRABBITS SEEKING ONE MORE VICTORY FOR TRIP

TO DISTRICT, the headline read. There was a caption below the photo: *Rebel QB Cole Logan continues to prove the skeptics wrong, see story on 6A.* Cole already knew the story and knew he'd like his own version of it better. He tossed the paper into the oil drum–cum–ash can beside the door.

The air was bitter and carried a dampness that ate through clothing and seeped into bones like acid. He slipped into his jacket and zipped it up under his chin. He pulled his boots up over wet socks, then leaned against the door, finished off the milk, and ate the Pop-Tart in three bites. He was debating having one more smoke before hitting the road when he heard a noise to his right—wet leaves shifting underfoot at the side of the house. There were multiple footfalls. He cursed. Word of the bologna sandwich must have spread through the local feline population. He feared that tomorrow the whole pride would show up expecting a buffet if he didn't put a stop to things right now.

He went down the steps, picked up the rain-warped football that had lived in his yard since the fourth grade, and circled a wide arc across the gravel drive. He set his fingers on the laces, hoping one tightly thrown spiral into the middle of the pack would be enough to send the cats scurrying away for good.

But when the side of the trailer came into view, he saw only one cat, just below his bedroom window. It was the same cat he had fed moments before, only now it lay on its back, split open from chin to tail, its innards spilling onto the mud. A narrow ribbon of steam rose from the gaping wound.

The football fell from his limp hands. He spun around in place, not quite sure what he was looking for. A coyote most likely. Maybe a bobcat; they were rare in these parts, but not unheard of. He was more worried that it had been a dog. Mr. Garner down the street had a pair of pit bulls that were known to get loose from time to time. And unlike a coyote or bobcat, a pit bull wouldn't hesitate to attack a man in the same ferocious manner it had attacked a help-less housecat.

He saw no movement in the surrounding woods, animal or otherwise.

His eyes went back to the cat. He approached it slowly, covering his nose to fend off the smell. Standing over it, he realized that the cat had not been ripped open by animal teeth. In fact, it hadn't been ripped open at all, but rather sliced. The cut was clean, symmetrical. Nothing jagged. It almost looked to be the work of . . .

The first blow struck him across the back of the neck.

Before the pain even registered, the attackers spun him around, pinning his back against the side of the trailer. A stomach punch robbed him of the chance to cry out. Through swimming spots he saw two men before him and a third in the distance. All three wore jeans, sneakers, and ski masks under hooded sweatshirts.

The biggest of the three planted a forearm against Cole's neck.

Cole tried to speak but only managed a strangled gasp.

"Keep your fucking mouth shut!" The shorter man picked up the dead cat with a gloved hand and mashed the carcass into Cole's face.

Cole gagged and pitched forward, spitting gore.

"We'll do the talking here, Logan," hissed the taller man. His voice was calm, level. His breath was hot against Cole's cheek. "Our message is real simple, asshole. If you walk onto that field tonight, you'll be the next one that gets cut. We'll gut you like a fucking fish if you even suit up. Understood?"

Cole shook his head, struggling against his restraints.

Another stomach punch halted his resistance.

The arm pressed harder against Cole's neck. "Today you take a dive, Logan. It's real simple. You find a reason not to play, or we'll give you one. And then we'll go after the rest of the team. Understand?"

Cole managed to draw a breath. A coppery taste trickled down his throat. Through clenched teeth, he told the men to go fuck themselves.

The attackers shared a glance.

A grin parted the taller man's mouth. "I kinda hoped you'd say that." His lips brushed against Cole's ear. "Because there's nothing better in this world than putting the hurt on a candy-ass quarterback." He pressed a hand over Cole's mouth. With the other hand he pulled a hatchet from under his sweatshirt.

His accomplice pinned Cole's wrist to the side of the house.

The hatchet came up.

"Let's see you play now, motherfucker."

Then the blade came down hard on its mark.

CHAPTER 2

"Y ⊏⊔ type like a man."

Savannah Hickham lifted her hands from the iBook keyboard and spun around on her stool. Kip Sampson, a regular at the Buttered Bean Diner, sat in his usual booth, having what he liked to refer to as his breakfast of champions: three over easy, black coffee, and a Winston unfiltered.

"What do you mean?" she asked.

"Index fingers only, pounding the piss out of the thing." Kip gestured accordingly.

"Is that so?"

"It's not a criticism. Way it should be done, you ask me."

"Thanks for the tip. I never took you for a writer."

"I'm not a writer, but I read the paper every day. I know what's good and what ain't. Had an old buddy in Korea, wrote for *Stars and Stripes*. I used to watch him pound on his little Remington all the time. He told me once that if your fingers aren't bruised when you finish grinding out a story, chances are it's crap."

"That's fascinating. Look, I don't mean to be rude, but I'm on a deadline."

"What are you working on?"

Savannah went back to typing. "Piece on the Archaeology Club's field trip to Glen Rose."

"Where the dinosaur tracks are?"

"That's the one."

"What'd I miss?" Don Paul Klevin, fellow regular, returned from the men's room and took his seat in the booth, opposite Kip.

"Savannah here's doing a Lois Lane on dinosaur prints for the school paper."

"No kiddin'?"

Savannah started to run a spell check on her finished article.

Kip said, "Look, I'm sure you got a good piece there and all, but it seems to me if you're writin' for the high school fish wrapper, you might as well be covering the biggest story in town."

"I know what you're going to say, and even if it was my beat, which it isn't, I'm not interested."

Kip jabbed a thumb in her direction and looked to Don Paul. "For the first time in Killington High School history, the Jackrabbits are one win away from the district championship game and she ain't interested."

Don Paul shook his head ruefully.

The jukebox exchanged a Johnny Paycheck for a Hank Williams. Kip crushed out his cigarette and joined Savannah at the counter. "How the hell could you not be interested?"

"I want to be a real reporter, not a sportswriter."

"Gonna be a hell of a story. Already is."

"Yeah, I can see the headline now: 'Jackrabbits Choke Again, See You Next September.' Not really much there."

"Gotta dig, woman. Gotta dig."

"Look, I'm the first to admit that my portfolio is in desperate need of some more newsworthy topics. But I'm sure something will come along that's more significant than a stupid football game."

"But this is more than just a news story. This is town history. Could be anyway."

Savannah approved a spelling change. "Don't know a thing about it."

"Right, you're fairly new in town. Well, if you got a few minutes for a quick history lesson . . ."

"I don't."

"Fine. I'll nutshell it for you. Might make a difference to you later. See, it's like this: as far as football goes, the Killington Jack-*rabbits* have a history of playing like Jack-*shit*."

"Not listening . . ."

"Sixty-nine losing seasons in seventy-eight years."

"You don't say . . ."

"Just to pull a few gems from the highlight reel: in sixty-two they didn't make a first down until game seven . . ."

"Still not listening . . ."

". . . and that was only because a desperation pass wedged itself into the tight end's face mask."

"Boy, did that one bring 'em to their feet," Don Paul said, reminiscing.

Savannah steered her mouse back and forth across the countertop, pointing and clicking.

"Last year against Lamar we had to put our punter on supplemental oxygen because of exhaustion. Our *punter* for chrissake! What's that tell you about the Jackrabbits' understanding of forward progress?"

Savannah clicked again. "Does pterodactyl really start with a *p*?"

"But now we're eight and one going into tonight's final game against Stanton High. Winner of that meets the Elmwood Badgers in the district championship game. That's *the* Elmwood Badgers. The titans of two-A. Take into account the bad blood between the two towns, and we're talking 'bout a real barn-burner."

Savannah hit Save, powered down, and slammed the laptop shut. She checked her watch and smiled. "With time to spare . . . as always. One more coffee, Bernice, before I head to school?"

Bernice McFay put down her sudoku book, buried her pencil in her hair bun, and crossed over to Savannah with a fresh pot. "You headin' back for the pep rally, honey?"

"I wouldn't be caught dead there. Anyway, I have to set a layout for the paper."

"Isn't any of what I've been sayin' getting through to you?" Kip asked.

"Not a word."

"Well, why the hell not? I just don't get it."

"Oh, leave the girl alone, Kip," Bernice said. "Can't you see she ain't interested?"

Kip threw his arms up. "All right, you go ahead and be the Woodward and Bernstein of field trips, but I'm telling you, you're missing the big story."

"I got an idea," Bernice said. "How 'bout doing a profile on that quarterback, the Logan boy. You know, a human-interest kind of thing. Been startin' for us all season, and he's still pretty much a mystery."

"Cole Logan?" Savanah shuddered. "What would I call it, 'The Man Behind the Tattoo'?"

"I think the tattoo is kind of sexy."

Savannah rolled her eyes. "Which one, the dagger or the grim reaper?"

"Sexy? Christ, Bernice, you're old enough to be the boy's grandmother!" Don Paul exclaimed.

"Well, hell, Don Paul, I'm not dead yet. Not blind, either. You take six inches and fifteen pounds off Cole Logan and you got yourself a spittin' image of Montgomery Clift. I used to carry pictures of Monty Clift around in my bra."

"Cole Logan is a pig," Savannah said. "He sits behind me in economics. He looks like a vagrant and smells like Pennzoil."

"That's probably from that motorbike he tears around on," Kip said. "I'll concede the kid's a little rough around the edges."

"White trash is what he is," said Don Paul.

Kip shrugged. "Okay, so he's from the wrong side of the tracks, but what chance did he have? His daddy was just plain sorry; up and run off last fall. And his mama's since become the town whore."

"Oh, Kip . . ."

"Well, I'm sorry, Bernice, but it's true. Anyhow, the boy wasn't exactly dealt a flush hand, was he?"

"But I'll tell you one thing," said Don Paul. "He can throw like Elway and scramble like ole what's-his-name . . . the little fella out of BC."

"Flutie."

"Right, Kip, the kid scrambles just like Doug Flutie. And he's six-three! Runs the forty in four-point-one. Just imagine what he could do if he cut down to a pack a day. He's fast, all right."

"He's also a mouth breather," Savannah said.

Kip lit another Winston. "Well, that mouth breather has led our boys to their best record ever. Of course, it didn't hurt that we finally got us a good coach."

"I'm not interested in the coach," Savannah snapped.

"I'm just saying . . ."

"I told you, I'm not interested."

For a few seconds Hank Williams was the only one in the room saying anything. Bernice popped her Doublemint to break the silence. "I hear he's a loner," she said. "Cole Logan, I mean. Usually not a good thing for a quarterback."

"Not unusual for a criminal, though."

Kip sighed. "Not that again, Don Paul."

"Well, it's true, ain't it?"

Savannah's eyes shifted from one man to the other. "What? He's a criminal? Like, *seriously*?"

"Ah, the boy got in a little trouble last year," Kip answered. "Weren't no big thing."

"Only if you consider grand larceny little," said Don Paul.

Kip shrugged. "This is old news, Don Paul. Logan was still seventeen at the time, couldn't even be tried as an adult. They gave him the standard swift kick in the ass, threatened him with a one-way ticket to Parris Island if he didn't straighten hisself out, and it was case closed."

Savannah asked Kip what Cole had stolen.

"A set of TaylorMades and a Buick Reatta."

"From the mayor," Don Paul added.

"Can we move past this now?" Kip asked.

"Yeah," Don Paul agreed. "Hell, I could care less if Logan's a criminal, long as he can run a good bootleg." He stood and went to plug the jukebox.

The chimes clanged above the front door. A woman entered, apparently already dressed for Halloween.

"Who is she?" Savannah asked.

"You don't know Black Mona?" Bernice said. "She's been a regular here for years. Stay in this town long enough, you'll hear a lot about her. She's an odd one, I'll tell you that."

"Odd?" Kip put on a fake smile, offered the old woman a wave. Through clenched teeth he muttered, "She's crazier than a rat in a shithouse."

Savannah watched the woman slide into the first booth by the window. She looked like a cross between a sideshow Gypsy and Norma Desmond. Even at a distance Savannah could hear the rattle of her earrings, which looked like tiny gold chandeliers dangling from sagging lobes. A tangled mass of matching necklaces hung from her neck.

"What's her story, Kip?"

"All I know is that she's a crazy old spinster that lives across the tracks and spends most of her time talking to her cats. Rumor in town is that she's into black magic. You know, voodoo-mojo types of stuff."

"Do you really believe any of that, Kip?" Bernice asked.

"Well, I don't put much stock in it, but I can tell you one thing: Couple years back, old Chip Simmons accidentally scratched her station wagon with a shopping cart in the Kroger parking lot. Tight bastard that Chip is, he didn't even leave a note. Next morning he wakes up with an unfortunate combination of shingles and lockjaw."

"Coincidence?" Savannah asked.

Kip rolled his shoulders. "You tell me. Only other thing I know about her is that she never misses a Jackrabbits football game. The woman loves her football."

"Well, I better go take her order," Bernice said. "Keep the hexes away." She winked at Savannah. "Coffee's on the house, honey. Just make sure I get a copy of that dinosaur story, you hear?"

"Sure, thanks." Savannah turned to Kip. "It's been riveting, as always, but I have to get to school. See you tomorrow." She slid the laptop into her backpack, then took out her iPod and fiddled with the dial.

"One more game, Savannah, just one more game. We win tonight against Stanton High and we're finally in the big one—the district championship game against Elmwood Heights."

"You've said as much."

"Elmwood Heights is out for blood."

"You said that, too."

"Tell me something. What do you know about the history of these two towns?"

"As much as I want to."

"That's what I thought. Allow me to paint you a picture."

"Kip, I don't have time for—"

"We may share a border and a water supply, but the towns of Elmwood and Killington couldn't be more different. They were both named for wildcatters back in the Great Boom of the thirties. Slocum Elmwood and T. K. Killington had been lifelong friends when they pooled their pennies together, dug two wells eight miles apart, and agreed to share the profits if one of them hit. Guess which one hit? I'll give you a hint: it wasn't the one tapped into the dirt under our asses.

"You can probably figure out the rest. Opulent wealth suited Slocum Elmwood so well, he decided to screw T. K. Killington out of his share. Not long after, Mr. Killington hung hisself from an abandoned derrick. Slocum Elmwood, on the other hand, went on to lord happily over a thriving boomtown until the day he died some nine years later, choking on a rare leg of lamb. To say that us Killingtonians are still carrying a bit of a grudge would be an understatement. To this day, Slocum Elmwood has heirs walking the streets over there in the town named after him.

"They're still a rich town. With a damn rich school, too. Elmwood Heights's stadium holds sixteen thousand. Their weight room is state-of-the-art. This year they're planning on sending a handful of graduating seniors to little corners of the football world like Notre Dame, Penn State, and Michigan on full scholarships. Elmwood students often drive Beemers, wear shirts with alligators on 'em, go to the mall every day and spend their parents' money on things like surround-sound theaters for their SUVs."

"Sounds like a heck of a deal to me."

"Sure enough." Kip looked over both shoulders, then leaned in closer. "But I'm of the opinion that the Elmwood football players are spending daddy's money on something else, too."

"And what would that be?"

He started to say something but changed his mind. "I've read your stuff, you know. You write good. It's your story selection that needs work. You want a real story, find out what it is that's turned them Elmwood Heights players into such savages this year."

"What are you talking about?"

"Maybe nothing. But one look at their players' stats from last season compared with their stats now, and I think you'll see a glaring difference in the size and performance of these boys. They've been dishing out concussions and compound fractures all season. Last week a hit from their middle linebacker caused a collapsed lung in one player and a ruptured spleen in another . . . on the same play. Did I mention that they're also undefeated?"

"Your point?"

"I'd say the Badgers football team might be doing more than just eating their Wheaties."

Savannah rolled her eyes again. She slung her backpack over her shoulder and started to go, but stopped. "Hold on. Just what *are* you saying?"

Kip lit another Winston. "I ain't saying nothin'. But if we do get to that district championship game, I'd sure hate to see any of our Jackrabbits get hurt the way them Elmwood Badgers have been putting the hurt on other teams. Before long, somebody's gonna get hisself kilt."

Savannah gnawed on the inside of her cheek. "You really think there's something shady going on?"

Kip met her gaze. "Don't matter none, does it? You ain't interested."

She started to press him further, but decided against it. Instead she cranked up Avril Lavigne on her iPod, slapped Kip on the back, and told him she'd catch him later.

Kip watched Savannah until she was out the door. He sent a few smoke rings toward the ceiling as Bernice topped off his coffee.

"You finally let the poor child go?"

"Not now, Bernice. I'm thinking."

"Well, think about going easy on her, will you?"

"Ah, she can take it. You ask me, that kid's tough as nails."

"Yes, tough as nails and wise beyond her years, but she's still an only child from a single-parent household, trying to make it in a new town."

"She'll be just fine, Bernice. Nice gal with her looks . . ."

"Oh, she's a doll. Red hair. Green eyes. That adorable figure."

"Nice freckles, too . . ."

"She'll have no trouble turning heads, Kip, but that's not what I'm talking about. Things still aren't going to be easy on her at first, and you know what I mean. Anyway, I'd hate to lose her business, not to mention her company, so you and Don Paul both need to give her some breathin' room."

"What'd I do? I was schoolin' her on a thing or two is all. Sue me."

"You shouldn't have brought it up."

"Brought it up? Hell, woman, that football team is the only thing in this town anyone is talking about. We sure as hell don't have anything else going for us."

"I meant you shouldn't have brought up the coach."

"Oh, that. Well, I didn't mean anything by that. Just forgot is all." He pulled a couple of wrinkled bills from the pocket of his Dickies and tossed them onto the counter. "It's just that she seems so disconnected from that football team, I sometimes forget that her daddy's the coach."

CHAPTER 3

THE crowd at the Killington High pep rally was already in a frenzy by the time the stampede of football players burst out of the locker room and charged onto the basketball court. The band welcomed the charge with a thunderous rendition of the school fight song. Bleachers rocked under a thousand scuffed sneakers, stomping time with the music. Stands filled to capacity and checkered jet-black and bloodred flanked both sides of the court. The smells of buttered popcorn and teenage sweat hung thick in the air.

Head Coach Jimmy Hickham wished he were anywhere else.

Still, as he traversed the court with his players and coaching staff, he masked his lack of enthusiasm with the occasional fist-pump here, thumbs-up there. He didn't begin to relax until the team reached the chairs set up along the baseline at the opposite end of the court. He sat at the end of the front row as his staff fanned out to his right. The players sat in sequential order according to jersey number.

As the last player took his seat, head cheerleader Maxine Wiley took center stage, flinging a cloud of confetti out of her megaphone in perfect sync with a rimshot from the drum section. Red and black paper clippings fluttered down over the team as Maxine sank seductively to the floor in a full split, pom-poms raised high.

When the approving hoots and whistles finally faded, Principal Wyndle Hodges stepped up to the microphone at center court. His tassled loafers shone almost as brightly as the Brylcreem in his comb-over. He hitched his polyester pants into the crevice under his stomach and tapped the mike. The squeal of feedback brought a hush over the room.

"Students . . . faculty . . . *Jackrabbits!*"

The crowd erupted again. Trombonists swung their instruments up and down like legs in a Rockettes kick line. The percussion section pounded machine-gun fire on the snare drums.

"Welcome back, one and all," Mr. Hodges said. "I got just four words for you people right now. *We . . . are . . . district . . . bound!*"

Two pigtailed cheerleaders punctuated the statement by launching into the air like twin rockets, legs split, pom-poms flying. A blonde in a sequined leotard sent a twirling baton sailing toward the rafters. Popcorn fell in a blizzard over the stands.

Mr. Hodges wiped spittle from shining lips. "Now, Monday through Friday may be the time for schoolin' around here. Saturday may be for family, and Sunday may be for Jesus. But, folks, I'm here to tell you that tonight . . . Friday night . . . is the time for what?"

"*Football!*"

"Say again . . ."

"*Football!*"

"I can't hear you . . ."

"*Football!*"

"You bet your red and black butts, football! And not just a time for football, but a time for us to wage war on any school—any *team*—that thinks they can stand across a chalked line from those boys over there and walk away with all their bones intact!"

Veins swelled in the principal's neck. He was now shouting over cheers of *"Kill-ing-ton! Kill-ing-ton! Kill-ing-ton!"* He ripped the clip-on tie from his collar and tossed it over his shoulder. He removed the microphone from its cradle in a manner that Mick Jagger would have admired and paced the length of the court.

"Now, lately we've taken our share of hits in this town, both on the field and off. But I'm here to tell y'all that these tough times can take our money, they can close our businesses, and they can send our soldiers away from their families . . . but they can't take away our spirit, and they sure as hell can't take away this football team that's gonna lift us above it all!"

More applause.

"They said we were too *small* . . ."

Boos rumbled through the stands.

"They said we were too *slow* . . ."

"Booo!"

"They said we just weren't *good enough* to be a real factor in this thing they call Texas high school football. . . . Were they right?"

The crowd's answer vibrated in Coach Hickham's toes.

Mr. Hodges continued. "Now, I know there's a lot of talk around here about the district championship game. I know Elmwood Heights has already secured their own position in that game . . ."

The mention of Elmwood Heights brought jeers from the student section:

"Fuck the Badgers!"

"Elmwood Heights can suck me!"

Mr. Hodges pressed on. "Now, I know that before we get to that district championship game, we still gotta win tonight against Stanton High. I also know that we're *gonna* win that game tonight. And I know we're *gonna* make it to that district championship game 'cause we finally got the *coach* we need to do it, we finally got the *team* we need to do it, and by God, we certainly got the *fans* we need to finally bring glory to the Killington High School Jackrabbits!"

A large stuffed animal sailed from the stands, landing on the parquet floor near Coach Hickham's feet. The giant teddy bear wore a Stanton High football jersey. A plastic knife pierced its heart through a jersey splattered with fake blood. Freddy Delveccio, the Jackrabbits mascot, immediately pounced on the offending toy. Zipped into his furry bodysuit and floppy-eared headpiece, Freddy made quite a show of ripping the bear's limbs off in a spray of cotton stuffing, much to the delight of the crowd.

Hermie Tucker, the defensive line coach, chuckled beside Hickham. "Gotta admit, that's pretty damn funny."

Hickham nodded but couldn't bring himself to join in the laughter.

"Say, you all right, Jimmy? You look a little—"

"I'm fine," Hickham replied. "Just got game film I could be watching."

Coach Tucker straightened in his chair. He leaned in closer to be heard over the crowd. "Hell, I know this part ain't really your thing, Coach. But I've been at this school for a long time. I ain't never seen this town as worked up as they are right now. Just look at 'em. If you can't take any pleasure from the rally, I hope you can at least take pride in the fact that things had never been as exciting around here till you came along."

Hickham looked at him.

Coach Tucker grinned, then spat tobacco juice into the Gatorade cup in his lap. "Not to change the subject, Jimmy, but I don't suppose you know where Logan is, do you?"

Hickham peered down the row to his right. Cole Logan, who wore jersey number 8, should have been the second player in the row after the placekicker. Hickham hadn't noticed the empty chair until then.

"He wasn't at roll call?"

Coach Tucker shrugged. "I thought maybe he was in your office watching film. Want me to go make a call or something?"

Hickham shook his head. "Let's give him a few minutes. When he does show, make sure he comes to see me right after the rally."

"Will do."

Bedlam reigned in the gym for the next few minutes. The crowd was treated in quick succession to a cheer from the pom-pom girls, a dance number from the drill team, and a head-pounding performance from the drum line. Things didn't even begin to settle until the baton twirler started her spotlight solo.

It was toward the end of the twirling routine—the gym still bathed in darkness and wrapped in Brahms's Lullaby—that an exterior door burst open, piercing the darkness with a shard of white light.

The baton fell hard to the floor. The music stopped. All eyes turned to the silhouette in the doorway. The crowd held its silence as the overhead lights flickered to life and Cole Logan stepped into the gym.

"Sweet Jiminy Jesus," Coach Tucker whispered.

Hickham came to his feet as his starting quarterback moved across the floor on unsteady legs, a blood-soaked bandanna wrapped around his hand.

Cole offered no acknowledgment to the crowd. He walked up to a slack-jawed Principal Hodges, who still stood at center court. The principal looked Cole up and down, then stepped back to keep his loafers clear of the blood that trickled in steady drops from the glistening bandanna.

Cole told the man he had something to say.

Mr. Hodges blinked out of his trance long enough to say, "Uh . . . sure thing, Cole." He raised the microphone. "Well, um . . . ladies and gentleman, I know this man needs no introduc—"

Cole ripped the mike from the principal's fingers and angled his body toward the team.

Hickham saw more fury than fear in his quarterback's eyes.

Cole unwrapped the cloth and raised his bloody hand overhead.

There were two gaping holes where his fourth and fifth fingers should have been. Gasps swept the crowd.

Cole said, "I just want to show you what we're up against tonight. . . . People who would do something like this without a second thought to keep us from winning." He twisted the hand slowly under bright fluorescent light. "I'm also here to tell you that they're gonna have to take more than two of my fingers to keep me from leading you onto that field tonight."

Hickham heard the pain in Cole's wavering voice.

Cole continued, "But I also want you to realize that it's gonna take a hell of a lot more than popcorn and cheerleaders for us to pull out a victory. It's kill or be killed tonight, Jackrabbits. I hope to hell you're all with me."

The explosions occurred as soon as he finished the statement.

And blood rained down from the rafters.

CHAPTER 4

"Touch my balls," Booker Flamont whispered hungrily.

"Touch your own balls," Nina Hernandez replied, pushing him off her. She stuck her Bubble Yum back in her mouth and came off the bed, rehooking a neon pink bra strap under her skintight tank top.

Booker watched with longing as she inched her miniskirt back down over a pair of red lace panties with the Rolling Stones' tongue-and-lips logo on the crotch. "I don't see what's the problem," he said.

"I want to take things slow."

"Slow? We've been together three weeks!"

"First of all, we're not *together.* And second, you haven't even taken me out or anything."

Booker came off his parents' bed feeling the need to punch something breakable, but he managed to calm his temper. "So if I take you to a movie Saturday night, will you let me go further?"

"I don't like movies."

"Well, whatever. We'll play putt-putt or some shit."

"Putt-putt? I think not-not."

Booker took her hand. "But . . . I think I love you."

Nina jerked her hand back. "What-ever."

This is how it had gone for most of their fledgling courtship. They had first become acquainted in the Elmwood Heights after-school detention program. Booker had been midway through a six-day stint for urinating in the teachers' lounge water fountain, and Nina was serving three days for smoking in the drama room prop closet. Nina would soon be granted an early release on good behavior, but not before Booker had made his move, offering to carry her books to study hall at the end of her first day.

They had wound up making out in the janitor's closet on the way.

For a few days Booker was certain he had hooked a live one. Unfortunately, that spontaneous whim of passion against the stacked cans of vomit-absorption powder had been a singular occurrence. Since then, Nina had scarcely allowed Booker to lay a hand on her, and things were now becoming as painful as they were frustrating.

"It hurts, you know," Booker said.

"What, your pride?"

"No, my balls. They're going to kill me if things don't get taken care of."

"Why don't you take care of *things* yourself? I thought that's what you guys did all the time anyway."

"Coach won't let us."

"Excuse me?"

"Coach won't let us beat off. Says it makes us soft."

"I thought that was the idea."

"You know what I mean. Coach says we'll lose our edge if we do that. Made us all sign a pledge promising we wouldn't do it for the good of the team."

"That's a joke, right?"

He shook his head. "Got us into the district championship game, didn't it? Undefeated, too."

Nina flung her hands up. "No wonder all you football players have turned psycho. You've become animals this year, all of you."

"What's that supposed to mean?"

"Look in the mirror, you'll find your answer."

"You told me you thought I was good-looking."

"Right. *Thought.* Past tense. Last year you weren't bad. Maybe even semihot. Just my luck I caught you on the down slope."

Nina was beginning to put a serious damper on Booker's good mood.

He'd been walking in the clouds all morning until now. The assault on Cole Logan had gone off even better than expected. Especially that business with the cat, which had been an unplanned yet inspired alteration to their original plot. All told, he, Manny, and Elray had pulled off everything without a hitch. The hatchet had gone through Logan's fingers like they were sticks of warm butter.

Now all Booker had to do was wait around for Manny and Elray to report in on how things had gone at the Killington pep rally. He'd hoped to kill the time sticking it to Nina, but of course she had gone all prude on him again.

"So what's the hang up here?" he asked. "I mean . . . I'd wear a rubber."

"Don't make me sick." She opened a compact and reapplied her glitter-flecked lip gloss. "Where are your parents, anyway?"

"Dad's at work till six. My stepmom is visiting her cousin in Fort Worth till Sunday, and my real mom's asleep in her room. But she don't care if we're messing around. She's real liberal."

"Your real mom still lives here? With your dad and stepmom?"

"She hasn't found a place to stay yet."

"How long since they divorced?"

"Three years."

Nina shifted her eyes from the compact. "Can you say dysfunctional?"

Booker thought about it. "Do what?"

Booker Flamont was now the starting middle linebacker for the Elmwood Heights Badgers, which was quite a leap from the previous three years, during which he had served as a third-string backup on special teams.

He currently stood six-four, 248, with chiseled muscles from head to toe. This, too, was quite a change from the previous seasons, in which he had weighed in at a paltry 157 wrapped in a wet towel. The dramatic increase in size and strength was due to two contributing factors: intensification of his weight-lifting routine and a newfound affinity for steroid use, which he and most of his teammates had developed during the off-season.

It was Booker's best friend, Manny Deluccio, the Elmwood Badgers flanker, who kept the team well stocked with juice. Manny had been dealing in various narcotics since the eighth grade, but it wasn't until last spring that he hooked up with El Toro Grande, his Mexican connection, whose primary export had in a matter of months drastically altered the size—and personalities—of the majority of the Badgers' roster.

El Toro Grande manufactured and distributed his product from a deserted shoe factory just across the Rio Grande from El Paso. The product for which he had become famous in underground circles was a performance-enhancing drug commonly known as Hombre Muchacho. The only thing anyone in Elmwood, Texas knew of Hombre Muchacho was that it looked like urine, smelled like brine, and was about twice as potent as your run-of-the-mill steroid favored by a large number of today's world-class athletes.

Realizing the benefits of just one dose was all it took for Booker Flamont to begin indulging in the drug with abandon.

Within two weeks of his first injection, he'd increased his bench press by twenty pounds and knocked two and a half seconds off his forty-yard sprint. Such results were so seductive that he managed to exhaust his initial six-week supply of the drug in only seventeen days.

The results spoke for themselves. It took him only two pre-season practices to move from the end of the bench to defensive captain. Soon his abilities became so extreme, his teammates were left with no choice but to increase their own dosages just to keep up.

Following the Badgers' third consecutive shutout win, the local press labeled them the most feared team in the state. And for the first time in Booker's life, people were finally taking notice of him—fans, media, college scouts, even Nina Hernandez.

"So are we gonna go at it, or what?" he asked, casually inching closer to Nina.

"In your dreams, Flamont." She snapped the compact closed and dropped it into her purse. "Look, call me when you get rid of all that shit on your face."

"What shit?"

"That acne. Your whole face is like some wicked gross moon-scape."

Booker turned to the mirror. "Oh, that. That's nothing. Just a rash."

"Well, then you better get it looked at. I think it's spreading across your back. Oh, yeah, and your ass, too."

"Why are you talking to me like this?"

"I'm only doing you a favor, pointing out the things that others won't. And while we're on the subject . . . aren't you getting a bit thin up top all of a sudden?"

"Huh?"

"I mean, don't let it get you down or anything. Some girls really go for the whole balding thing." She winked and made a clicking sound with her cheek. "Unfortunately, I'm not one of them."

Booker's fists clenched. "I'm not going bald. I've just been stressed—you know, with the season and all."

"Yeah. Sure. Right. Look, I gotta go."

"Already? You can't go now."

"Yeah, why?"

He was about to tell her that watching her apply her lip gloss had given him an erection, but as it turned out, he didn't have to.

"What the hell is that?!" She pointed at the protrusion in his gym shorts.

Booker smiled lovingly. "You gave me a boner."

"Well, keep it away from me."

"But it's *because* of you, baby."

"I'm leaving."

"But you can't. Not now!"

"You're a freak! Your whole family is freaks! Juicer!" She left the room.

"I'm not a juicer!"

A voice called out from down the hall. "Booker, is that you?"

"Go back to sleep, Mom!" Booker started after Nina, but it was too late. The front door slammed.

The phone rang on the dresser behind him. "Christ, Manny!" He swiveled around to pick up the receiver and knocked over a picture of his stepmother with his aroused manhood. The frame tumbled off the nightstand and shattered on the floor. "Shit!"

"Booker, what's going on?"

"I said go back to sleep, Mom!" He fumbled with the receiver before it got to his ear. "Hello, goddamnit!"

"Booker, it's me, Manny. What's up, bro?"

"My dick!"

Manny laughed. "Nina still playing Mother Teresa with you?"

"Speaking of mothers, can you hold on while I pull out of yours?"

"Real funny, bro."

"So how'd it go at the pep rally?"

"Perfect. I think. From our spot in the bushes across the street, the explosions sounded like fucking Hiroshima."

"Like what?"

"You know, that bomb we dropped on the Nam. Anyway, our

little prank might have taken half the damn night to set up, but I think it was well worth the trouble."

"Did you and Elray get away clean?"

"Clean as a homecoming queen, bro."

"Anyone see you?"

"I just told you, bro, we're clean." Booker heard Manny and Elray exchange a high five on the other end of the line. Manny said, "Me and Elray watched the whole crowd run out of that gym like scared, blood-splattered little pussies. It was S-W-E-E-T."

Booker knew that Manny was high on Mexican reefer. For some reason it always made him want to spell out his words. "Great," he said. "With Logan out, and with the scare we put into the rest of the team, there's no way Killington can beat us in district now. Hell, the Jackrabbits might not even play Stanton High tonight after all we've done. They'll probably forfeit the game. But even if they do play, and Killington somehow manages to beat Stanton without Logan, there's no way in hell they can beat *us* without him."

"S-M-O-O-T-H sailing now," Manny agreed. Booker heard the exchange of another high five. "Listen, bro, I'll catch you later."

"Where you going?"

"School. It *is* a school day, you know."

"You can't. I need you to come over here."

"Why?"

"I need to juice."

"But we ain't even playing tonight. Have you forgotten that it's our off-week? Plus, I think you need to go easy for a while. Hombre Muchacho is strong stuff, you know. You can always double up next week for district."

"Just get over here and stick my ass."

CHAPTER 5

GET the hell off me!" Cole jerked his hand away from the young medic attempting to apply fresh gauze to his hand.

The medic recoiled and cast his eyes up to the sheriff. Sheriff Curtis Clark nodded and the man moved away in a huff, stripping off his rubber gloves in Cole's face as if to say, *It's your funeral, asshole.*

Cole sat on the bumper of the ambulance parked outside the gym and rewrapped the bandanna over his wounds. The pain was bad enough to cause his ears to ring, but he refused to let it show.

O'Dell Lamar, the Jackrabbits tailback, and Willard Blunt, free safety, brushed past the sheriff and hovered over Cole. Both boys were fellow starters on the team, and they had been the first to rush to Cole's side when he had finished his speech at the pep rally.

O'Dell placed a hand on Cole's shoulder. "Hey, Logan, ease up there, man. I know you've been through the shit today, but that hand needs—"

"I don't need a nurse, O'Dell, but thanks."

Willard and O'Dell shared a look.

Willard said, "That may be, Logan, but *we* need a healthy quarterback . . . and in just a few hours. I think you'd best just let the doctors do their thing. We're counting on you, man . . . but we're also here to help."

"Well, I appreciate that, but what say you guys worry about holding up your end and let me hold up mine?"

A tense beat passed. O'Dell shook his head and offered a humorless chuckle. "Yeah. Sure thing, Logan. Don't let us get in your way. Just trying to help, you know?"

By the time Cole brought his head up, his teammates were moving away, shrugging their broad shoulders.

A half hour had passed since the explosions in the gymnasium put a quick end to the Killington pep rally. The parking lot still buzzed with emergency vehicles, medical personnel, media, school faculty, and stunned Jackrabbits fans caked in wet pumpkin meat and blood—or what appeared to be blood. Horns honked in all directions. Gridlock jammed the exit of the lot, where students were attempting to make a clean break from campus before any school official could instruct them otherwise. Over the sheriff's shoulder, Cole saw that a sizable crowd of students still remained. Enduring the cold drizzle, they had gathered about twenty feet behind the sheriff to listen in on the questioning, which Cole was desperate to bring to a close.

"So are we done here, Curtis, or what?"

Curtis flipped his notebook closed. "For now. We can finish this up at the hospital. Right now I want you to go get yourself fixed up."

"I'm not going to the hospital."

The sheriff raised an eyebrow. "Say again?"

"No hospital."

"You got someplace more important to be?"

"Yeah, home, getting ready for tonight."

"Tonight? I hope you don't think you're gonna play a football game tonight after what's happened."

"The hell I'm not, Curtis."

"Sheriff Clark."

"I'm not gonna chicken out, *Curtis*. That's exactly what they want."

"What who wants?"

"Who do you think? The assholes who did this to me."

"I thought you just told me they didn't say *anything* to you."

Cole backpedaled, having almost been caught in a lie.

"They *didn't* say anything to me. But it doesn't take a genius to know that whoever did this was trying to keep me off the field tonight. Well, fuck 'em. I'm playing." The comment brought cheers from the crowd. "It's gonna take more than a couple missing fingers to keep me off that field."

"Yeah, you've said as much. I heard you made quite a show of yourself at the rally."

"You got a problem with what I said?" Before Curtis could answer, Cole spotted Coach Hickham weaving his way through the onlookers. "Coach! Can I talk to you for a minute?"

Hickham and the sheriff exchanged a nod.

"I just want you to know that I'm okay to play tonight, Coach." Cole held up his hand. "This is nothing a few Advil can't take care of, at least until after the game. 'Least it's not my throwing hand. If I can just get home and work with the ball a little, I'm sure I can—"

"Cole, just settle down for a minute," Hickham said. "We can talk about this after you get your hand looked at."

"Please, Coach. Just give me the chance, and I'm sure I can—"

"Looks like it was cherry bombs and ketchup, Sheriff."

The three of them turned to the deputy who had spoken.

"Come again?" said the sheriff.

"Firecrackers, Sheriff. Pretty good trick, you ask me. According to the Killington FD, they stuffed the pumpkins with clusters of cherry bombs and water balloons . . . that's to say, *ketchup* balloons. Looks like they broke into the gym and put the pumpkins up in the rafters sometime overnight, probably real early this morning. KFD estimates there were ten or twelve of them scattered around for optimal coverage."

"Eight hundred people in that gym and no one noticed that there were pumpkins in the rafters?"

The deputy swallowed hard. "Well, sir, it *is* Halloween."

Curtis moved a chewed-on matchstick from one corner of his mouth to the other. "You can't light cherry bombs by remote control."

The deputy nodded. "That's what I was thinkin', too, sir. But the fire chief told me they could have used punks."

"Punks?" Coach Hickham asked.

"That's right, Coach. They're these slow-burning sticklike things, look sort of like incense. Tape a few of them together, end to end, and it's possible they could take a couple hours to burn down far enough to ignite a fuse."

"Don't they give off smoke, some kind of burning smell?" asked Curtis.

"Very little smoke, and I guess not enough of a smell to overpower the popcorn and hot dogs cookin'."

Curtis chewed this over. "All right. Thanks, Hubie. I'll see you back inside in a minute."

Cole stood. "I'll just leave you to it, then, Curtis."

"Sit down, son."

"Why? I've got things to do, too, you know."

A news photographer shoved his way through the crowd and trained his lens on Cole. Cole subtly gave him the finger just as the flash went off, then turned back to Hickham. "Coach, will you just tell the sheriff that I'm fine so we can both get back to work?"

More commotion from the crowd. Now it was Savannah Hickham shoving her way through, tape recorder in hand.

"Savannah? What are you doing here?" Coach Hickham asked.

Ignoring her father's question, Savannah marched up to the sheriff. "Would you care to make a statement?"

"Young lady, I'm not sure who you are, but—"

"Savannah Hickham of the *Paws and Whiskers.*"

"The what?"

"The school paper," Coach Hickham said. "This is my daughter, Sheriff. Savannah, I'm not sure this is the right time for this."

She moved the recorder closer to Curtis's mouth. "Sheriff, would you care to comment on the embarrassing breech in school security displayed here today?"

Hickham rubbed at his temples. "Savannah, please. This isn't the time."

Cole stood again. "Actually, it's a great time."

Savannah turned and gasped at the sight of the blood on Cole's hand. "Omigod! Is that . . . I mean, are you . . ."

"What I am is outta here," Cole said. "Coach, don't worry about me. I'll be on that bus tonight, ready to play."

Curtis took hold of his elbow. "Cole, you're gonna get your butt in that ambulance and go to the hospital. And you're gonna wait until I get there so you can answer the rest of my questions. I want to know exactly what happened in your front yard this morning."

"Speaking of questions, Sheriff, what say you answer mine?" Savannah intervened.

The sheriff shook his head. "Not now, missy."

Savannah looked at her father. "Fine. How 'bout a statement from you, then, Coach?"

"I'm not your coach, I'm your father, and I'm telling you to give it a rest."

Cole broke free of Curtis's grasp.

Curtis said, "Get in that ambulance now, Cole! It's not a request."

"Hey, Cole!"

All eyes turned to Maxine Wiley. The varsity head cheerleader stood at the front of the crowd, one hip cocked strategically, her skirt riding high.

"I know how to make that hand feel better," she said. "I think you'll remember what I'm talkin' about."

Laughter and whistles all around.

Savannah rolled her eyes and jabbed the recorder into Cole's face. "So why the reluctance to seek medical attention, Mr. Logan?"

"No comment, sweet . . ." He started to say *sweet tits*, but remembered that he was addressing his coach's daughter. "Sorry, Ms. Hickham. No comment at this time."

"It's a simple question," she persisted. "Why would a football player with a big game only hours away be so reluctant to receive medical attention?"

The answer was that getting into the ambulance would mean going to the hospital, which would also mean stitches, sedatives, and more questions about the attack at his house—all things that could prevent him from playing tonight. He knew that even a suggestion of the threats made to him—and to his teammates—might mean a cancellation of the game.

"All right, fine. I'll go to the hospital," he said, feigning surrender. "But let me drive myself."

"You think I was born yesterday, Cole?"

"Curtis, I'll go straight to the emergency room, I promise. I just don't like ambulances and would prefer to take my bike, that's all."

"Cole, it's not safe for you to ride a motorbike with your hand like that," Hickham said.

"I'll be fine."

Curtis shook his head. "I said no." He made a move for his handcuffs.

Savannah jumped between them. "I'll take him."

All eyes went to her.

"Sure," she said. "I'll take him. I've got my car here. It'll be no problem."

"And why, may I ask, are you volunteering?" Hickham said.

She took her time answering. "Call it school spirit and giving back to the community. You don't mind, do you, Mr. Logan?"

The truth was he *did* mind. The coach's daughter had never been anything but a bitch to him since the day he'd been assigned to the desk behind hers in economics. Secondly, the last thing he wanted to do at the moment was talk to a reporter, even if she was only writing for the school paper, and even if she did, in fact, have sweet tits. But at the moment, he was out of options. What he really needed to do was get home, do a Frankenstein job on his hand, and reteach himself to play football with only eight fingers.

"No, I don't mind," he said. "Whatever. Long as I get to the hospital, right, Curtis?"

The sheriff gnawed on the matchstick, swapping glances between Cole and Savannah. He jabbed the soggy end of it into Cole's face. "If I don't find you at that hospital in half an hour, it's your ass. Is that clear?"

Cole nodded. "Crystal."

"You have my word, Sheriff," Savannah said. "I'll have him there in five minutes."

"This isn't a joke, you two," Hickham said. "Straight to the hospital."

Savannah gave her father a saccharine smile, jangling the car keys in her hand.

Cole moved past her. "Hey, Coach?"

"What is it, Logan?"

"I just want you to know that I'll be ready. I promise you, I'm not gonna let you down."

Savannah pulled Cole away before Hickham could reply.

CHAPTER 6

COLE lit a cigarette before Savannah even got the key in the ignition.

"Do you mind?" she said.

"Oh, sorry." He extended the pack toward her. "You want one?"

She bit her tongue, struggling to keep her revulsion of him in check. "Will you at least crack the window?"

He did. Then he slid out of his jacket and used it to wrap his bleeding hand, a gesture she assumed was more out of necessity than courtesy.

Neither of them spoke until they were off the lot. Savannah knew she needed to break the ice quickly. It was a short drive to the hospital, and she would have to get him talking fast if she was going to get what she needed . . . which at this point was pretty much anything printable.

"No need to thank me," she said. "Really." It probably wasn't the best opening line for buttering him up, but it was the first thing that came out.

"Thank you for what?"

"Kept you out of that ambulance, didn't I? Isn't that what you wanted?"

Cole blew smoke into the velour ceiling. "You and I both know you didn't do that for me."

"What's that supposed to mean?"

"It means that for a journalist you make a great chauffeur."

"I beg your—"

"The biggest story to ever hit Killington just exploded, literally, in the high school gym, and you were the only student in the school who didn't see it. Now you wanna use me to play catch-up for your little news article. God forbid you lose your position at the *Ears and Whiskers*."

"It's the *Paws and Whiskers,* and how did you know I missed the pep rally?"

"Because if you had been there, you wouldn't have been so shocked to see my hand. Plus, we both know there's no way in hell you'd have me in your car right now if you didn't want something from me, and I got a feeling you're not looking for a date to the homecoming dance. Well, you can forget it because I'm not gonna be your goddamn news story."

His next exhalation sent smoke in her direction.

"Okay, Cole, you got me."

"So it's Cole now? What happened to Mr. Logan?"

"Look, are you going to tell me what happened to you, or are you going to sit there and be an asshole?"

"The asshole thing has always worked for me in the past." He pointed through the windshield. "Turn left up there."

"But the hospital is to the right."

"Exactly. Hang a left."

She hit the brakes hard.

Cole's head somehow missed the dashboard, but the sudden jolt sent his cigarette flying from his lips. He was still flailing in his seat, slapping at his lap, when she got the car pulled over to the shoulder.

"Jesus!" He brushed sparks off his jeans. "What the hell are you trying to do?"

She put the car in park. "All right, here's the deal, Logan. I know that even if I drop you off at the hospital, you're just going to walk right out when I pull away. So your choices are simple: you either answer a few questions while I drive you to wherever it is you want to go, or you keep silent while I drive you to the police station."

"So that's the deal?" A grin crept over his face. "You know something, sweet tits, you're kinda hot when you're demanding."

Savannah's knuckles went white on the steering wheel, but she kept her calm. "What did you say to me, Cole Logan?"

"I said, you're dreaming, sweet tits, if you think I'm gonna answer any of your questions."

"One more time . . ."

"What are you, deaf? I said I'm not . . ." He stopped. The color drained from his face. "Where's that damn tape recorder?"

She smiled. "What do you think my father—your coach—will say when he hears the way you're speaking to me?"

Cole searched the car—under the seats, beneath the floor mats, in the glove compartment and console.

When he reached into the backseat and started rifling through her purse, she told him to give it up.

"Where the hell is it?"

"In my bra."

His eyes came up fiery.

"That's right, Logan. Pressed right up against what you have so eloquently referred to as my *sweet tits*. I don't recommend you go looking for it there, however, seeing as how your hands are dripping a blood trail and both my father and the sheriff know you're in the car with me."

His complexion paled a little more. She took pleasure in it.

He came back around in his seat. She reached under her sweater, brought the recorder out, stopped the tape, and slid the machine under her leg. "Now do you feel like talking?"

"Enough of this shit." He reached for the door handle. "I'll fuckin' walk."

Savannah hit the door-lock button and the gas pedal simultaneously. "You might want to buckle up; my braking foot seems to be a bit itchy."

"Ah, hell." He flicked the cigarette out the window. "What do you want from me?"

"Directions for starters. Where are we headed?"

"Fuckin' home!"

"Fine. Where's *fuckin'* home?"

"Left on Cummings!" he barked. "Another left at the dead end, all the way down Maple to the tracks."

"That's the trailer park, right?" She cringed, immediately wishing she hadn't said it.

"Yeah. Orchard Village. But if you reach either an orchard or a village, trust me, you've gone too far."

She turned left at the light and checked her rearview mirror to make sure the sheriff wasn't having them followed.

Confident that they were in the clear, she said, "Okay, Logan, we're off the record now, so relax. This won't sting. If it'll make any difference, I'll admit that you were right. I *did* miss the biggest event in this school's history, and I *am* trying to save my ass. I didn't even hear about the explosions until twenty minutes after the fact because I was in the photo lab, and I didn't know about your injuries until just a minute ago. So, yes, I'm playing catch-up."

"Hard to believe that shitty school paper could mean this much to you."

"It doesn't. But if I can write a couple good articles for that shitty school paper—something with a little more intrigue than field trips and book fairs—I might get an internship at the *Daily*. I get the internship, and it could go a long way toward helping me get into a good journalism school, preferably somewhere as far from this godforsaken town as possible. You can relate to that, can't you, Logan? Isn't that your plan, too, to let football be your ticket the hell out of here?" He didn't answer. "I mean, why else would you be so adamant to play tonight, considering what's happened to you?"

He lit another Marlboro. "Are these the questions you got me in here to ask?"

"No. So is it true you were attacked? I'm guessing you didn't lose your fingers in a pencil sharpener."

"Look, I'll tell you the same thing I told the sheriff. Three masked men jumped me outside my house this morning. They roughed me up a little, then put the hatchet to two of my fingers."

"And?"

"And? That's it."

"They didn't say anything?"

"Not a word."

"Not *one* word?"

"Nope."

"Any idea who it was?"

"Nope."

"And if you had to take a guess?"

He raked his fingers through his hair. "Well, hell, where were you early this morning? Your dad keep a hatchet lying around the garage by chance?"

"Can we be serious?"

"I am. I mean, it makes sense, doesn't it? I seem to remember just last week you threatened to cut off my foot if I didn't get my boot off your damn purse strap."

She had to concede the point. "Fair enough. But assuming it *wasn't* me . . . any ideas?"

Cole shook his head. "Could have been the bogeyman or the

mailman for all I know. Tell you the truth, it doesn't concern me right now. All that concerns me is winning two more football games. After we win district, then I'll go find the assholes that did this to me."

"So are you frightened?"

"About what?"

"You're the starting quarterback of a team that's one win away from the district championship game against the undefeated Elmwood Badgers . . ."

"Hey, not bad for a girl who hasn't been seen anywhere near the team all season. Why is that, anyway? I mean, your old man is *only* the head coach."

"Let's stick to the subject. Clearly someone wants to keep you from playing . . ."

"Yeah, maybe even the mailman . . ."

"So if you really want to play so badly, why did you reject professional medical care? Why were you so adamant about staying out of that ambulance?"

"Uh . . . I'm claustrophobic. Yeah, I don't like anyth—" He cringed.

"What? Does it hurt?"

"No, I'm wincing in pleasure. Yeah, it hurts like shit."

"You sure you don't want to go to the hospital?"

"I'll be fine. Just step on it before I bleed out here." He tightened the jacket around his hand.

Savannah pressed the pedal to the floor. "So aren't you concerned with what they might do next? I mean, if you do play tonight?"

He appeared uneasy with the question.

"Look," he said. "I've told you everything I know, which is not a damn thing. For all I know the ones that did this don't give a shit about football and just mistook me for a neighborhood prowler."

Savannah had yet to believe a word he'd said. She was about to call him on it when he told her to veer right past the railroad tracks. She swerved the car hard. The tires skidded as the road went from asphalt to dirt.

They passed the rusted skeleton of a playground on the left and a weed-choked vacant lot on the right where two mongrel dogs wrestled in a coital knot at the base of a towering heap of garbage and burned leaves. They entered Orchard Village a quarter mile farther along. Mobile homes dotted the hilly, heavily wooded terrain. The homes looked like discarded freight cars that had fallen from the sky at odd intervals and taken root wherever they landed.

Another mile on Cole indicated his own home. It sat on at least an acre. The nearest neighbors were some hundred yards away on either side. The trailer was white, or at least had been at one time. Strewn tools, tires, and sofas (or were those slashed-up car seats?) cluttered an elevated porch that stretched the length of the facade.

"Good," Cole said, peering through the windshield. "They're gone."

"Who?"

"Forget it. Doesn't matter."

Savannah weaved between potholes on the muddy drive. She parked a few feet away from a Trans Am that looked like it had been on cinder blocks for a decade.

Cole opened his door. "Well, Suzanna, it's been real."

"It's Savannah, and we're not finished yet." He tried to get out, but she took hold of his arm. "We didn't even get to talk about the pep rally."

"There were a thousand people in that gym who can tell you about it. Take your pick."

She released his arm but continued to stall. "Well . . . um, so what happens now?"

"Now you get the hell off my land."

"No, I mean . . . it's only a matter of time before the sheriff finds out you're not at the hospital. Don't you think he'll come looking for you here?"

"Yes, which is why I have to work fast and get the fuck outta here." He stood and slammed the door behind him.

"What kind of work?"

"I said go."

She came out of the car. "But where will you go?"

"You think I'd tell you?" He stepped onto the porch.

"Well, you can't stay here if the cops are going to come. You gotta go somewhere. But your bike's at school. So unless there are some wheels around here that I don't see"—she indicated the Trans Am—"or unless you're one hell of a mechanic . . . you're pretty much afoot, right?"

"What part of *fuck off* are you not getting?" He rummaged through a pile of tools in an old ice chest.

"I could drive you." She hoped the suggestion hadn't sounded as desperate as it felt.

"I don't need you to do shit for me. I do have friends, you know."

"That's not what I hear."

"Well, how 'bout thirty-six teammates who depend on me for their success? Trust me, if I need a lift, I can get one."

She considered this, then shook her head. "No. Sorry. I don't buy it. You don't want to have to speak with anyone today, Logan, and I'll tell you why. Because you don't want to tell anyone what really happened this morning."

He came up holding a tangled extension cord. "Look, either get the hell out of here, or—"

"What? You'll call the cops?" She moved to the bottom of the steps. "Look, Logan, I'll make you another deal. I'll take you anywhere in town you want to go, keeping you clear of the police and anyone else you want to avoid until it's time for you to get on that bus. In return, you let me write about everything that you do today, from this minute until the final tick of the clock in tonight's game."

"Hell no. I told you, I'm not gonna be your damn news story." He pointed at her with some kind of electrical tool that she couldn't name.

"Fine. Have it your way." She pulled her cell phone out of her jeans pocket. "Let's see now, what's the sheriff's number? Oh, silly me, nine-one-one, right?" She started to dial.

"Ah, hell!" He descended the steps. "Why are you doing this?"

"Because I happen to be in need of a news story and you happen to be one."

"You think anybody in this town gives a shit about anything I do outside of throwing touchdown passes?"

"I think a lot of people in this town would love to read about how their heroic quarterback began a day by losing two of his fingers and finished it by leading his team into the district championship game."

Cole winced again. His hand dribbled red at his feet. Painful tears watered his eyes.

"All right," he said in surrender, jabbing a finger toward her. "But you don't print shit until after the game. Got it?"

"Fine."

"After the *district* game, not just tonight's game. I don't want to read a word about me until the season's over."

"You have my word."

"But first you have to do something else for me." He doubled over at the waist.

"What's that?"

He raised the tool in his hand. "The ironing."

CHAPTER 7

E XCUSE me?"

"You heard me."

"Heard, yes. Understood, no." Savannah indicated the rusty tool in his hand. "What is that thing?"

"A soldering iron."

"What do you do with it?"

"Solder stuff."

She followed him onto the porch, where he plugged the extension cord into an exterior outlet and attached it to the iron. "You're not really going to use that thing on your hand?"

"No," he answered. "*You* are. Long as you're here, I'd rather not have to do it myself."

"Have you lost your mind?"

"No, just my fingers."

"Please just let me take you to the hospital."

"This'll work."

"How do you know?"

"I saw it in *Braveheart*."

"*Braveheart*? Are you kidding?"

"You burn the wounds, they close right up." He spat on the tip of the iron, waited twenty seconds, then spat again. This time there was a hiss. He sat on the top step and held out the iron to her. "We'll do 'em one at a time. Press hard. And be quick about it."

"Oh, right. As if." She folded her arms across her chest and turned away.

"Come on," he said. "It'll give your story a nice little gory detail." He slipped his belt from the loops of his jeans and folded it over on itself. "Come on, I don't have all day!"

"I said I'm not doing it! I don't want to be responsible for permanently damaging your hand."

"It's permanently damaged already. If you don't help me close up these wounds, I can't play tonight. Would you rather be responsible for that?"

"Cole, there are plastic surgeons these days who can reattach your fingers, make you good as new."

"I don't think that's gonna happen."

"Why?"

"Because the shitheads that did this took my fingers with them. And no plastic surgeon can take care of this before kickoff tonight, so come on."

Savannah just shook her head.

"Fine. I'll do it myself."

He squeezed his wrist between his knees to keep his arm from recoiling when the iron made contact. He placed the belt between his teeth and bit down hard enough to hear the leather crack. Then he brought the iron down toward his hand. It was less than an inch away, close enough to feel its heat, when Savannah spoke.

"Hey, Braveheart."

He spat out the belt. "Jesus, what is it now?"

She nodded toward the trees. Cole followed her gaze. A squad car was approaching quickly, just a couple of hundred yards up the road.

"Damnit!" He ripped the cord from the wall and flung it and the soldering iron down the porch.

"What do we do now?" she asked.

"*We?*"

"I'm in as much trouble here as you, remember?"

There wasn't time to argue the point. "Shit, come on!"

He led her down the steps. They sprinted across the drive and into the woods to the top of a rise about forty yards inside the tree line. When they were over the crest, Cole pulled her to the ground beside him. He rolled onto his stomach and stayed low as the squad car pulled up next to her Honda. Curtis's Stetson was easy to recognize behind the wheel.

Savannah tried to speak. Cole covered her mouth with his good hand and pushed her face into the leaves.

Curtis shut off his engine. He came out of the squad car and looked inside the Honda.

Cole lowered his head to avoid being seen, and kept his cheek pressed to the ground until he heard the sheriff knock on his front door.

Savannah murmured something again. Cole pushed her face deeper into the leaves. "Shh. Shut up!"

Curtis peered through the trailer's windows, then turned and looked toward the woods. Cole had no doubt that the sheriff knew he was being watched. He also knew that Curtis wasn't about to give him the pleasure of watching him snoop around the place like a blind man in search of his ass.

The sheriff was already on his way back to the squad car when Savannah's wiggling became convulsive.

"Hold still!" Cole hissed. He had to climb onto her back to finally restrain her, but by then her struggle had betrayed their position.

"I know y'all are out there," Curtis hollered, "so you might as well just come on out, make this easier on all of us."

They froze. Cole felt Savannah's heart stammering in sync with his own.

A minute passed.

"Fine, then," Curtis said. "We'll do this your way. I'm not gonna stand around here all day and play hide and seek with you. But just know that before the day is out, I'm gonna have both of your butts down at the station house, so help me. And I can assure you it ain't gonna be pleasant. Y'all have now officially broken the law, I hope you realize that."

Cole didn't exhale until the engine fired back up. Curtis's car peeled away, kicking up clumps of dirt behind it.

When it was out of sight, Savannah sank her teeth into Cole's hand.

"Ow! What was that for?!"

"Get the hell off of me!"

"What's the matter with you? Why'd you have to start squirmin' around?"

"I said get off, you asshole!"

Cole rolled off her. "You just got us busted."

"Well, forgive me, but I don't appreciate being tackled to the ground and having a wild animal crawl all over me."

"Trust me, I took no pleasure from it, sweetheart, so don't flatter yourself."

"Not you, you idiot! The *other* animal. That thing!"

Cole turned. The animal she was referring to lay a few feet away. "It's just a damn house cat. What's the big deal?"

"Well, I didn't know it was a house cat, did I? My face was being mashed into the dirt. But the thing was crawling all over my legs. For all I knew it was a snake or a wolverine or something. You really know how to treat a lady, don't you, Logan?"

Cole didn't answer. His focus was on the gray tabby cat looking back at him with mismatched eyes. One eye was black, the other blue—just like the eyes of the cat he had fed at his bedroom window that morning; the cat whose guts had been spilled over his yard soon thereafter.

Cole would have chalked it up to coincidence were it not for the blood. The cat's chest was caked with it. And yet there was no sign of the wound Cole had seen on the cat that morning.

"Logan? Excuse me? Hey, asshole." Savannah snapped her fingers. "You still with me?"

"It's not possible," he whispered.

"That you're an asshole? Believe me, it is."

He moved past her and crawled slowly toward the cat. Its tail went rigid and its ears folded back with caution, but it didn't run away. Cole reached out and delicately stroked the animal's head.

"What's that stuff all over it?" Savannah asked.

"Blood."

"God, is there anything around here that's not bleeding?"

"It isn't bleeding."

"But you just said—"

"It's got blood on it. But it's not *bleeding*." He spoke more to himself than to her. "There's . . . there's nothing wrong with it."

"Well, get away from it. It might be rabid or something."

The cat inched closer. Cole read the tag suspended from its plaid collar. The tag was smeared with red, but the letters were legible: coodles.

"Impossible," he whispered again.

"Why do you keep saying that? Come on, get away from it. It's just a mangy stray."

"It's not a stray. It belongs to Mona."

"Mona? You mean *Black* Mona, the crazy Gypsy witch-lady everyone's so afraid of?"

"She's my next-door neighbor."

"Why does that not surprise me?"

Cole peered through the foliage toward Mona's trailer in the distance. He reached under the cat and brought its forepaws off the ground. Aside from the blood, he saw nothing that would indicate the animal had ever been harmed. He tucked the cat into the crook of his elbow and stood.

Savannah rose beside him, brushing wet leaves off her jeans. "So are you gonna tell me what's got you looking so freaked-out?"

"Come on." He started down the hill.

"Where are we going?"

A distant roll of thunder cut off his answer. The drizzle graduated to a light rain. Cole moved Coodles under his shirt and quickened his pace. They jogged to the bottom of the hill, then turned onto Mona's property. The old woman was sitting in a rocking chair on the corner of her covered porch, a narrow trickle of cigarette smoke rising above her head.

"Sorry to bother you," Cole said when they reached the base of the porch, "but I think we found something that belongs to you." He presented the cat.

Mona studied the animal with narrow eyes. If the blood on its undercarriage shocked her, she didn't show it.

"I think you are mistaken, Mr. Logan." Her yellowed fingers lit a fresh cigarette and she smiled. "I think it was Coodles that brought you to me."

CHAPTER 8

"You two gonna stand there gettin' soaked, or y'all gonna come on up?"

They stepped onto the covered porch. Cole handed Coodles over to Mona, then moved away. Savannah stayed close on his heels. Some twenty more cats wandered the porch all around them, brushing against their legs.

Battered tools and yard equipment littered the area, not unlike Cole's own porch. A rusted bug zapper hung in a far corner of the overhang. Below it, a faded sofa sat on three legs. Loose springs poked out of its slashed cushions. Overhead, handmade wind chimes built of chicken bones and fishing line clicked in the breeze.

Cole extended a hand. "I suppose I should introduce mys—"

"No need to do that, Cole Logan. I know you well enough. I'm as big a Jackrabbits fan as they come, you know?" She didn't shake his hand.

"Yeah. I've heard. And we've always appreciated it."

"I never miss a game, rain or shine. Already got my ticket for Stanton High tonight."

"This is Savannah," Cole said. "Savannah Hickham."

"Ah, the coach's daughter? Knew he had one. Didn't know what she looked like." Mona leaned forward in her chair. She eyed Savannah the way one might appraise a cut of beef.

Cole sensed Savannah's reluctance to be there. He, too, had no desire to hang around any longer than necessary. "Well, I hope we didn't distur—"

"Spit it, boy."

"Excuse me?" he said, taken aback.

"Say what you came here to say."

He shared a glance with Savannah, but said nothing.

Mona said, "Why don't we start by you showing me your hand?"

Cole had been holding his injured hand behind his back. He slowly brought it around and held it out. Mona wasted no time in unwrapping the bloody bandanna, despite Cole's painful winces as she did it. She looked neither surprised nor repulsed by the sight of his wounds.

"Gotcha good, didn't they?"

His eyes came up. "Did you see them?"

"See who?"

"The ones who did this."

"No. Should I have?"

"Well, how did you know that someone—"

"Heard it on the radio. Your *fanger* loss and all that tomfoolery at the pep rally have been all over the local airwaves for the past hour now. Question is, What are we gonna do about this situation?"

"Cole, I think we should probably go get that looked at now." Savannah pointedly cocked her head toward the stairs.

"Yeah," he said. "Maybe I should go get it looked at."

"It's getting looked at now, ain't it?" Mona said.

"I meant that—"

"I know what you meant, Logan. Something's gotta get done about this before tonight, right? You *are* playing, ain'tcha?"

"I want to, but I'm not sure how I can like this."

"Well, no local sawbones is gonna be able to fix you up by kick-off time, that's for sure."

"No. I don't think so."

Mona drew off her cigarette. "Well, I haven't waited all these years to see my beloved Jackrabbits' best chance at a district championship end with the loss of a couple measly fangers, I can tell you that."

Under different circumstances, Cole might have found the remark funny. He wasn't laughing now.

Mona studied the wounds with a surgeon's gaze, turning his hand over and over between her own arthritic fingers.

This was the closest Cole had ever been to the woman who had been his neighbor his entire life. Cole's exchanges with her over the years had been limited to the occasional wave and kind word spoken across their property line. Otherwise she was as much an enigma to him as she was to the rest of the town. It was clear that she preferred her solitude. He knew that she had been a widow since before he was born, but he had never known her to entertain guests, gentleman callers or otherwise. And to his knowledge her only entry into any social setting was at the football games. Even then he knew her to always sit alone, watching the games from a distant vantage point in the stands.

She released his hand and went back to stroking Coodles, who now slept peacefully in her lap.

Savannah tugged the back of Cole's shirt, prodding him to leave. Much as he wanted to go, he couldn't. Not yet.

"Ms. Mona . . ." he said.

"Just Mona."

"Mona . . . some *things* happened in front of my house this morning."

"Come closer, my ears ain't what they used to be." She motioned for him to kneel beside her. "There, that's better. Now, you were saying?"

"I was just saying that . . . before I was attacked this morning, one of your cats came . . ."

"You feed my cats sometimes, don't you?"

"Yes, I do. That's why I feel sort of responsib—"

"Bologna, isn't it? I've seen a few bologna sandwiches turn up on my porch here lately. I can't stand the stuff, so I know they aren't getting it from me."

"I'm sorry. I know it isn't my place."

"It's quite all right. I suppose I'm indebted to you."

Cole shook his head. "No. You see . . ." He searched for the right words. "Somebody wanted to send me a message today."

Mona chuckled. "I'll say."

"But it wasn't just my hand that they hurt. See, one of your cats . . ."

"Coodles."

"Right. Coodles. I read the name on her collar this morning."

"*His* collar. Coodles is a boy."

"Sorry. I didn't know it was a male."

"*Is.*"

"Ma'am?"

"Coodles *is* a male. Not *was* a male." She indicated the cat in her lap. "I'd prove it to you, but I swear that in sixty years of looking, I've never once been able to locate a cat's pecker. You ever wondered why that is?"

Cole didn't answer the question. He looked at the animal in Mona's lap. "So you have two cats named Coodles?"

"Why would I have two cats with the same name?"

"I don't think I'm explaining myself." He decided to hell with tact. "Mona, your cat Coodles was injured badly this morning. Killed actually. I saw him. He was gutted right up the middle, probably with the same hatchet that was used to chop off my fingers."

Mona nodded. "Ghastly, wasn't it? Poor little thing." She lifted the cat from her lap, held it in front of her face, and kissed it on the nose. She raised her pitch into a sort of baby talk. "You just got the fright of your life, didn't you, boy?"

Cole now had no doubt that the rumors about Mona were true. She really was stark-raving mad. "Mona, you're not really suggesting that this cat is—"

"They will pay for what they did to my little baby," she said. "Have no doubts about that."

She burned down a third of her cigarette with one inhalation.

Cole was at a loss for words. It was clear that Mona was unwilling or unable to accept the fact that one of her animals had been mutilated. Part of him felt he owed it to her to explain further. Another part wondered what good could actually come of that. If she wanted to believe the cat in her lap was the same good ole Mr. Coodles he had seen that morning, then who was he to tell her differently? At the moment he just wanted to get the hell out of there.

He tried to stand, but Mona quickly took hold of his hand again. "It isn't right, what happened to you today, Cole. It appears your talent and success have created enemies for you, wouldn't you say?"

"Yeah, I guess." He grew uncomfortable with her touch, and fought the urge to pull his hand back.

"Question is, How far are you willing to go to make things right?"

He shrugged. "I just want to play football. That's all."

"Yes. Yes, of course. And that's why you're here, right? That's why destiny has brought you here."

"Destiny?"

She winked, then squeezed his hand hard between her palms.

Searing pain jolted through his body.

The wind began to swirl all around them. Trees swayed in the distance. The wind chimes swung and slammed into the overhang.

"What's happening?" Savannah said, her voice tinged with panic.

Cole tried to pull his hand free, but Mona increased her grip with strength he wouldn't have thought she possessed. Her eyes shut tightly. Her lips compressed. It was as if she had entered some kind of trance. The pain became unbearable. Cole began to shake uncontrollably. Just as he opened his mouth to cry out, Mona released him.

Cole coiled his hand to his chest and turned away. His head felt woozy. He coughed, struggling to catch his breath. Sweat streamed down his face.

A clap of thunder rocked the sky, and Mona laughed—a low, cryptic cackle. "They will pay, Cole Logan. Together we will make them pay for what they have done."

Cole looked down at his hand. The pain wasn't the only thing that had disappeared.

CHAPTER 9

"WHAT do you mean, there shouldn't be no game tonight, Gallbreth?"

"I mean precisely what I said, Principal Hodges. As your immediate subordinate, I trust you will give my suggestion serious consideration."

Mr. Hodges crossed the floor of Coach Hickham's cramped office to come face-to-face with the vice principal. "But I just got off the phone with the principal over at Stanton High. He said he had no reason to believe that either the attack on Cole Logan or the stunt at the pep rally involved anyone associated with his school. He told me that from where he sits it's game on. He's waiting by the phone right now for our decision."

"In light of today's events, I don't feel that it would be prudent to play this evening's competition as scheduled."

"This evening's competition? It's the goddamn season-deciding final game. What do you mean, we're not gonna play?"

"I see no reason why the game can't be rescheduled for a later date."

"This ain't a goddamn squash match, Gallbreth. We don't show up, it's a forfeit."

Vice Principal Kenneth Gallbreth used a handkerchief to rid his glasses of the spray that had flown from Mr. Hodges's lips. "It is my opinion, Mr. Hodges, that in light of all that has transpired this morning, all athletic events should be postponed until a time when we can guarantee the safety of our players and student body. There will, after all, always be next season."

"Is that right? Well, this ain't even your decision. Last time I checked, I was still your boss."

"That is correct, but I am afraid that if you insist on fighting me on this, I will have no choice but to go over your head, and you know precisely what I am talking about."

"Gallbreth, just because the lieutenant governor is plugging your aunt don't mean you can raise this issue to a higher political level. You go over my head and I'll have your ass."

"I make one phone call and I'll have your job, Mr. Hodges. You know this to be true."

Mr. Hodges's face flushed with rage, but he had no choice but to stand down. He turned to Coach Hickham, who was sitting behind his desk, silently studying a play chart. "Uh, you know, Jimmy, if you got anything to add here, now might be a good time."

Hickham glanced over the top of his reading glasses. "You gentlemen seem to be doing just fine as it is." He went back to the charts.

Mr. Hodges said, "Gallbreth, did you see what happened to Cole Logan today? Do you know what it took for him to show up at that rally and say what he said?"

"I am afraid I wasn't in attendance."

"Of course not. You were too busy sitting in your office, coming up with rules and shit."

"I was in my office tending to the business of running this school. I thought that perhaps someone should, seeing as how you were preoccupied on the basketball court, parading around with a microphone. I did, in fact, read the police report in full, and it is on that report that I am basing my judgment.

"You're not really suggesting that I tell the people of this town that we're tucking tail because a couple vandals decided to get cute with us."

Mr. Gallbreth raked a hand across the lip of his flattop. "That is precisely what I am suggesting."

"But—"

"But what, Mr. Hodges?"

"Everybody'll think we're cowards!"

"There is nothing cowardly about prudence."

"Prudence? Whoever did this is pissin' in our faces. Whether it was someone from Stanton High or not, I say we go over there to-night and tear the limbs off the entire goddamn team!"

"That attitude, Mr. Hodges, is precisely the problem with this school: misguided priorities. May I remind you that this is first and foremost a learning institution?"

"Sure, but that don't mean football shouldn't get its share."

"I suppose it is that sort of thinking that allows you to justify the misappropriation of funds you agreed to in July?"

"What are you talking about?"

"I am talking about the seventeen hundred dollars that was transferred from a worthy philanthropic endeavor to the purchasing of new game jerseys for a football team that received identical new jerseys just last season."

Mr. Hodges frowned. "Are you talking about that bird thing?"

"It is not just a bird, Mr. Hodges; it is an Atlantic Puffin, a threatened species. Those funds had been painstakingly collected by the Environmental Science Club to help pay for its survival."

"Well, forgive me, Gallbreth, but if you ask most folks around here what's more important, our boys looking sharp on the field or the survival of some goddamn bird that they can't even hunt in these parts—"

"For the last time, it is *not* just a bird; it is an Atlantic Puffin."

"I don't give a fuck if it's Pegasus! I ain't pissing away a red cent on it as long as I'm—"

There was a knock at the door. Curtis entered.

"Welcome to the party, Sheriff," said Coach Hickham dryly. He removed his glasses and rubbed the bridge of his nose. "What can I do for you?"

"I just came by to tell you that your starting quarterback is AWOL, and that I'm pretty sure he's rolling around in the woods with your daughter. So what's happenin' here?"

Hickham sighed. "I'm trying to figure out how to break down a strong nickel defense with an extremely inexperienced quarterback."

Mr. Hodges spun around. "Who you talkin' 'bout, Jimmy?"

"Our backup. He's a little green."

"You mean Smoot? You're not gonna start Teddy Smoot, are you? He's a damn freshman, had hardly any PT all season."

"Mr. Hodges, what say you run this school and let me run my team?"

The principal stood down. "Yeah, Jimmy. Sure. Of course. But . . . well, what about Logan?"

"Cole Logan lost two of his fingers this morning, Mr. Hodges. While I appreciate his courage and determination, I'm sure you can understand why I might question his effectiveness on the field tonight."

"Especially considering that he hasn't had any medical attention," added the sheriff.

Mr. Hodges looked around the room. "So . . . what are y'all sayin'? We're just gonna piss away the damn game?"

"I thought we had just decided that there wasn't going to be a game," said Mr. Gallbreth.

"There *is* going to be a game." All eyes suddenly turned to Cole, who was standing at the door with Savannah. "And I *am* going to play."

. . .

Cole stepped into the cramped room, sensing the tension immediately. Savannah remained at the door.

"There's the man of the hour," Mr. Hodges said, smiling. "See, Coach, I told you he was fine."

"Nice of you two to show up," Curtis said. "I hope you don't think this means you're off the hook."

Hickham stood and came around the desk. "Savannah, would you care to tell me what you're up to?"

Cole answered for her. "We're just here to tell you that I'm fine to play tonight, Coach. Just like I told you I'd be."

Mr. Gallbreth cleared his throat. "Before we go any further, I am going to insist that Mr. Logan remove the ornamentation from his ear. He is, after all, on school grounds."

"Christ, Gallbreth, put a cork in it," said Mr. Hodges. "Can't you see there's more important issues at hand here?"

"It's all right," Cole said. He removed the earring and slid it into the hip pocket of his jeans. "I can still give it everything tonight, Coach, so don't worry about me."

Hickham's eyes went to Cole's hand, now concealed under a black biker's glove.

"Hot damn!" Mr. Hodges clapped his meaty palms together. "Now that's what I'm talking about, Gallbreth. That's school spirit. You could learn a thing or two from this kid."

"Mr. Logan's condition is beside the point," said Mr. Gallbreth. "It was my understanding that the decision had been made to call off the game."

"My ass it had. This boy wants to play, we're gonna play," Mr. Hodges declared.

"On whose authority?" Gallbreth asked.

"On Coach Hickham's." Mr. Hodges turned to the coach. "That's right, ain't it, Jimmy? I mean, the kid seems fit enough, don't he?"

Cole and Hickham eyed each other as though they were the only ones in the room.

"You're right, Mr. Hodges," Hickham said, keeping his eyes on Cole. "It *is* my team, and therefore my decision whether or not we play. And we *are* playing tonight as scheduled."

Mr. Hodges beamed. "Coach, I knew when you got here you were gonna be the answer to all our prayers. Now, come on, boys, let's get outta here and let the coach get back to work."

"Thanks, Coach," Cole said. "I won't let you down." He started to file out of the room with the others.

"Hold on just a second, Cole." Hickham took him by the elbow. "We're going to play tonight . . . but I think maybe you ought to sit this one out."

Silence fell over the room.

"But why, Coach?"

"Son, you lost two fingers."

"On my left hand. I can still throw, still hand off the ball."

"I'm not just concerned about your physical health, Cole. You were the victim of a violent attack."

"So? I can assure you it wasn't my first brush with violence in my neighborhood."

"What are you so worried about, Coach?" asked Mr. Hodges.

"I'm responsible for the safety of my players. And I'm not going to put anyone at risk unnecessarily."

"Jimmy, I know you're in charge of this show and all, but this ain't exactly an *unnecessary* risk," Mr. Hodges said. "I mean, your backup quarterback has had about thirty-six seconds of playing time in the season. I'm not sure he's up to snuff, if you know what I mean."

"He'll be fine."

"What makes you so sure?"

"Because Logan is going to help him."

"What?" Cole said, aghast.

"From the sideline. As the leader of this team, I expect you to help your backup QB."

"You're joking, right?"

"My decision is final." Hickham glanced at each dumbstruck face. "You are all excused now."

Everyone spoke up at once, but none more loudly than Savannah, who had kept silent until now.

She stepped into the room. "Just show him, Cole."

"Show me what?"

"Cole is telling the truth, Dad. He's fine to play. Go ahead and show him, Cole."

After a moment's hesitation, Cole removed the glove. Mr. Hodges gasped. The others stood frozen. The fingers were still gone, but the wounds had healed completely, clear of even the faintest scar.

Curtis slipped on his bifocals and went in for a closer look.

"But that's . . . that's impossible!" exclaimed Mr. Hodges.

"Cole, would you mind telling me how in the Sam Hill you got healed up so quick?" Curtis said.

Cole knew that a truthful answer would almost certainly get him sent to the hospital—probably into a room with padded walls. He had hoped that his demeanor alone would be enough to convince the coach that he was okay to play, without his actually having to remove the glove. Now that the hand had been revealed, he wasn't sure how to answer the question.

"Cole?" Curtis pressed. "I'd like an answer."

"He soldered it!" Savannah blurted. "Isn't that right, Cole?"

Cole met her gaze. "Yeah. Miraculous as it may seem . . . and stupid a stunt as it was, I put a soldering iron to it." He shrugged. "I guess I'm just a quick healer."

"I can't believe it," said Mr. Hodges.

"I smell bullshit," Curtis said. "But never in my life have I doubted my own eyes. And you sure look healed up to me."

Cole turned to the coach. "So it's okay, then? Right, Coach?"

Hickham's expression remained like stone. "I'll be expecting you on the bus at six sharp, Cole."

Cole nodded. "I'll be there."

"In street clothes." Hickham turned and went back behind the desk.

Cole was sure he'd heard wrong. "Say that again, Coach?"

"Logan, I admire your determination. And again, I'm sorry about what happened to you. But I think you'll best serve this team from the sideline tonight."

Mr. Hodges cleared his throat. "Now, Jimmy, I'm not sure you're seeing this—"

Cole took the principal by the collar and yanked him out of the way. He leaned across Hickham's desk. "I bust my ass for you all season, take this team farther than they've ever gone before, and you hang me out to dry?"

"That's the way it is, Cole. My decision is final."

"Your decision is fucked!"

Hickham came out of the chair.

"All right, Cole," said the sheriff, "just take it easy now."

"Fuck easy."

Savannah took hold of his arm, but he shrugged free of her grasp.

"Cole, because I know how upsetting today has been for you, I'm going to excuse your outburst," Hickham said coolly. "But I am ordering you to leave this office immediately. Go simmer down. And I expect to see you on that bus at six. Your team needs you."

"Is that right? Did it ever occur to you that I might need this team?"

"Cole, I understand where you're coming from—"

Cole slammed a fist onto the desk. "Bullshit! You *don't* know where I'm coming from. I'm coming from a house that sits on three cinder blocks and a spare tire. I'm coming from a drunk mother who whores herself out to anyone who might help pay the rent and a father who skipped town a year ago with a bottle of gin and every dime we had. You want to hear more about where I'm coming from?

"In seven months I'll be a high school graduate with a C average and a criminal record. Because some motherfucker with a mask cut off two of my fingers, I can forget about the college scholarship I've been working toward for the past four years. You really wanna know where I'm coming from, Coach? I'm coming from a place where sixty minutes on a scoreboard clock is the only thing I've got to give a shit about and you're telling me I can't have it. So you know what? Fuck the game, fuck this team, and fuck you!"

His arm swept the desktop, clearing it in a flutter of flying papers. He stormed out the door.

Cole was halfway across the parking lot by the time Savannah made it out of the building. She ran after him, calling him, but he didn't stop.

A few cars were still scattered across the lot. At the north end, a group of students clad in Jackrabbits sweatshirts and ball caps stood around a battered pickup, smoking and laughing. One of them spotted Cole, reached into the bed of the truck, and came up with a football.

"Hey, Logan!" he yelled. "Kick Stanton's ass tonight, ya hear!" He tossed the ball to Cole, then held out his hands for a return pass.

Cole just looked at him. Then he turned his back on the man, cocked the ball over his shoulder, and let it fly. It sailed some sixty yards before slamming into the windshield of a Volkswagen parked clear across the lot. The glass shattered with a splintering crack.

Savannah couldn't believe what she'd just witnessed. When her eyes returned to Cole, he was already dropping his weight onto the kick start of his bike. He was out of the lot seconds later.

CHAPTER 10

BOOKER had just bludgeoned a toddler with a bicycle chain and was about to shoot a crack whore in the face with an assault rifle when the phone rang.

He hit Pause on the video game controller and picked up the receiver.

"Yeah?"

"Are you sitting down, bro?"

"Manny, where the hell are you? You were supposed to be here two hours ago."

"I told you I'd be over later."

"Well, get your ass over here now!"

"Booker, who is it?" called a voice from down the hall.

Booker covered the phone with his hand. "Go back to sleep, Mom!" Then to Manny: "I told you I need you here to help me juice."

"Well, after you hear what I got to tell you, we might want to up your dosage again."

"What are you talking about?"

"The Killington-Stanton game is still on . . . and Logan's playing."

"What? Fuck! How?"

"My cousin got the whole story."

"Elray?"

"No, my stepcousin Tina. She's a candy striper at the hospital over in Killington. She called a few minutes ago to order up some weed. I figured, long as I had her on the line, I'd ask if she had by chance heard any news on Logan."

"Are you crazy? What if she gets suspicious?"

"Don't worry, bro, I didn't give anything away. Besides, Tina's cool, she's family. Anyway, she told me that Logan never even checked into the hospital."

"We hack two fingers off the sonofabitch, and he doesn't even go to the hospital?"

"But it gets worse. Wait till you hear what Slim Freddy told her."

"Who the fuck is Slim Freddy?"

"Slim Freddy's this guy Tina's been dating off and on, goes to Killington High. He was hanging out in the Killington parking lot a while ago and saw Logan throw a football through a goddamn car windshield. Sure sounds to me like the guy can still play."

"Fuck. So we know all this for certain?"

"Trust me, this is all coming from solid sources. And I just heard on the radio that the school administrators have announced that the game is definitely still on."

Booker threw the game controller against the wall. "I told you we should have cut off Logan's foot. This is going to fuck up everything."

"Look, bro, I thought this whole thing through. Even if Logan plays tonight, he can't possibly be in top mental form. I'm sure Killington will lose tonight. But even if they pull off a win and we end up playing them in the district championship, that only means you'll get to kick Logan's ass all over again. Only this time it'll be on the playing field. That's better than all this sneaking around anyway, don't you think?"

"I can't risk it."

"You're not really scared of him stealing your thunder, are you?"

"Fuck no," Booker lied. "Shit! How the hell can Logan still throw that good with two missing fingers?"

There was a pause. "Listen, bro, there is just one other thing I need to tell you."

"What now?"

"I think I grabbed the wrong arm."

"What are you talking about?"

"This morning, when I pinned Logan's arm up so you could do the choppin', I think I grabbed his left arm."

"So?"

"Well, the thing is, Logan's right-handed."

"Goddamnit, Manny!" Booker picked up a cowboy boot and hurled it through the TV screen.

"Chill, bro. This is no time for a 'roid rage."

"I'm gonna 'roid rage your ass!"

"It ain't my fault! There was a lot of confusion, you know? I don't think so good in pressure situations. You didn't notice it either in the heat of the moment, did you? Logan was kicking up a storm."

"It might have helped if that mongoloid cousin of yours had helped us restrain him instead of standing in the background with his dick in his hand."

"For the last time, Elray's not a mongoloid. He's just thick."

"Well, what the hell are we supposed to do now?"

"We need a plan."

"No shit we need a plan!" As Booker looked around for something else to break, he was suddenly struck with an idea. "Wait a minute. Wait just a damn minute."

"What is it?"

"You know what we've got to do, Manny?"

"I'm listening."

"We're gonna have to break out the chain."

The line went silent.

"You don't mean . . . *the* chain."

"Shit, yeah. The chain'll fix all this."

"You're serious?"

"We got no other choice."

"Last time we brought out the chain, someone nearly got kilt."

"Exactly. And if we're lucky, someone will *nearly* get killed again. Know what I'm saying?"

"It's pretty risky, bro."

Booker considered this. The chain *was* risky and a difficult thing to pull off alone. "I'll tell you what I'm gonna do, Manny. I'm gonna bring the whole damn team into our operation."

"You think they'll do it?"

"Hell yeah, they'll do it. This is in their best interest as much as ours. No one on this team can afford anything less than total victory. Have you forgotten Brackenwall?"

"Booker, don't. Please."

"Don't what?"

"Don't say that word. We all agreed never to mention Brackenwall again. It's in the past. We buried it. I don't want to talk about that shit ever again."

"Fine. But I can promise you the memory of it will ensure the rest of the guys' participation. Trust me."

CHAPTER 11

JIMMY Hickham was the only head coach in the district who arrived at visiting fields with a fully dressed and padded team. He had been quoted as saying that dressing for away games in a home locker room carried a psychological advantage, offering players a home-field mentality during their pregame preparation. It was a custom that had begun early in his career and been sustained throughout.

It was now a quarter of six. Dusk had fallen, and the rainfall could be heard through the ceiling of the Killington High School locker room as the players suited up.

A few members of the team had gathered in a far corner of the room to swap stories as they finished dressing, taking advantage of the fact that Coach Hickham had yet to emerge from his office since the heated meeting with Cole Logan a few hours before. The particulars of the meeting had already sent a flood of rumors and conjecture throughout the Jackrabbits roster.

"Fucked is what we are," whispered Kevin O'Flannery, left offensive tackle. He squeezed his head through the hole of his shoulder pads. "Without Logan we're toast. For two months we've been riding on an offense geared around that arm of his. So where's that leave us? Everyone in the district knows we can't always rely on our defense."

"Eat me," said Phil Meekin, middle linebacker, who had just rounded the corner.

Shane Butler, strong-side receiver, put a finger to his lips. "You guys want to keep your voices down? If the coaches hear us jawing on, it's our asses."

"I'm just saying," Kevin continued, "we might really be screwed here. Logan says he wants to play, so why wouldn't Coach at least let him try? Now we're stuck with Teddy Smoot at QB. My sister can throw better than that limp-wristed pansy."

"Fuck you *and* your sister," Teddy Smoot said, joining the group. Wearing only a jockstrap and gym socks, the second-stringer looked more like a junior high towel boy than a varsity quarterback. "I don't need to hear that kind of talk right now."

Teddy had already thrown up twice since learning that he had ascended to the starting spot.

"Well, you're gonna hear it," said Sam Toony, tight end. He jammed a finger into Teddy's chest. "I didn't risk my neck all season catching passes across the middle just to get dog-assed in the final game because some freshman couldn't get me the ball. I sure as hell hope you got your head and ass wired together tonight."

"Don't worry about me," Teddy said. "Coach Tucker told me that Logan's gonna be with me on the sidelines, keeping things in check."

"My ass he will," Phil said. "Butler and I were sitting right here this afternoon, listening to the spat in the coach's office. No one knew we were in here, but we heard the whole damn thing. Last thing we heard Logan say before he stormed out the door was something along the lines of *fuck all this!*"

Teddy paled. "Well, where else would he go tonight?"

Shane shrugged. "Might go slip it to Kevin's sister for all we know."

Marvin Bumbgardner, deep safety, piped in. "I just don't under-stand why Coach would do this to us. Not if Logan says he wants to play."

"I bet y'all anything Logan ends up playing in the end," Shane said.

Marvin asked what made him so sure.

"'Cause my old man is not only the richest SOB in town, he's also head of the booster club. It's Dad's signature on the checks that supplement the coach's salary. And Dad agrees with all of us: the coach is making a big mistake benching Logan. Dad called the coach and told him so, too, said that Coach had better just watch his butt, 'cause the last thing he wants to do is get sideways of the booster club."

"That ain't no lie," said Dale Haggertay, right offensive tackle, who punctuated the remark with a fart.

"Anyway," Shane went on, "if Logan doesn't play, we're gonna have to keep the ball on the ground, which means that O'Dell Lamar better finally step up and play like he's got a pair."

The remark was met with a chorus of shushes.

"Come on, give O'Dell a break," Marvin hissed. "He's a good guy. He just needs a little time to develop, find his game. Hell, he's just a sophomore . . . and he's a tailback playing on a *passing* team."

Across the room a urinal flushed. Backs and receivers coach Doke Clements hollered, "Bus pulls out in five, boys! Fix your socks and strap your jocks!"

"Look, I wasn't meanin' to insult O'Dell," Shane Butler said, spreading tape over his shoelaces with a pair of hands that were sure to put him on the all-state list. "I was just saying it's high time he starts puttin' up some numbers. Sophomore or not, so far he's proven to be a lot of raw talent and speed that ain't done shit for this team."

O'Dell stepped around the corner behind Shane. The other players fell silent as the tailback trained cold eyes on the back of

Shane's head. It was clear he had heard every word. O'Dell was already in full dress, his jersey stretched tightly over his pads. Only the flawless black skin of his slick bald head was exposed.

"What's the matter?" Shane said, noting his teammates' expressions. "You fellas look like you've just seen a spook."

It was an unfortunate choice of words.

The brawl ignited quickly. O'Dell Lamar threw the first blow, swinging his helmet into Shane Butler's skull. After that it would be hard for anyone to remember exactly who had hit whom. Several players tried to break up the fight only to get involved in their own scuffles. Teddy Smoot cowered under a bench and covered his head with a thigh pad. Kevin O'Flannery went on a punching spree, hitting anyone who'd ever mentioned his sister. Marvin Bumbgardner flung bodies from his hulking frame like he was swatting flies. And through it all, O'Dell Lamar continued to jackhammer Shane Butler's face with a gloved fist.

Sixty seconds passed before the scrap ended, as quickly as it had begun, with the shriek of a coach's whistle. All went silent. The players froze. Every eye went to Hermie Tucker, who stood in front of the chalkboard, his whistle clenched between tobacco-stained lips.

"Knock off the goddamn ass-grabbin'!" he said.

The players were sluggish coming off the floor until Coach Hickham marched into the room seconds later and stepped up to the pile of players.

The players leaped to attention. Those who were standing quickly hoisted up those who were not.

"We got some kind of problem here, gentleman?" Hickham asked.

The question was met with a smattering of uninspired *no sirs!*

"Does it mean more to us now to hurt each other than to hurt our opponents?"

A few heads shook.

"What!" Hickham yelled. Every person jumped.

"No, sir!"

"I asked you a question!"

"No, sir!"

The coach circled around them, gazing into every pair of eyes as he passed. "Gentlemen, we have a job to do tonight. I can assure you that you will all achieve greater heights and suffer more crushing defeats in life than what is reflected by the score of tonight's game. But *tonight* it matters. This team matters, and this game matters. It is a night that will stay with you for the rest of your lives. So I want you men to think about what you want to carry off that field when the final whistle blows. Will you be satisfied knowing that you played with fear and hesitation? That you played carrying a grudge for fellow teammates . . . for your coach? Or are you prepared to walk off the field knowing that you played with pure hearts and minds?"

He stepped up to Shane Butler, who was still trying to stanch the blood streaming from his nose. "Mr. Butler, do you think we have players on this team performing beneath their potential?"

"No, sir!"

"I didn't think so. We are not a team of individuals, gentlemen. We are a unified body . . . a chain, held together by equal links. Is that understood?"

Some players nodded. Others locked elbows. Hands came up to teammates' shoulders. A wave of restlessness passed through the group.

"I know there is talk right now," Hickham continued. "I know there are those who may question the decisions I make for this team. To that I will only say that if anyone has a problem with any choice I make as your coach, he is free to walk out the door right now. That is all, gentlemen."

"Let's do it, boys!" yelled Phil Meekin, following the coach's exit.

The players broke into a frenzy of foot stomping and pad slapping.

"Who are we?" shouted Marvin Bumbgardner.

"*Jackrabbits, Jackrabbits . . . fight, fight, fight!*"

"I can't hear you!"

"*Jackrabbits, Jackrabbits . . . fight, fight, fight!*"

Again, Coach Tucker silenced them with his whistle. "All right, goddamnit, let's circle in for a prayer!"

The players knelt. Every head bowed; every hand found a shoulder. They spoke the Lord's Prayer as one humble and determined voice.

When it was finished Coach Tucker sent the team thundering toward the bus.

Cole Logan was nowhere in sight.

CHAPTER 12

THE sound of breaking glass brought Cole up off the mattress. He hadn't been sleeping, but it wasn't until he sat up that he realized darkness had fallen outside. He crushed out his cigarette and went to the door. Cracking it open a few inches, he listened down the darkened hall, but heard nothing.

"Mom? What was that?"

"Come here, boy."

He stepped into the living area. His mother sat on the sofa in a bathrobe and socks. Her bloodshot eyes stared through darkness at the glowing television. Last night's makeup streaked her face. Her hair was pulled into a ponytail, held with the rubber band that had wrapped the morning paper. A broken glass lay next to an open bottle of Southern Comfort on the coffee table.

"You okay?"

Her eyes cut away from *Judge Judy.* "Glass slipped."

Her speech was slurred. Cole didn't know how long she had been there; at least long enough to get through a third of the bottle. She hadn't been home when he'd returned several hours before. He had passed the time in his room, on his back, burning through

Marlboros and Metallica albums. Neither had done much to quell his anger.

"Come sit by me," she said.

"Not now."

"Why?"

"Just . . . not now."

"We don't talk anymore."

"Are you going out tonight, Mom?"

"No. I don't know. Maybe." She drank from the bottle, then fell heavily back into the sofa.

Cole spotted her car keys on top of the television and put them in his pocket. If she saw him do it, she made no protest. "Mom, I think you should go to bed."

"What time is it?"

"Early."

"Well, then, there's no reason to . . ." Her words trailed off on a yawn. Her chin fell to her chest.

Cole went to her. He took the cigarette from her hand, crushed it out, and lifted her from the sofa. "It's all right, Mom. You'll feel better tomorrow."

He carried her to her room and set her gently on the bed, placing a pillow beneath her head and pulling the comforter up to her chin.

"Wait," she said when he started to leave. She took hold of his gloved hand, paying no notice to the empty fingers. "It's Friday, isn't it?"

"Yes."

"Isn't there a game?"

"Yeah, Mom, there's a game."

Her eyes closed. "You do real good, then, Cole. You hear?"

"Yeah. I hear." He slipped from her grasp and moved to the door.

"Cole?"

"What is it?"

"Be sweet, boy."

"I will. Go to sleep now, Mom."

Lightning flashed, and he saw that she had already drifted off.

He stepped out of the room, shut the door, and went to retrieve the bottle.

He tucked it under his jacket on the way outside, where his bike was parked in the pelting rain.

CHAPTER 13

ELRAY, just to be safe, we're gonna put you in charge of the shotgun."

Elray grunted and tipped a bag of corn nuts into his mouth.

"Manny, are you crazy?" Booker said. "You wanna put Elray on the gun detail?"

"Elray can hit a gnat's ass from a hundred yards in high wind. I've seen him do it."

"Yeah, but . . ."

"Bro, don't worry about Elray, he's family."

Booker peered down the length of the rain-swept bridge in both directions. He turned a full circle in place, scanning the surrounding hills. Lightning lit up the sky across both sides of the ravine. "Let's go through this one more time, Manny. Where are you gonna be again?"

"I gotta set the barricade across the road once the bus passes by. You know, to block other cars from following. We gotta make sure no one sees nothin' until we're done with our business." Manny checked his watch. "Where the hell are the rest of the guys?"

"Don't worry, they'll be here," Booker said. "The whole team is coming. Now, you talked to Tommy Larkin, right?"

"Yeah, Tommy's all squared away." Manny pointed out headlights approaching up the road. "Car's coming."

Booker turned. "That Tommy?"

"No. Looks too small. We better take cover."

The three of them sprinted off the bridge and cowered on the embankment underneath until the car passed overhead.

When they returned topside Booker cinched the collar of his letterman jacket around his neck to keep the rain off his chest. It was coming down harder by the minute. He felt cold and anxious, and with a fresh dose of Hombre Muchacho coursing through his veins, he was starting to get irritable. He just wanted this to be over with soon so he could go looking for Nina, maybe charm his way into a hand job.

Manny handed the shotgun over to Elray, who took it greedily and tucked it under his orange slicker.

"Elray, you better be damn sure you don't shoot that thing at nothing that don't need to be shot at, you hear me?" Booker said.

Elray grunted and smiled around a mouthful of chomped-up corn nuts.

Manny lit a joint between cupped hands, then knelt to examine the chain they had stretched across the width of the bridge.

"You sure it'll do the trick?" Booker asked.

"This is the strongest chain on the market. They hang ship anchors from these fuckers. Trust me, it'll do the trick."

"And the truck?"

"Tommy is bringing his old man's Ford four-wheel-drive King Ranch Dooley. The sumbitch has three twenty-five under the hood. That enough muscle to set your mind at ease, bro?"

"So everything's set?"

"Bro, relax. Our plan is S-O-L-I-D, long as the rest of the guys get here quick." The reefer already had Manny spelling out his words. He looked at his watch again. "Where the hell are they? We're getting down to crunch time."

"They'll be here. They know if they don't, it's their ass."

Manny and Elray fell into step behind Booker as he walked the length of the bridge. Leightner Bridge was an unsupported truss built during the oil boom of the twenties to transport crude and rigging equipment across the Trebock River, a branch of the Trinity. An impressive undertaking at the time of its construction, it had long since begun to show its age. The truss was rusted and corroded, most of its girders hidden under a blanket of moss. For this reason, most commercial traffic had shifted to the new Highway 7, which crossed the Trebock nine miles upriver.

Booker hoped that Manny was right about setting up on Wilma Way instead of the highway. Though rough, rutted, and sparsely lit, the road was still the most direct route between the towns of Killington and Stanton.

Booker leaned over the railing. Water surged sixty feet below. "So no doubt this is the best place to do it, huh?"

"This is the right place, bro, sure as S-H-I-T. Think about it. It's in the middle of nowhere. No lights and no witnesses. Plus, our plan requires the strength of these steel beams. These babies are grade A, bro. Carnegie shit. I can't think of anything else that would be strong enough for our purpose."

Although Manny was making some good sense, Booker was still apprehensive. To take the edge off, he cracked open the beer he'd been carrying in his jacket pocket, drank it down in two gulps, and tossed the can over the railing.

"Give me another."

"Bro, you just juiced a pretty high dose less than an hour ago. You sure you wanna mix Hombre Muchacho with booze? Last time you did that you threw a pool table through a car windshield."

"Just give me the fuckin' beer."

Manny handed Booker another Shiner Bock from the six-pack strapped to his belt loop. He opened another one for himself.

Elray tucked the shotgun under his arm, unzipped his fly, and began to urinate off the bridge. With his free hand, he sipped from a can of cream soda.

"Now, supposing they do take the other route . . ." Booker said.

Manny sighed. "Bro, relax already. Trust me. If you want to take a football team to Stanton High from Killington High without fucking with the game traffic on Highway Seven, you head east on Wilma Way. It's the route the Jackrabbits have been taking for years." He looked at his watch. "Damn, the bus should be here any minute now. Kickoff is in less than an hour. Where are the guys?"

Another engine rumbled up the road. Headlights shone through the trees, approaching at a good clip. It sounded more like a speedboat than a car.

Manny smiled. "Come to D-A-D-D-Y."

The headlights washed over Elray's face. He zipped up midstream and finished the rest of his business in his overalls.

The vehicle swerved around the corner and they heard the first cackles of laughter from the boys piled into the bed of the truck. The mammoth Ford accelerated onto the bridge, then screeched to a halt in front of Booker. The KC lights above the cab switched on, looking like something out of a science fiction movie.

"Turn those fuckers off!" Booker yelled. "We don't want to attract any attention."

The lights switched off and twenty members of the Elmwood Badgers football team spilled out of the truck bed . . . along with a blizzard of empty beer cans.

"Whooo doggie!" one of the boys yelled.

"Where are those Killington pussies?" yelled another.

"Bring 'em on, baby!"

"Shit yeah!"

Booker saw more headlights approaching up the road—two cars, coming fast. "Shit, we got company!"

Tommy Larkin stepped down from his dad's truck and put a hand on Booker's shoulder. "It's fine, Book. That's just the rest of the team."

"Everyone's coming?"

"You got it, my man. No one wanted to miss this."

The two cars skidded in behind Tommy's truck. One was a yellow Mercedes, the other a silver Lexus—parent-bought cars. *Badgers Rule!* was painted in white shoe polish on the inside of the Lexus's windshield. Seven boys spilled out of each vehicle.

The scene was like a winner's circle celebration at the Daytona 500. Shaken beer cans exploded everywhere. Fist-pumps, high fives, and man hugs were exchanged all around. It was clear to Booker that his teammates had been attacking the booze with abandon.

Tommy Larkin, left tackle and co–defensive captain, came back to Booker. "Just tell me what I got to do, chief."

Booker downed his second beer, tossed it, belched, and gave Tommy a high five. "Manny briefed you already, right?"

"Yeah, man. But how do I know when to let her fly?"

"You hear Elray fire off that twelve-gauge, and you'll know it's time."

Elray pumped the shotgun and smiled.

Tommy Larkin nodded approvingly. "Fuckin' A, chief." He leaned in toward Booker's ear. "Say, you sure it's cool giving that ole boy a gun? I always thought there was somethin' the matter with him."

"Take it up with Manny," Booker said. "It's his family." He placed his fingers between his lips and whistled. "All right, listen up, assholes. I'll need all you sumbitches on my defensive squad in the bed of the truck for weight, so get your asses in there soon as I'm done talking. We don't have much time. The rest of y'all hop back in the cars, park over there in the trees, shut the fuck up, and enjoy the show. And goddamnit, keep quiet." He looked at Manny, who was dumping a bag of sand over the chain for camouflage. "You set?"

Manny flashed an okay signal. "We're good, bro."

"Now, when the deed is done," Booker said, "we gotta get the hell outta Dodge quick. We'll lay low for a while, then meet back at the Shake and Scoop around midnight, got it?"

"Yeah, baby!"

"Yeeehhhawww!"

"We're fixin' to kick us some Killington ass, baby!"

The boys dispersed to their assigned vehicles.

Manny moved off to his position fifty yards up the road, where he had hidden the barricade.

Elray checked the chamber of the shotgun, then climbed down to the embankment to await Booker's signal.

Booker retreated to his own post in the weeds near the foot of the bridge. He watched the Mercedes and Lexus creep into the woods. Tommy Larkin reversed the pickup off the bridge and headed into the trees across the road. When he was parked safely among the shadows, he killed the lights but kept the engine running as instructed. Then he stepped out of the truck, retrieved the open end of the chain, and hooked it to his trailer hitch.

Booker looked over at Elray, who sat with the shotgun across his lap, wrapping his mouth around a MoonPie. Booker snapped his fingers to get Elray's attention. Elray flashed a thumbs-up and smiled through marshmallow and chocolate.

Booker said a silent prayer that Elray wouldn't fuck up.

He felt pretty good about the situation now, and it wasn't just because of the beer, although that was helping.

He pressed himself lower into the weeds and waited for the first sign of the Jackrabbits' bus.

Hermie Tucker's cell phone vibrated against Hickham's hip. Coach Tucker flipped open the phone and smiled at the screen.

"I thought we outlawed cell phones on the team bus," Hickham said in jest.

Coach Tucker snapped the phone closed. "Little good-luck message from the wife."

"I remember those. You've got yourself a real sweetheart there, Coach Tucker."

Coach Tucker blushed as he plugged a wad of Levi Garrett into his cheek.

Hickham looked back at his players and wondered whether school buses were getting smaller, or high school boys were getting bigger. He thought that perhaps his tradition of dressing his team in their home locker room before road games might be doing more harm than good. The players were jammed into the seats like sardines with shoulder pads. But he was pleased to see that they looked calm and focused. Most sat with their heads back, eyes closed. The rest stared into the night through the rain-splattered windows.

Hickham came back around, closed his eyes, and listened to the dull moan of the engine.

"You thinking about Logan?" Coach Tucker asked minutes later.

"No."

"Bullshit. You're gnawing the inside of your cheek. You only do that when something's bothering you."

"Yeah. Maybe I was thinking about him."

"You think he'll show?"

"Doesn't matter if he shows now or not. The rule stands. He doesn't make the bus, he doesn't join the team on the field."

"Did you really expect him to show?"

"No," Hickham said. His eyes moved to the window. "Hell, I'm not sure I would have, either."

Coach Tucker tapped a fist on Hickham's knee. "Don't worry about it, Jimmy. I'm sure you did the right thing."

"Yeah? So you're the one."

"Relax. These things have a way of working out. Besides, I think Teddy Smoot is gonna fill in just fine as QB."

Teddy Smoot vomited into his helmet.

Seated in the back row of the bus, he had been struggling to hold his sickness down since they had pulled out of the high school parking lot. His nerves had finally gotten the best of him.

Shane Butler's head appeared over the seat in front of him. "Oh, this is perfect!"

"Who farted?" Phil Meeken whispered from a few rows ahead.

"It's not a fart. The freshman's back here pukin' his tits up. This is just what we need. Our quarterback's scared shitless!"

"You worry about your own self," Teddy spat. "I'll be fine."

"You better be, freshman."

"Bite me, Butler."

"Cut out the chatter back there," Coach Tucker barked from the front seat.

The boys went silent.

Shane Butler turned back around in his seat.

Teddy Smoot threw up again.

Cole popped the clutch and revved the throttle, raising the bike's front wheel off the pavement as he came out of a tight corner. He rode the wheelie for a quarter mile, came down, and punched the throttle harder. The speedometer needle passed fifty, then sixty.

When he got to the road marker he was looking for, he veered off Wilma Way and rode onto a wooded trail. It was a trail he could ride blindfolded—one he had first tackled on his Schwinn in grade school. What was usually a sandy path was now soft mud, slick as ice. Dirt clots pelted his chest. Stray tree limbs whipped his legs. He fishtailed up the narrow single-track until it broke through the tree line and came to a dead end where the ravine opened up at the edge of a sheer cliff. He squeezed the brake and swung his rear wheel around, stopping just inches from the edge. A fan of mud sailed toward the river far below.

He killed the engine and opened the visor of his helmet. Cold rain stung his face.

He gazed down at the water. The residual vibration of the engine tingled his extremities and he felt at peace for the first time all day. Since childhood, this had been his favorite place—the place he went when he wanted to get away, to think, to be alone.

To drink.

He came off the bike and sat at the cliff's edge, dangling mud-caked boots over the side. He took the bottle out from under his jacket and knocked back a long swig. The warm liquor stung his throat and burned even more as it trickled down his chest.

It tasted great and felt even better.

He huddled against the cold wind and watched the white foam churning below. The storm had already brought up the water level considerably.

Lightning flashed, revealing Leightner Bridge about a hundred yards upriver. He smeared the mud from the face of his watch. The bus should be passing by any time now, if it hadn't already. He hoped he hadn't missed it. He wanted to offer a toast to the Jackrabbits as they headed off to their slaughter without him.

He took another drink, and his mind went back to the conversation in Hickham's office. He still couldn't understand why Coach wouldn't at least let him suit up, let him play one offensive series to prove that he could still do it. Put him on a field in front of three thousand people, with the adrenaline pumping and the season on the line, and the last thing he would have been thinking about was a couple of missing fingers.

He took off the glove and made a fist with the remaining fingers. There was no pain; the mobility was completely intact. He punched the fist into his other palm. Still no pain. Whatever Mona had done to him was nothing short of a miracle.

He stood and looked upriver. Still no sign of the bus.

He took another drink and waited.

Booker was fixin' to get pissed.

The bus was past due now. The wet ground had saturated his clothes. He was cold and stiff. He felt a 'roid rage coming on, and there wasn't a damn thing around that he could hit except for Elray, and he still needed Elray conscious.

Kickoff was in forty-three minutes. He was starting to believe that Manny had been mistaken. Perhaps because of the storm the bus had taken the long route to Highway 7 after all.

Then what?

Then all this would be for nothing.

Then he'd look like a dumb shit in front of the guys.

Then Cole Logan would get another chance to play football.

Fuck.

He seethed at the thought as another set of lights appeared up the road. The headlights were spread far apart and looked high off the ground.

This could be it. *Had* to be it.

The vehicle lumbered around the corner, giving Booker his first glimpse of bright yellow steel.

This was *definitely* it.

The bus accelerated out of the final turn leading up to the bridge. *Good. The more speed, the better.*

Booker figured Manny should have set the barricade behind the bus by now.

Across the road, Tommy Larkin revved the pickup's engine—the signal that he saw the bus, too, and was ready. Everything was set. The bus was only an eighth of a mile up the road now.

Booker turned toward the embankment to give Elray the signal.

Elray was gnawing on a strip of Laffy Taffy and staring at the sky.

"Elray! Pssst! This is it!"

But Elray was lost in his own thoughts.

The bus was seventy-five yards from the bridge now.

"Elray!" Booker snapped his fingers.

Fifty yards.

"Elray! Snap out of it, you dumb fuck!"

Elray did. He turned to Booker, gave a thumbs-up, and set the shotgun at his shoulder.

Twenty-five yards.

The bus was still accelerating.

Fifteen.

Booker raised a hand out of the weeds.

Ten yards.

Five.

Booker slammed his palm to the ground. *"Now!"*

Elray fired the shotgun.

Tommy Larkin hit the gas. The pickup wailed. Its tires spun to find purchase in the mud. The truck finally shot forward, lifting the chain off the pavement and out of the concealing sand. Pulled taut between the pickup and the truss, the chain rose straight across the bus's path.

The bus driver slammed the brakes. The wheels locked and the vehicle went into a skid. It was still moving at full speed when the chain slashed its grille. The chain kept cutting, like a fillet knife slicing down the length of a trout.

Frightened screams rang out of the truck bed as the bus dragged Tommy's pickup toward the cliff. They were less than two feet from the edge when the chain snapped in an explosion of flying steel.

Now free of the pickup's weight, the bus lurched forward onto the bridge, completely out of control. It was perpendicular to the road by the time it crashed into the truss. Steel girders snapped and fell like dominoes for twenty yards before the bus screeched to a stop midway across the ravine.

Its front half hung in open air off the side of the bridge.

Another girder snapped, pitching the bus out even farther. The rear wheels came off the ground. Both halves of the vehicle hung suspended, balancing over the edge.

The engine sputtered and died. The wheels creaked to a stop.

Booker heard screams and ran onto the bridge, his heart racing.

It had happened so fast that he could hardly take it all in, but by all accounts, everything had gone off perfectly. The crash had been spectacular!

He stopped about seventy-five feet short of the bus to avoid being seen. Even at a distance, the damage to the vehicle was evident. Wheels were bent on twisted axles. The bus's front end hemorrhaged fluid from a gaping wound of warped metal and loose hoses. Half of the rear bumper had peeled away and become twisted under the rear axle.

Arms waved out of broken windows. Upended seats had pinned players against the glass. Other windows were white webs of shattered glass, many of them marked with sprays of red. Through the wind Booker heard painful groans, frightened curses, and cries for help.

A smile tugged the corners of his mouth. He hoped one of the screams belonged to Cole Logan. With any luck, Logan had lost another finger or two, maybe even an arm.

Elray appeared beside him, the strip of Laffy Taffy in one hand and the smoking 12-gauge in the other. Booker felt so good about things, he decided to hold off asking why Elray had fired the fucking signal shot into his face instead of straight into the air as instructed. Booker reached up and touched his birdshot-riddled cheek. Fortunately he was so high on booze, adrenaline, and Hombre Muchacho that he couldn't feel the pain yet.

There would be plenty of time to kick Elray's ass later. Right now he just wanted to relish the moment.

Behind him, his teammates piled out of the pickup, hugging one another and jumping around in drunken elation.

Booker started toward them, but stopped when he heard metal creak again.

Turning back, he saw the bus pitch forward once more and fall nose-first into the raging water below.

Elray then spoke the first words Booker had ever heard him say: "I don't think that was part of the plan."

Mona looked up from her game program with a start.

Seated in the top row of the Stanton High football stadium, she had just been struck with a strange feeling—a sharp prickling at the base of her spine.

Something in the cosmos had changed.

Dark forces had awoken.

"Holy shit!"

The bottle fell from Cole's hand. He swept rain from his eyes and looked upriver again.

It had all happened so fast—the shotgun blast, the roar of the pickup, the crash.

For a moment he had thought everything might be okay. By some miracle the bus had managed to stop before going over the side of the bridge.

Then, in the next instant, it was gone.

"Holy fucking shit!"

He leaned out over the cliff. The bus had hit the water front-end first, then righted itself, wheels down. It was moving downriver now, toward him, pitching back and forth against the rocks like driftwood.

Cole jumped onto the bike. If he hurried down to the main road, he could head off the bus farther downriver. Then he could . . . what? He'd have to figure it out when he got there.

He kicked the starter. The engine fired up immediately . . . then gurgled and died. He kicked it again to no effect.

"Shit!"

He ran back to the cliff. The screams were clearer now, closer. The bus was almost even with him.

There was no time to think.

He took three steps back, sprinted forward, and leaped off the edge.

His legs buckled like twigs when he hit the water. Liquid filled his lungs as he plunged deeper and deeper. He finally made it back to open air coughing and sputtering. He thrashed his limbs to keep his head above the surface, catching only intermittent glimpses of the bus, fast approaching. Fighting the current, he swam toward midstream, trying to reach it before it passed.

The current changed direction and rammed him against the blunt edge of a boulder. When he came back up, the bus was right over him. He lunged away to avoid being plowed over. A wall of water blocked his view as the vehicle moved past. He reached out blindly and took hold of an open window. He held on as the bus dragged him along.

A hand shot out of the window and seized Cole's arm. Then a face appeared, the eyes wide with terror.

"Help me, Logan! Oh, God, help me!"

It was O'Dell Lamar. Cole recognized the shaven head, now spilling blood from a deep gash at the crown.

Behind O'Dell was a scattering of black-uniformed men, trapped under bus seats that had been ripped from their bolts. The players were twisted into impossible positions. Their limbs flailed as they fought to keep their heads above the rising water. Their cries were relentless. Helmets, gloves, towels, sweatbands, bandages, tape rolls, and play charts floated all around.

Looking down the length of the bus, Cole saw other players, like O'Dell, whose shoulder pads hindered their escape through the windows. Only their heads fit through the small openings. Coach

Tucker, at the front of the bus, was prevented escape by his girth alone.

The bus succumbed quickly to the weight of the water. Its windows were now only inches above the surface.

"Please, Logan!" O'Dell cried. He yanked on Cole's arm with both hands. "Help me! Help me!"

Cole drove his shoulder against the current, planting his feet on the side of the bus for leverage. He pulled with everything he had, but the effort was futile.

"Your pads!" Cole screamed.

"Help me, please . . ."

"Your shoulder pads! You have to get out of your pads!"

O'Dell just shook his head in panic. "Help me, Cole! Help!"

The windows fell below the surface. A wave of water rushed into the vehicle. O'Dell fought to keep his head above the waterline, but the bus sank too quickly. The tailback went under. Still, his grip held firmly on Cole's arm.

Within seconds the roof was submerged.

Cole squirmed to break free but couldn't. He was pulled under. The bus sank deeper as Cole thrashed feverishly at its side. A gurgling scream depleted his lungs of his last breath.

Total darkness had surrounded him by the time O'Dell's hands finally went limp and fell away.

Now free, Cole clawed for the surface, sucking in water with every stroke. Seconds passed. When he was sure he couldn't go any farther, lightning flashed, revealing the surface only a few feet above him. Complete panic spurred his limbs into a single final stroke.

He broke the surface.

Fighting to stay conscious, he rolled onto his back. His lungs burned. His strangled coughs purged water from his chest.

He gave himself over to the river, floating listlessly at its mercy.

The rapids eventually subsided where the river peeled into a gradual bend. Minutes later the drift steered Cole toward the bank. When he felt earth beneath him, he turned onto his stomach and crawled the rest of the way onto the flat sandbar.

The last thing he saw before blacking out was a lone figure rushing toward him along the bank.

CHAPTER 14

WE'RE all gonna get the chair for this!" Tommy Larkin said, squeezing a fistful of his hair in each hand.

Booker put a finger to his lips. "Shh. No, we're not! Not if we play our cards right. And keep your voice down, you dumb shit. Act cool!"

"Act cool? We just murdered an entire goddamn football team! I thought Manny said the bridge was sound . . . remember, Carnegie and all that shit!"

"Kiss my ass, Tommy," Manny said. "I knew exactly what I was doing. It wasn't my fault that bus driver had no control over his vehicle. He must have been a damn maniac."

"Manny's right," Booker said. "That fucker must have been crazy."

Tommy was hearing none of it. "They drowned, you idiots! We just drowned forty people!"

"And that's another thing," Booker said. "What kind of assholes wear full pads on a damn school bus? It's no wonder they drowned. You wanna talk about a safety hazard . . ."

"We're all gonna fry! Fuckin' fry . . ."

Booker took Tommy by the shoulders. "Tommy, get a grip, man. Stop being such a pussy."

Tommy shook free of Booker's grasp and kicked a beer can across The Shake and Scoop parking lot.

"It wasn't our fault they drowned," Booker said. "Those Jackrabbits were taking way too many risks in getting to that ball game."

"You told us you just wanted to stop the bus," Tommy said. "Put a little scare into the Jackrabbits and prevent them from making it to the Stanton High game. You never mentioned anything about killing anyone!"

What Tommy said was true. Their plan had never actually included the bus going off the bridge. That part had been an accident. But now that the sons of bitches were dead, Booker knew he had to prevent his teammates from coming unglued.

"You're right, Tommy," he said. "But the most important thing is we're a team and we back each other up—always. And let's not forget who died . . . we're talking the Killington Jackrabbits here."

The statement extracted halfhearted grunts of agreement from some of the boys. Wet and shivering in the biting wind, most of them were still huddled on top of the empty beer cans in the bed of Tommy's truck. The rest were pacing around, smoking cigarettes, and trying to either sober up or get drunker. They looked like combat soldiers who had just come out on the losing end of an ambush. Most of them were still in various states of shock and had scarcely said a word since the moment the bus fell from the bridge.

Booker eyed the frightened faces before him. "Look, guys, we did what we had to do. Any of you fellas want to experience another Brackenwall?" All eyes came up. Booker held their stare. "That's what I thought. Now, what's done is done. So let's cut this crybaby shit."

"You better be right, Flamont," Tommy said. "I didn't sign up for this shit just to spend the rest of my life behind bars!"

Booker shushed him again. "Keep your voice down! Nobody is

going to prison. Let's all just stay calm; there are people around."
Booker glanced over both shoulders. "It's important that we look like
we're just out having a good time. Somebody laugh or something."

The order was met with blank stares.

Manny said, "Not to change the subject, bro, but what's up with
your acne? Looks like it's bleeding all over your face."

"It's not my acne," Booker said. "That cousin of yours, ace
sniper that he is, somehow managed to miss the goddamn sky."

"What do you mean?"

"I mean his signal shot hit me in the fuckin' face!" Booker
touched his tender cheek. Now that the Shiner Bock/Hombre
Muchacho buzz had worn off, the wounds stung like hellfire.

Manny stepped in for a closer look. He shrugged. "Well, one
good thing about your acne; it hides the pellet wounds. That's in
our favor. It's important you don't tell anybody about getting shot
in the face. That could raise suspicion. Anyway, you'll heal up in no
time. Ain't that right, Elray?"

Elray nodded and bit into his corn dog.

"So what's the plan now, genius?" Tommy asked.

"It's like this," Booker said. "After you guys got out of there, me
and Manny and Elray went about covering our tracks. Literally. We
picked up all the busted chain links and we smoothed over the tire
tracks from your daddy's truck. Now seeing as how all the witnesses
are sitting tight at the bottom of the river, the whole deal will look
like an accident just like we planned. So y'all see now? Everything's
cool."

"Cool?" Tommy threw his arms up, exasperated. "Are you kidding? Did you cover up your footprints, too?"

"Yes, Tommy, for chrissake. We stepped over every one of them,"
Booker said.

"Oh, Jesus!"

"Calm down," Manny said. "All we got to do now is come up
with an alibi."

"Right. We need an alibi." Booker paced for a minute. "How 'bout this: we were quail hunting."

"At night?" Manny asked.

"In the rain?" Tommy intoned.

"I'm not so sure our alibi should involve guns," Manny said. "Especially seein' as how Elray shot you in the face."

A car turned into the parking lot. Headlights bathed the group.

"Everyone act happy," Booker said through a false grin.

No one did.

The car passed by without incident.

It was just past midnight. The rain had let up to a soft drizzle, but the wind was still gusting and the temperature hovered just above freezing. News of the bus crash had spread quickly throughout the region. Television and radio bulletins ran on every station. The streets were virtually empty, save for emergency vehicles. Distant sirens screamed across town in every direction. Even The Shake and Scoop drive-in, usually a hot spot on Friday nights, was a ghost town except for the odd customer and a handful of employees.

"I got it," Booker said, snapping his fingers. "We'll just say we were having a study session for school."

"You really don't understand the strategy behind this whole alibi thing, do you?" Tommy said. "The idea is to make it actually *believable*."

"Come on, fellas, this ain't that hard." Manny said. He asked who had parents out of town. Two of the players raised their hands. Manny pointed to Dougie Scagnetty.

"Dougie, you'll do best 'cause you don't have any siblings. So here's our story: we all went over to Dougie's for pizza and Xbox."

"I only got Nintendo."

"What's the damn difference?" Booker asked.

"No, Booker, that's important," Manny said. "We need to keep our details straight. So we went to Dougie's for pizza and *Nintendo*. I'll call in a pizza delivery right now. That'll leave a paper trail, which is good. 'Lotta criminals get the chair 'cause they don't have an alibi with a paper trail. Now, I say we all just head over to Dougie's, eat a pie, play some Shootout and wait for this whole thing to blow over. And remember, anyone asks, we spent this Halloween at Dougie's, resting up for the big game next week."

Booker smiled. "That sounds good. You boys go and do that."

"Where the hell are you going?" Tommy asked.

"I got my own alibi. Her name is Nina Hernandez."

CHAPTER 15

KIP set his fork down on the plate. "You gonna keep blubbering all morning, Bernice? I mean, I'm heartbroke, too, but I *am* trying to eat here."

"I can't help it." Bernice wiped tears from her cheek as she topped off Kip's coffee. "It's just too awful to even think about."

The trucker rush at the Buttered Bean Diner, which usually appeared with the sun, was still a half hour away. It was coming up on 5 a.m., and Kip, Bernice, and Don Paul still had the place to themselves.

Kip offered Bernice a wadded bandanna to dry her tears with, then he subtly dabbed some moisture from his own eyes with a napkin. "Still can't believe it happened," he said. "What a waste. Just an awful damn waste."

Don Paul nodded. "Yeah . . . best football season in Jackrabbits history, pissed away in an instant."

Bernice slapped Don Paul on the back of the head. "He's not talking about the damn season, you insensitive ass. What about those boys' very lives?"

"I'm just sayin' is all! Geez, good morning to you, too. Say, where's my patty sausage anyway?"

Bernice ignored him. Turning to Kip, she asked, "What do they even do in this kind of situation?"

Kip leaned back in his seat, thought about it for a minute. "Well, I suppose they'll just consider it a forfeit, give the win to Stanton High."

Bernice beat a fist on the counter. "For chrissake, Kip, you're no better than Don Paul. I'm not talking about the football season!"

"Hell, woman, we know that! Can't you see we're as tore up about those boys dyin' as you? It's just . . . well, we all grieve different. Maybe it's just easier for me and Don Paul to deal with it in terms we're comfortable with."

Bernice allowed his words to sink in. "You're right, Kip. My apologies to both of you. I just . . ." She collapsed onto a stool at the counter. "I just don't know how we'll ever recover from this. I don't think we ever will."

Kip slid his half-eaten eggs away and lit a Winston. "I'll tell you one thing: that wrecked bridge *was* a damn sight to behold."

"You mean you went there?" Bernice asked. "You saw it?"

"We both did," Don Paul said. "Why do you think we're here so early, smelling like a damn sewer? Been knee deep in that river all night."

"What were you doing there?"

"I've been a card-carrying member of the volunteer fire department for twenty-three years," Don Paul said. "Kip for seventeen. We both got the call on our cell phones while we were sitting there in the stadium, wondering where the hell the Jackrabbits were, just like everyone else. By the time the team was a half hour late, some school officials decided they'd best go looking for 'em. Didn't take them long to discover the busted-up bridge. The VFD had Kip and me on the horn before they even made the announcement over the stadium

PA. I figure we were the first ones in that stadium that knew what happened. Kip and I got to the crash site about twenty minutes later."

"It must have been just ghastly, seein' those poor boys pulled outta that river."

The men exchanged a look.

"Uh, nobody got pulled from the river, honey."

"What? Kip, don't tell me they're just gonna leave them down there."

"Not indefinitely. But according to the news, last night's flash flood was the worst these parts have seen in a half century. Said it dumped nine inches of rain in less than an hour. The banks where the bus finally sank are pretty steep, and right now they're too soft to get the necessary equipment in. Pulling a body from a river is one thing; pullin' forty of 'em out of a sunk school bus is another."

Don Paul lit a Salem. "They even brought in a tropigaffer."

"Topographer," Kip corrected.

"Yeah, right, one a them. This fella said the bus went down in the deepest section of river within fifty miles. Talk about your damn luck."

"They sent a couple of frogmen down there to inspect things, see if they might be able to get some of the kids out," Kip said.

"And?"

"They said it was such a tangled, gory mess down there, there was no way they could get *any* of 'em out."

"But why?"

Kip looked at her. "You really want me to paint a picture for you?"

Bernice shuddered. "So what did you do there all night?"

"I smoked mostly," Don Paul admitted. "There wasn't a whole lot that *could* be done. We're just gonna have to wait a few days until the water recedes. Forgive my sayin' so, but if those boys look bad now, imagine how they're gonna look after a few days underwater?

There's alligator gar the size of bathtubs in that river. It'll be a god-damn buffet. Say, how 'bout that patty sausage, Bernice?"

Bernice had quit smoking fourteen years ago. She took a Winston from Kip's pack without bothering to ask, lit it, sat back down, and wiped away another tear. "It's just the worse thing I ever heard of. Such a terrible accident."

"I'm not so sure," Kip said, thumbing the rim of his cup.

"What do you mean?"

He looked at her. "Nothing. Forget it."

"Aw, go on, Kip, might as well tell her."

Kip sighed. "Well, we were down on the bank at the base of the ravine all night. We weren't allowed up on the bridge 'cause they had it blocked off for law enforcement personnel only. Sheriff Clark had near enough his whole force up there for a good while. When they finally came down to the bank, I overheard the sheriff talking to one of his deputies about footprints. *Lots* of footprints up there near the bridge."

"Sneaker footprints, like the teenagers wear," Don Paul added. "And tell her about the shell, Kip."

"I was just getting to that. I also heard Curtis say something about a spent shotgun shell lying around. Also some fresh candy bar wrappers, stuff like that. Signs of a recent human presence."

"What are you trying to say?" Bernice asked.

"I'm saying I think the police suspect foul play. What's more, apparently someone called in to report that they had tried to cross the bridge around the same time that the crash happened, but found the road barricaded off about a quarter mile short of the ravine. The highway department claims they hadn't blocked off any roads within a ten-mile radius of that area. You ask me, it sounds like someone didn't want any witnesses around, don't it?"

"Yeah, but they got one, don't they?" Don Paul winked.

"Appears so," Kip concurred.

Bernice motioned for him to elaborate.

"Cole Logan," Kip said.

"What about Cole Logan?"

Don Paul told her about Cole being found unconscious on the riverbank.

"My god, what was he doing there?"

"That's the first thing Curtis and his deputies wanted to know," Kip said. "Seemed a little suspicious, seeing as how red-assed Logan had been about being benched, and how he had made quite a scene in the coach's office yesterday afternoon, telling everyone where they could stick their football team. Add to that the fact that Logan has a prior criminal record . . ."

". . . and was piss drunk when they found him . . ."

". . . and it makes sense that johnny law thought some hard questions were in order."

"They don't really suspect that Cole would do anything to harm his teammates?" Bernice said. "Criminal record or not, surely they don't think he's a murderer."

Kip shook his head. "Not anymore. Quite the opposite, in fact. Turns out the boy's a hero . . . or at least he tried his damnest to become one."

"You lost me," Bernice said. She crushed her cigarette into Kip's egg yoke.

"Well, this is all hearsay, but it seems that for whatever reason, Cole Logan was at that river last night and actually saw the bus go off the side of the bridge."

"But that's not all," Don Paul said. "We heard Logan pulled a Geronimo right off the goddamn cliff, trying to save everyone!"

"You're kidding!"

"That's the word," Kip said. "The boy swam right through the rapids and did all he could to save his teammates, only to have the bus nearly take him down with it."

"I'll be damned!" Bernice said. "Wait . . . you mean the cops believed his story? I thought Logan was their primary suspect?"

"Not for long. They were able to corroborate Logan's story pretty quick."

"How?"

"Think about it."

"I don't see how they could," Bernice said, "unless there was *another* witness."

"Bingo," Kip said. "But not just any witness. A *survivor*. The only one who got off the bus alive."

"Right," Don Paul said. "The only one not wearing pads . . . or not too fat to fit through the window."

Bernice thought about it. Her eyes widened. "You mean the coach?"

Kip nodded. "Jimmy Hickham his own self."

"I don't believe it!"

"Is this a crazy town, or what?" Don Paul said.

No one answered the question. The three of them were already caught up in their own thoughts.

Kip stirred circles in his coffee.

Bernice lit another Winston.

Don Paul went to take a leak.

On the jukebox Marty Robbins sang about a Mexican girl in El Paso.

No one spoke until Don Paul returned from the john and asked again for his patty sausage.

CHAPTER 16

THE Killington Sheriff's Office had buzzed all night with deputies coming and going and fielding calls from emergency services, reporters, lawyers, and worried friends and relatives.

Almost eleven hours had passed since the bus crash. Curtis had been on the move from the moment he'd gotten the initial call. He'd spent most of the night on the radio—ordering, delegating, questioning, and cursing. He had drunk enough coffee to float a tugboat and had chewed fifteen matchsticks down to their sulfur tips.

After leaving the scene at the river around 3 a.m., he had gone to the hospital to check on Cole. He'd found the quarterback standing in the waiting room, cursing the staff and refusing to be admitted. Curtis had been astonished by the turnaround in Cole's condition.

At the riverside, Cole's body temperature had measured 95 degrees—a level the sheriff was sure had dulled the young man's intellect. Cole's account of the crash and attempted rescue sounded like the ramblings of a person in shock. His mumblings had been almost incoherent. Even after Coach Hickham—whose disposition hadn't been much better—precisely corroborated Cole's account, the sheriff still found the story impossible to swallow.

Cole's story still hadn't changed by the time Curtis made it to the hospital. His demeanor, however, had altered dramatically. He was completely lucid and wound up tight as a drum.

Curtis had tried to send Cole home, but the quarterback refused, insisting instead on being taken to the sheriff's office to see how the authorities were following up on his testimony.

Curtis had finally agreed to bring both Cole and Hickham into his office for further discussion. It went against his better judgment, given what the men had been through, but he took a chance. Thirty-one years on the force had taught him that witness testimony usually proved most beneficial when taken as soon after an incident as possible.

It was just past dawn now. Curtis had finished taking the men's deposition and was now occupied with trying to simmer Cole down. He had just told Cole for the third time to sit down when the door opened.

Savannah poked her head into the room.

"Answer my question, Curtis!" Cole scowled at the sheriff from his position against the far wall.

"I don't have to answer a damn thing I don't feel you need to know at this time."

"That's bullshit. Just tell me what you know!"

"Cole, for the last time, either sit down or I'm taking you to a cell to cool off."

Cole turned away in a huff.

"Can I come in?"

Curtis turned to Savannah. Tension fell from his tight shoulders. "Of course, honey, please." He seemed glad for the intrusion. Unshaven and glassy-eyed, the sheriff hardly resembled the man Savannah had hidden from in the woods the day before.

She shut the door behind her and raised the cardboard tray in her hands. "Thought maybe y'all could use some coffee."

Curtis nodded. "That's real good of you, thanks. I think we were just finishing up in here, anyway. Isn't that right, Cole?"

Savannah set the coffee on the sheriff's desk. No one made a move for it.

Her father sat slumped in a chair next to the water cooler, looking as haggard as she'd ever seen him. Miraculously, he had suffered only superficial cuts and bruises in the crash. Hours before, she had heard him tell the sheriff that he'd escaped through a window only seconds after the bus hit the water, and was pinned against a cluster of rocks until he finally managed to swim away. It seemed that his daily predawn walks around the high school track had served him well. The rest of his coaching staff, with their fast food diets and bulging stomachs, had not fared so well.

Savannah knew she'd entered a hornets' nest, but she was glad to be back in the room. Two hours before, she had been excused from the questioning, against much protestation on her part. Curtis and her father had hoped to spare her hearing any gory details. It had been a brutal interim. She had been forced to pass the time with her ears glued to the local radio station and her eyes on her laptop.

Before anyone could excuse her again, she slipped off her backpack and crossed to Cole. He still wore his wet clothes and smelled like river water. His eyes were sunken, his hair matted with mud. A small cut above his eyebrow had been tended to with a clear salve and a butterfly bandage.

"Thought you could use these." She pulled from the backpack a pair of her father's jeans and a flannel shirt. Cole took only the shirt without so much as a nod of thanks.

Savannah moved to her father and handed him a clean sweatshirt.

They all listened to the clock tick as Savannah tried not to watch Cole change his shirt. His chest was lean and taut, much less muscled than she would have thought. The skin from his neck to his waist was marked with cuts and scrapes, but nothing too deep.

There was a tattoo on his left pec—a naked woman with angel wings riding a motorcycle out of a cloud.

Savannah was still staring when Cole closed the last button. He looked up. Their eyes met for a split second before she looked away.

Curtis cleared a raspy throat. "Well, I think we're all done here. Just know that I've got every badge on my force working on this. We're gonna get to the bottom of it as quick as possible."

"Hold on, Curtis," Hickham said. "I think I'd like you to answer Cole's question. You've heard our side. Now it's your turn. What kind of leads do you have?"

"Jimmy, please understand, we have to follow procedure."

"Curtis, my starting quarterback was brutally assaulted, and the rest of my team and coaching staff are at the bottom of a river. I think we're both entitled to some answers."

A long stare down ensued. Curtis went to lock the door, then returned to the front edge of his desk. "Okay. I'll tell you what I can on two conditions: First, nothing I'm about to say leaves this room. If there's one thing that will throw a wrench into any investigation it's the wrong person saying the wrong thing at the wrong time. One slipup and even an open-and-shut case can be overturned in court for the slightest breach in proper procedure. Second, I don't want anybody acting on this except my men, who are all working under my authority. You want justice to be served, you just let us do our jobs. Is that understood?"

Hickham nodded.

Cole merely shifted his weight and crossed his arms over his chest.

"All right, then." Curtis slipped a fresh matchstick into his mouth. "We know that this wasn't an accident. A bus crash like that—especially following the attack on Cole and all that business at the pep rally—clearly there's some foul play involved. Taking into account your testimony and what we found at the scene, it looks like some kind of industrial-strength chain was set in the bus's path. We found a few busted links scattered around the scene. We believe it was meant to disable the bus violently, but we can't prove that they meant to send it off the bridge. Looks to us like a harebrained prank gone terribly wrong."

"And the pickup?" Hickham said. "I saw a Ford through the bus window, a blue one."

"I saw it, too." Cole said. "Whose was it?"

Curtis didn't answer.

"Come on, Curtis, the thing was a monster," Cole said. "A big four-wheel-drive pickup with a lift kit and tires four feet high. You said there were tracks. There can't be too many vehicles like that around."

Curtis held Cole's stare. "Before I answer anything else about the bridge, what say we do a little quid pro quo? How 'bout you tell me what really happened at your house yesterday morning."

"I thought I did that."

"Cut the crap, Cole. What are you hiding?"

It was a question Savannah wanted answered as well. She'd suspected all along that he was withholding information about the attack.

Cole lowered his chin but said nothing.

Curtis waited. "Cole, I can't help you unless you help—"

"They told me not to play, all right? They said that if I didn't find a reason to sit out, they would give me one."

Curtis came off the desk. "What did you say to them?"

"I told them to go to hell. Then they chopped off my fingers."

"Is that all?"

Cole raised his head. "They also said that if I didn't stay away . . . they would hurt the rest of the team."

Savannah read the torment on his face. "Surely you don't blame yourself for what happened on that bridge, Cole," she said.

Cole looked over at her. "I wouldn't call my little speech at the pep rally standing down, would you?" His eyes returned to Curtis.

"So there it is. I was afraid that if I mentioned the threats to anyone, the game would be called off. If it *had* been called off, none of us would have been at that river last night. Whoever did this, whether they thought I was on that bus or not, still wanted to make sure that the Jackrabbits didn't take the field last night."

"And you really have no idea who attacked you?"

"Curtis, it doesn't take a genius to suspect that it was someone connected to one of our opponents in some way. Stanton High? Elmwood Heights? Who knows? I'm pretty sure they were my age, high school guys. As for who it was, your guess is as good as mine." He told the sheriff it was his turn to talk now.

Curtis slowly sat back down and lifted a file folder from his desk. "The ones who caused that bus crash didn't do a hell of a lot to cover up the crime. In fact, they were downright stupid. We found footprints all over the place, at least twenty, twenty-five sets of them. With the exception of a few, they all had the same tread pattern. Leads one to wonder what kind of group wears the same type of athletic shoes."

"A football team," Savannah said.

Curtis nodded, then read from the file. "We believe that pickup you saw is registered to one Edmond Larkin, father of Tommy Larkin—one of the captains of the Elmwood Badgers."

Cole threw his wet T-shirt against the wall. "The fuckin' Badgers! Figures."

"It was their off-week," Curtis said. "They were the only team not scheduled to play last night."

It was a conclusion Savannah had come to on her own over the past two hours. Combining Internet research with what Kip Sampson had told her about the Badgers, she had boned up quickly on the subject of local high school football. The fact that Elmwood wasn't scheduled to play last night made it easy to suspect their involvement.

"We all know how well the Badgers have played this season,"

Curtis said. "I'm guessing that with all the media attention they're receiving, and the interest their players are getting from big-time college scouts, some of those boys didn't want to risk having to meet the Jackrabbits in the district game. 'Course, we can also take into account the bad blood between the two towns."

Hickham crossed the room. His pensive eyes stared distantly out the window.

"What is it, Dad?"

"This Tommy Larkin. Are we to assume he's responsible for the whole thing?"

"Jimmy, it's my job not to assume anything," Curtis said.

Hickham turned to Cole. "You got any personal beef with this kid? Any reason to believe he was one of the ones that jumped you?"

Cole shook his head. "Nothing personal. There were three of them, but only one of them spoke. It's like I said before: he threatened me, then threatened the team. I think he said something about loving to put the hurt on candy-ass quarterbacks, something like that."

Savannah looked up. "He said that?"

"What?"

"That he loved to put the hurt on quarterbacks? *Candy-ass* quarterbacks. That's exactly what he said?"

Cole shrugged. "I don't know. Maybe not exactly, but something like that."

"Mind if I use your computer, Sheriff?"

"What for?"

She crossed behind the desk and sat before Curtis's desktop. She punched a few keystrokes, found what she was looking for, and turned the monitor around to face the room.

"I'll be damned," Curtis said.

On the screen was a sports-page article from the *Elmwood Tribune* dated six weeks before. There was a picture of Booker Flamont standing on the Badgers' sideline, a smear of blood across his jersey.

The caption below the photo read: *Star middle linebacker Booker Flamont speaks his mind—"I like nothing more than putting the hurt on candy-ass quarterbacks!"*

Cole's eyes shifted from the screen. "Where's my bike, Curtis?"

"Why do you ask?"

"Curious."

"Where do you think you're going?"

"Nowhere. Home."

"Cole, remember what I said. You are not to get involved in this."

"I'm just going home, okay? I swear. Is my bike here?"

"We'll have someone drive you."

Cole went to the window and looked out to the parking lot. Over his shoulder Savannah saw the motorcycle parked among the squad cars.

"Is it running?"

"I said we'll have someone drive you."

"No. I'll be fine."

He grabbed his jacket off the chair and started for the door. Curtis called after him, but Cole was already gone.

The motorcycle roared seconds later. Tires skidded across the pavement.

Curtis pressed the intercom button on his desk and ordered that Cole be followed.

Savannah knew he wouldn't be caught.

CHAPTER 17

MANNY gave Booker a high five. "That's sweet, bro. So then what happened?"

"Then she touched my balls."

"She touched your balls?"

"No lie," Booker lied. "Nina can't get enough of my balls." He took a bite of his breakfast burrito.

"That's because she's a skank," Manny said.

Booker grabbed Manny by the back of the neck. "You say another thing like that about my girl and I'll kick your ass across this parking lot."

The tarmac at the Circle K was empty save for an old man pulling his Chevy away from the pump.

Manny held up his hands in surrender. "Chill, bro. I'm just jerking your chain. And since when is Nina Hernandez your girl?"

"Since I paid her a little visit last night at her stepdad's house. The old man was out bowling. Nina must have touched my balls for an hour."

"Well, just remember, anyone asks, you were at Dougie's."

Booker cracked open a gallon jug of whole milk, took a long swallow, and belched. "I know. Our alibi, right?"

"Right."

They were sitting on the concrete step in front of the convenience store, trying to put a dent in their hangovers. It was coming up on ten in the morning. The sun had burned away the morning fog and now gleamed brightly off the wet pavement. It was turning out to be a stellar autumn day. As Elray chunked rocks at the Reddy Ice machine nearby, Manny bit into a Ding Dong, washed it down with grape soda, then unfolded the *Killington Daily* and scanned the front page.

"Says here they may not be able to dredge the bus out for a week 'cause of all the flooding."

"That's a damn shame," Booker said.

They laughed and exchanged another high five. The laughter brought pain to Booker's swollen cheek. The pellet wounds had begun to crust over, forming little scabs among the whiteheads that already pocked his face. The pain reminded him that he hadn't yet gotten around to beating the shit out of Elray for shooting him. Not wanting to spoil his good mood, he elected to hold off a little while longer.

"We really did it, didn't we, Manny?"

"Looks like it. No more Killington High Jackrabbits, and no more Cole Logan." He read some more. "Says here that Stanton High will get the win by forfeit just like we thought. 'Course, we can't forget we still got a district game to win next week."

"I ain't worried about that," Booker said. "Stanton High ain't shit. We could beat them blindfolded. I can't wait for those college scouts to see what I got to show 'em next week."

Booker closed his eyes and got lost in a daydream about the big moment.

"Oh, shit . . ." Manny said a minute later.

"What?"

"You're not gonna like it."

"What's that?"

"Read this."

"You read it, I'm working on my tan."

"You sure you wanna hear it?"

"What, Manny? Spit it!"

"It says here that the Killington coach didn't die in the bus accident."

"What? How the fuck?"

"But that's not all. It also says that Cole Logan was found—"

Booker never heard the rest of the statement because a fist slammed into his jaw.

"What the fu—" was all he managed to get out before a second blow came across the opposite cheek. By the time the pain registered, he was being flung across the parking lot like a rag doll. When he finally cleared the stinging tears from his eyes, he got a fleeting glance at his attacker. "What the fu—"

Cole Logan silenced him again with a head butt.

"Stand up, you sonofabitch!"

Booker shook his head to remove the spots from his vision. "Logan, what the fuck is the matter with you?" He looked back toward the store. Manny lay supine across the front step, moaning in pain and gagging on a mouthful of Ding Dong.

Beyond Manny, Elray was still chunking rocks.

Cole kicked Booker in the ribs. "I said stand up!"

Booker made it to his feet on wobbly legs. "What the fuck is this all about?"

"You killed my friends, didn't you?"

"I don't know what you're talking about."

"Maybe this will help remind you!" Cole pulled a switchblade from his back pocket and flipped it open.

Booker wiped blood from a swelling lip and smiled. "Bring it on, Logan. I'll kick your ass right here."

Cole started for him, the knife clutched firmly in front of him.

They were almost within arm's reach of each other when Booker heard a squeal of tires. A red Honda appeared from around the corner, swerved into the parking lot, and skidded to a stop right between them.

A girl emerged from the driver-side door and stepped in front of Cole, shoving her hands into his chest.

"Cole, don't do this!"

Cole couldn't believe it. "Jesus, Savannah, what are you doing here?"

"I'm not going to let you do this."

"Get out of my way!"

"No."

"Damnit, move!"

"What are you going to do, Cole, stab me, too? I'm not moving. This isn't going to fix anything."

Booker clapped his hands. "This is priceless. Cole Logan . . . saved by a cold bitch in a hot car. Gotta say, that kind of fight in a woman gets me horny. Send her my way when you're done with her, Logan, will you?"

Savannah spun on her heels. "Bite me, Flamont."

Booker laughed. "Just tell me where, honey."

She came back to Cole. "Put it away, Cole."

Cole alternated glances between Booker and Savannah, the knife trembling at his side. He folded the blade into the handle and slipped it into his back pocket.

Booker came around to the front of the car and hiked a foot onto the hood. "Now let's us just have a little chat, see if we can't figure out what this is all about."

Savannah moved to Cole's side.

Cole kept his eyes on Booker. In the background he saw that the man working the store register had yet to look over his newspaper. He also saw Booker's friend bent double, chocolate oozing out of his mouth in ropy streams. Cole had disabled him with a kick to the gut as he'd simultaneously taken his first swing at Booker.

"Now why would you go assaulting me and my friend while we were just sitting here having our breakfast?"

"The cops know you did it, Booker. They've already nailed you. All of you."

"Did what exactly?"

"You know goddamn well what. You murdered my entire team."

Booker frowned. "Oh, you mean that bus accident? Yeah, me and Manny were just reading about that in the paper. Damn shame that was. We were just discussing that very thing, weren't we, Manny?"

Manny made it upright, but kept his distance.

"They have you, Booker. They've got footprints, and they've got a make on the pickup."

"Fuck you, Logan. I don't even know what you're talking about. I was at Dougie Scagnetti's playing Xbox."

"Nintendo," Manny sputtered.

"Yeah, right. Nintendo is what I meant to say."

"Why'd you do it, asshole? Why'd you have to go after the whole team? It wasn't enough that you cut off my fingers? You had to kill the whole team, too?"

"I told you, I didn't do shit."

Cole stepped closer. "You were too chickenshit to try and beat us on the field, so you had to stop us off it, right? You're a goddamn cheat!"

"I'm no cheat!"

"That why you got on steroids?" Savannah said.

Booker's lips tightened. "Shut up, bitch!"

"Made you a big strong man, didn't it?" she said. "Daddy must be proud."

"You don't know what the fuck you're talking about." Booker's face flushed red; his fingers coiled into fists.

Cole moved Savannah around behind him, shielding her. "You're going to pay for what you did to my team, Booker. Before the cops nail you, I'm going to get you worse. Count on it."

Booker spat a stream of blood at Cole's feet. "We'll just see about that, won't we?"

Savannah tugged Cole's jacket. "Let's just go."

Cole stepped backward to the Honda and opened the passenger door.

"You know, Logan, I just placed your girlfriend," Booker said. "I knew I had seen her somewhere. Coach's daughter, right?"

Savannah shook her head. "Just leave it, Cole . . ."

"Tell me something, Logan. Is she easy? 'Cause I'm guessing she is. I always heard that guys go after girls that remind them of their mothers. Does she remind you of your mama, Logan? I hear she's the town whore. I hear that since your old man ran out on y'all, she'll open her legs for just about anyone."

"Cole, let it go . . ."

The blade was already back in Cole's hand, but he knew that if he drew it now, he wouldn't be able to stop until he'd killed Booker. And while it was a tempting prospect, he already had a better plan in mind. He got into the car and shut the door.

Savannah slid in behind the wheel.

Booker kicked her door shut, then knelt beside the car, resting his chin in the open window. He fluttered his tongue next to Savannah's ear. "Speaking of daddies, you should count yourself lucky I didn't send yours to the bottom of that river with all the rest of the little pussies."

The steering wheel creaked under Savannah's tightening grip, but she kept her cool. "Is that so?"

"Don't look so shocked by what I said, bitch. It's like I told you. I got an alibi. And the cops got nothing."

"Drive," Cole said.

Savannah did, but not before slapping Booker hard across his swollen cheek as she hit the pedal.

CHAPTER 18

TURN left on Hubert."

"Where are we going?"

"I parked my bike a couple blocks over. How the hell did you find me?"

"Same way you found Booker, I guess. Elmwood's as small a town as Killington. Only so many places a person can go." She took a Kleenex out of her purse and wiped Booker's blood from her palm.

"Nice slap."

"Thanks. It was a pleasure."

He looked at her. "You shouldn't have followed me."

"Oh, yeah? If I hadn't shown up when I did, things would have gotten *really* rough. You'd be in as much trouble with the law as Booker is."

"That wasn't rough. Booker Flamont doesn't know rough yet."

"Cole, don't you think you should let the police handle this? Sounds to me like they're ready to start making arrests."

He told her to turn left at the next intersection. "I don't want them to make any arrests. Not yet."

"Look, you got your licks in. Why don't you just let it go?"

"That's it on the right."

She pulled to the curb behind the motorcycle.

"You're not going to follow me again, are you?"

"Depends," she said. "Where are you heading?"

"I don't want to be your news story anymore."

"This isn't about a news story anymore."

"Please, just back off. This doesn't concern you."

"Doesn't concern me?" She killed the engine and turned in her seat. "Go to hell, Logan! My father was almost killed last night."

"Yeah? Well, why the sudden concern? Until yesterday, I don't remember ever seeing you and your dad in the same room, much less talking."

"Whatever problems there are between my father and me is none of your business."

"So you got problems with him, too, huh? Well, I guess it's both of our bad luck he didn't go down with the bus."

Her punch was lightning quick and landed squarely on his nose.

Cole bent forward, his face in his hands. "Jesus!"

"You're an asshole, Logan."

He came up wiping blood. "Of the first order, princess. But then, you already knew that, didn't you?"

He stepped out of the car, climbed onto his bike, and was gone in seconds.

CHAPTER 19

SEATED in his study in a bathrobe and slippers, Vice Principal Kenneth Gallbreth set down his Audobon Society bird watcher's field guide and answered the ringing phone.

"Gallbreth residence."

"Kenneth? It's Wendle."

"Principal Hodges? To what do I owe the honor of speaking with you on a Saturday morning?"

"Cut the shit, Gallbreth. I know you heard about what happened last night."

"Yes, such a dreadful and *avoidable* shame. I understand foul play is suspected. I suppose now you wish that you had heeded my advice."

"I didn't call to get into a dick-swinging match with you, Kenneth. Our football team is at the bottom of the river and the whole school just went to shit. Now, for the moment can we just speak as colleagues?"

"Hmm."

"I think we should hold some kind of meeting."

"What sort of meeting?"

"I don't know yet. But I think it should be for the whole town. Lots of red and black everywhere. We'll get the Delveccio kid to suit up in the mascot outfit; maybe bring the marching band in to play "Amazing Grace" or some shit. It'll be like a pep rally . . . only, you know, without the pep. I could make a speech about healing, rebuilding. Christ, I just think we ought to do something."

"Do you need my permission?"

"No, your help. Call the paper. Place a full-page announcement. Say that classes are canceled Monday, Tuesday, and Wednesday for mourning. Let's make the meeting for Sunday, midday, after church. All are welcome. Call the radio station, too, get the message out. Goddamn, this is terrible, just terrible. So you got all that, Kenneth?"

"I suppose. And what may I ask are you going to do in preparation for this meeting, Mr. Hodges?"

"I'll let you know when I sober up."

"Who's this?"

"Booker, it's me, Tommy."

"Yeah, what is it?"

"We're all gonna fry! Fuckin' fry! The cops just called here. They were talking to my old man, asking him about his truck."

"What about it?"

"You know, where it was last night and shit."

"Did you get it washed like I told you?"

"Yeah, but . . ."

"Did your old man ask you about it?"

"Yeah, but . . ."

"What did you tell him?"

"I told him we were at Dougie's playing Nintendo."

"Xbox."

"I thought it was Ninten—"

"Whatever the fuck. Relax, man. Nobody's gonna . . . hold

on . . . let me call you back later. I think Nina's trying to click in. You know, she touched my balls last night."

"This is Clark. It better be important."

"Sheriff, it's Savannah Hickham."

"Savannah, forgive me. I didn't expect it to be you. Is something wrong? I figured you'd be getting some sleep. How's your dad?"

"Sheriff, I have something I think you should see. Are you going to be at the station for the next half hour?"

"Hello."

"Why are you telling people I touched your balls, you pinkie-dick juicer?"

"Nina?"

"I didn't go anywhere near your balls, Booker, and you know it."

"How did you . . ."

"Milly Beth Henshaw just heard from Homer Gladstone that I touched your balls. Who the hell are you telling this to?"

"Baby, you got the wrong idea."

"You're an asshole, Booker. It's over."

"Nina, wait. It's not what you—"

"Cole?"

"Yeah, Mom, it's me. I didn't expect you to answer the phone."

"My God, Cole! Are you all right? I just heard what happened. Is it true about the bus? About your *hand*? Cole, why didn't you tell me about your hand? My God, what time is it, and you're just calling me now?"

"Mom, calm down. I'm all right."

"Where are you? I've been sitting here watching the news and . . . oh, those poor boys . . . all those poor parents. Cole, come home . . ."

"Mom, calm down. I'll be home soon."

"Soon? Honey, you have to sleep . . ."

"Soon, Mom. I promise."

"Cole . . ."

"What is it?"

"I'm . . . I'm sorry you had to see me like that last night. And for all the other times. I'm so sorry for all of it. I want you to know that it's over. I promise. Cole, are you still there?"

"I gotta go, Mom."

"Honey?"

"Yeah?"

"I love you."

"Yeah. Thanks, Mom. I gotta go."

He hung up the pay phone and wondered if she really meant it, if the life she had lived since his father had left them was finally over. Had all that happened to him yesterday lit some kind of fire in her? Would that be the greater good to come out of all this?

There was no point speculating now. Much as he wanted to believe her, he couldn't. Much as he wanted to reflect on the first sober exchange he and his mother had shared in months, he forced it out of his mind—partly for fear of being let down, but mostly because his mind was already occupied with far too much.

He raked his fingers through his hair and rubbed his tired eyes. His mother had been right about one thing—he needed sleep. He had been awake for more than thirty hours. The only reason he hadn't gone home already was because he hadn't wanted to face his mother. Whether he would have found her hungover and snoring, or awake and panicked, he hadn't been prepared to deal with either. That's why he had broken the ice over the phone. That done, he wondered if he just might be able to stomach going home. He decided he couldn't do anything without a cup of coffee first.

He exited the Buttered Bean's rear vestibule and took a seat at the counter. The place smelled of buttermilk biscuits and pork sausage, but for some reason he wasn't hungry. He asked the waitress for a cup of coffee.

She looked up, and he thought her chewing gum might roll out of her slacked jaw.

"Coffee?" he said again.

"You're Cole Logan."

"And you're Bernice," he said, indicating her name tag.

"Always wondered when you were going to drop by."

"Well, better late than never."

"You look like hell."

"Feel even worse. Sugar, no cream."

Cole felt her stare as she poured from a steaming pot.

"I know what you've been through so I'm just gonna leave you be," she said. "Anything to eat? It's on the house."

"Nothing, thanks."

She pulled a pack of Winstons from her apron and set them on the counter beside his cup. "These might help. Call if you need anything."

"Thanks." Cole lit a cigarette, sipped his coffee, and tried not to make eye contact with anyone. In the reflection of the shake mixer, he saw a handful of people scattered among the booths behind him, their heads straining for a better look at him. He kept his head down and drank quickly, waiting in earnest for the caffeine to kick in.

He finished the first cup and looked up to signal Bernice for another. In his search for the waitress he discovered Mona sitting in the front booth by the window, sipping green sludge he assumed was pea soup. Her eyes were trained intently on the bowl in front of her.

Bernice returned a minute later. "Black Mona."

"Huh?"

"The woman you're pretending not to look at." Her voice lowered to a whisper. "It's Black Mona."

"I know that. She's my neighbor."

"Well, I'd be careful staring if I was you. Piss her off and you might get lockjaw."

"Yeah." Cole blew smoke toward the ceiling. "Or shingles or acne or herpes or athlete's foot. I've heard 'em all. I even hear she brings dead cats back to life. She come here often?"

"Almost every day for breakfast. She's usually here for Saturday lunch, too, 'cause she likes my split pea soup. Hardly says a word most times. Not a bad tipper, though. Loves football, you know?"

"Yeah . . . I know. Excuse me."

Cole crushed his Winston, picked up his coffee, and walked to the front of the room. "Can I join you?"

"Hi, Cole," Mona said without looking up. It was as if she'd been expecting him. "Yes, please, sit down."

She audibly slurped her soup. Cole slid into the booth, opposite her.

"I suppose you're here to talk about a little payback," she said.

The remark caught Cole off guard. "I came here to use the pay phone. Thought I'd grab a cup of coffee so I can stay awake long enough to ride home and go to sleep."

She nodded. "Long night."

"So you know what happened?"

"Doesn't everybody? I already told you, Cole, I'm the biggest Jackrabbits fan there is. I was in the stands with the rest of 'em last night, waiting for my boys to show up. Of course, they never did."

"Of course. Mind if I smoke?"

She slid her empty bowl away and wiped her lips with the back of her hand. "Only if you'll light one for me."

They smoked in silence for a while as Tammy Wynette stood by her man on the jukebox.

"How's Coodles?" Cole said.

"Fit as a fiddle."

He decided he was too tired not to cut to the chase. "Mona,

Coodles was lying dead on my front lawn yesterday morning, wasn't he?"

She smiled. "Yep, bled out like a stuck pig."

"And that was the same Coodles I brought to your porch yesterday afternoon, right?"

"Didn't I say as much yesterday?"

"How do you do it?"

"Do what?"

"You know what. How did you heal the cat? How did you do *this*?" He took off his glove and extended his hand across the table.

Mona looked at it and shrugged.

"What the hell did you do to me yesterday, Mona?"

"Isn't that obvious?"

"But how? It's not possible."

"Clearly it is."

Her flippancy was beginning to grate on him. "So it's true? Everything they say about you is true?"

"Well, I never gave anyone the clap if that's what you want to know—at least, not by way of mystical forces."

Cole looked over both shoulders, then leaned across the table. "So where do your powers come from? What is it, voodoo? Satan worship? Some kind of pagan mumbo jumbo or something?"

She looked offended by the suggestions. "I'm a Christian, God-fearing lady, young man. Never miss a Sunday service. Whatever powers I have, I consider to be by the grace of the Almighty."

"Fine. So how did you come by such blessings?"

"DNA. My mother had the gift. She was raised in a coven outside Shreveport. Some residual powers passed on to me through the genes. It's not common, but not unheard of, either."

"A coven?"

"You know, a group of gals who get together to explore the dark secrets of the supernatural." She said it like she was talking about a bridge club.

"So you're a witch?"

"No, my mama was a witch. I'm just a woman with a unique gift who enjoys her solitude. If dressing like a sideshow Gypsy and hanging chicken bones around my house keeps people away, I'm happy to do it." She patted his hand. "That's not to say that I don't enjoy a little company from time to time, and yours in particular. Anyway, I don't wear a pointy hat, I don't cook supper in a cauldron, and I certainly don't fly around on a broomstick."

"So what do you call these gifts? Like what you did to my hand, and what you did to Coodles?"

"I call them healing the injured and bringing the dead back to life."

"How often do you use your powers?"

"Only when there's good reason."

"And your cats? How many of them are . . ."

"Only a handful are BA."

"BA?"

"Born again." She leaned back and thought for a moment. "Let's see . . . yes, only three of my cats are BA at the moment: Fluffy, Hitler, and Wishbone. Of course, Coodles makes four."

"Hitler?"

"A black Persian. Mean little bastard, but he keeps the snakes away."

"Ever had any mishaps?"

"What kind of mishaps?"

"Like was there ever a case when a resurrection didn't quite take the way it was supposed to?"

"Did Coodles look all right to you yesterday?"

"Yes," Cole admitted. "He looked fine."

A proud smile cracked her lips. "Mama taught me well."

Cole tapped another Winston on the tabletop, packing the tobacco. Mona took another for herself. When both were lit, he peered through the smoke and said, "What other things have you, you know . . . brought back?"

"Oh, hummingbirds, jackrabbits, armadillos. Years ago I brought back a gerbil for a little boy in the neighborhood. Napoleon."

"That was his name?"

"The gerbil's, not the boy's. Napoleon got hold of a Hershey bar, croaked from a caffeine overdose."

Cole wasn't sure how to ask the real question he wanted to pose, although he sensed that she was expecting it. He decided on a roundabout approach. "Forgive me, but I know that your husband passed on some time ago. I was just wondering . . ."

"Why I didn't bring him back?"

"Yes. Could you have brought him back?"

"Well, him I was glad to see dead. Good-for-nothing bastard is what he was. And it'd have been tricky to bring him back even if I'd wanted to—he met his end with a tree shredder. Damn thing got hold of his shirttail and just kept chewing."

"But would it work? On humans, I mean."

"Don't see why not. Just might take a little more dead animal flesh to summon the forces."

"Animal flesh?"

"You know, for the"—she made quotation marks with her fingers—"*procedure*."

"Right. The procedure. Can I ask you something else?"

"Go ahead. I'm rather enjoying this. No one's had the balls to ask such questions before." She winked. "Afraid I'll make 'em fall off, I suppose."

"Mona, when I sat down, you asked if I was here to talk about payback."

"Uh-huh." She grinned at her reflection in the window, removed a pepper fleck from her teeth.

"What did you mean by that?"

She turned back and clasped her hands on the table. "Well, it's like this, Cole Logan. I'm not a vengeful person by nature, despite what the yokels in this town may say about me. I am, however, a cat lover. I don't like to see my kitties gutted like a dead trout any more than the next gal."

"I understand."

"I'm also a football fan, as you know. I hate to see my team lose, but I especially hate to see my team not even show up because their bus was sent into the river by a bunch of cat-murdering finger cutters."

"I understand that, too."

"You know who did this, don't you, Cole?"

He met her gaze. "Yes. I do."

"Figured you did." She gnawed on a black press-on nail, thinking. "Well, shit, we can't kill 'em, can we?"

"No. We can't."

"So we gotta beat 'em, right?"

"That's right, Mona. We gotta beat 'em."

She crushed out her cigarette and pounded a fist on the table. "So here's what I think, neighbor: if you're interested in getting back at the sons of bitches that did this to us, what say you get hold of a flashlight, a dead skunk, and a fresh pack of smokes, and meet me down on that riverbed tonight at a quarter of midnight."

CHAPTER 20

Hickham residence."
　　　"Savannah?"
"Who is this?"
"It's Cole."
"Good-bye . . ."
"Wait! Don't hang up."
"Give me one reason why I shouldn't."
"I need to see you."
"Please tell me you're joking."
"Tonight."
"Forget it."
"Listen, I'm sorry about everything I said. It was shitty. I just . . . I just needed to be alone for a while."
"I'm perfectly happy to grant you that wish. Good-bye."
"Wait! I also want to thank you."
"Thank me for what, Logan?"
"You were right about what you said. If you hadn't shown up at the gas station when you did, I think I'd be in a lot of trouble right now."

"Yeah, no kidding."

"That was a brave thing you did."

"Are you groveling?"

"Is it working?"

"Well, you're going to have to do a lot better job if you expect me to come out with you tonight."

"Does that mean you'll do it?"

"Logan, I hope you don't think I'm agreeing to some kind of date, 'cause you don't have a chance there, buddy."

"Just meet me in the school parking lot at eleven. Dress warm. Wear boots."

"Boots? What's this all about?"

"Maybe nothing. But if it's what I think it is, I'm gonna need somebody there to tell me I'm not crazy."

Cole came off his bike and released the bungee cord that held his gym bag to the seat. He lit up a smoke. The only other vehicle in the Killington High parking lot was an old Volkswagen facing the street, a FOR SALE sign taped to its windshield. He checked his watch: 11:03. Savannah was late. He didn't know if Mona's plan was dependent upon the clock, but he didn't want to risk it. He wanted to be on the riverbank at a quarter to midnight as instructed, and they still had a stop to make on the way.

He paced around, too tired to move and too keyed up to stand still. He had managed a few hours of sleep in the afternoon, but not until first passing through an onslaught of adoration from his mother. It had taken her ten minutes to release him after he'd walked in the front door. Her sobriety was going to take some getting used to. When he finally made it to his room, he collapsed onto his mattress without even bothering to undress. Still, his sleep had been fitful at best.

Headlights crested the hill on Jenkins Avenue. Seconds later Savannah's Honda peeled off the road and swerved into the lot. Cole flicked his cigarette away as she pulled up alongside him and rolled down her window.

"Sorry, I had to sneak out, took a while."

Cole went around to the passenger side and got in, placing the gym bag between his legs. "Sneak out? You're eighteen. And it's a Saturday night."

"I just didn't want to have to answer any questions, all right? I'm here, aren't I?"

Cole shut the door. "Head east on Jenkins."

"Care to tell me what this is all about?"

"I think I'm just gonna let things unfold, let you see them for yourself."

"So where are we headed?"

"Wilma Way."

She hit the brakes hard.

Cole planted his hands on the dashboard to keep from flying though the windshield. "God, I hate it when you do that."

"Wilma Way? Cole, what's going on?"

"Nothing." He reached for his seat belt. "You'll just have to see."

"Why would you want to go down there tonight?"

"I think I might be able to help."

"Help?" She flipped on the dome light. "Cole, it's late. It's freezing cold. And if professionals with industrial equipment can't accomplish anything down there, what makes you think you can?"

He only heard about every third word she had said. He'd gotten distracted when she hit the light, giving him his first good look at her. The tight faded Levi's, cowboy boots, and weathered Carhartt jacket were quite a switch from the baggy jeans–loose cardigan–Doc Martens wardrobe she usually favored. But it was working for her. Big-time.

Her snap-button denim shirt was open at the neck, just enough to reveal a light patch of freckles scattered across her chest. He also noted that her hair had been haphazardly pulled up and secured

with a plastic clip—another first. After sitting behind her in economics class for weeks, he regretted that it was only now that he'd
gotten a look at her nape, where light wisps of red hair brushed
against flawless ivory skin.

Even the gum she was chewing smelled good. He was pretty
sure the flavor was apple cinnamon, but he found himself wanting a
taste just to confirm it.

Also—somewhat perversely—the fact that she seemed pissed at
him only served to increase her appeal.

"Cole?"

"Huh?"

"Did you hear me?"

"No. Yeah. Hear you say what?"

"I said, call me old-fashioned, but I'm not really up to traipsing
through the dark where thirty of my classmates perished last night.
Can't we just catch a movie or something?"

He blinked back to full attention and smiled. "I thought this
wasn't a date."

She scoffed and switched off the light.

"Don't worry about the dark," Cole said. "I came prepared." He
reached into his gym bag and came out with a flashlight.

"Oh, I feel so much better now." She jammed the stick into first
and drove off the lot. "What else you got in that bag?"

"Nothing. Yet. We have to make a stop. You know where the
road bends sharply just past the lumber yard out on Fourteen?"

"Yeah. So?"

"Head that way. We've got to pick up something before we head
down to the river."

"What, some lumber?"

"No, a dead skunk."

The sharp curve on Route 14 near the Cravens Lumberyard had cut
short a number of young lives in violent car crashes over the years.

The turn came at the end of a flat, three-mile straightaway, where speed traps were rare and drag races were common. Due to its location outside the town limits, and the fact that it was a completely blind turn, it rarely lacked a scattering of road kill.

Cole told Savannah to slow down as they approached the curve. He leaned forward and peered through the windshield until he found what he was looking for. "There's one. Stop right here. Pull to the side."

"What is it?"

"Skunk, I think."

"Looks more like an armadillo."

"Yeah, maybe you're right. You think it'll make a difference?"

"I really can't answer that question, Logan, seeing as how you won't tell me what the hell we're doing."

Cole glanced at his watch. "It'll have to do. Wait here."

"With pleasure."

He stepped out of the car with the gym bag. When he got closer, he saw that the dead carcass was, in fact, an armadillo. The animal's textured shell was cracked open. Entrails spilled onto the wet pavement in a soupy glob. It looked like a fairly fresh kill. Cole buried his face in his jacket to stifle the stench. He took out a garbage bag from the gym bag and strategically picked up the animal in a manner that didn't require him to touch it with his bare hands. When it was properly contained, he tied the garbage bag, shoved it into the gym bag, and went back to the car.

"Don't even think about it."

"What?"

"That thing is not going in this car."

"Fine. Pop the trunk."

"No way. I have to use that trunk every day. The smell will never come out."

"We don't have time for this!"

Savannah shrugged, leaned back in her seat, and turned up Nora Jones on the radio. "I've got all night."

Cole cursed. He pulled the garbage bag back out and tied its plastic handles to the luggage rack on the car roof, leaving the animal dangling against the side rear window. "Happy now?"

"Ecstatic. Where to, soldier?"

"The river."

They drove on. Cole checked his watch often and wished Savannah would play something tolerable on the radio. When he couldn't take it any more, he took the liberty of switching off the music.

"I love that song."

"It's shit."

"Well, forgive me, I'm afraid I don't have any Megadeth."

"I'm more of a Guns N' Roses fan myself. Here's our turn. Go right."

She cut the wheel sharply. A quarter mile on, she said, "So you figure Booker's been booked yet?"

"Hope not."

"Why do you say that?"

"I told you, I don't want any of them booked. Not until I'm finished with them."

"Cole, please tell me what you've got in mind."

"You'll see."

Their eyes met in the rearview mirror. She said, "Look, I've got something to tell you."

"Go ahead."

She paused. "Never mind. It can wait."

They pressed on. Cole looked over his shoulder to make sure the bag was still secure. It was swinging around in the wind and thumping against the window, but so far it was holding.

"I couldn't sleep this afternoon, so I did a little more Internet research on the Badgers," she said. "Did you know Booker is three years older than us?"

"For real?"

"At first I assumed he had flunked a few grades, but it turns out his father didn't put him in kindergarten until he was eight."

"You're kidding. Why?"

"My guess? He wanted Booker to be physically superior to the rest of his peers."

"Makes sense."

"Didn't work, though. Booker never really did fill out. Until this year, that is . . . until he got on the juice."

Cole nodded. "It's pretty obvious, isn't it?"

"I'll say. The acne, the receding hair, the violent temper. All the signs are there. Not to mention the muscles. I checked his stats. He's put on just over ninety pounds since last season. Until this year, he was a nonentity for that football team. Now he's defensive captain."

"Sure sounds like juice to me."

"And I don't think he's the only Badger shooting up either. I checked a number of the players' weight gains since last season. You wouldn't believe it. It's like they're breeding bionic men over there in Elmwood."

"Well, they're a big school. High profile. Their players are always in contention for college scholarships."

"So?"

"So, I guess they figure they gotta do everything they can to compete with the big boys," Cole replied.

"So what are you saying, that it takes monsters to beat monsters?"

He looked at her. "The notion's not unheard of, you know. You ever watch *SportsCenter*? Ever hear of Barry Bonds?"

"Sounds like you're justifying it."

"The hell I am. It's probably the juice that cooked the whole team's brains, led them to pull all that shit yesterday. But I also think the reason the Badgers got on juice in the first place is because they felt it was the only way they could guarantee victory."

"I think there may be another reason as well."

Cole asked what she meant.

"Does the word *Brackenwall* mean anything to you?"

"Heard of it. I think it's a brand of steak or something."

"You're close. It's a meat-processing company—a local business. They have a plant on Elmwood's south side, outside of town."

"What's it got to do with anything?"

"Read this." She pulled out a folded sheet of printer paper from her jacket and handed it to him.

"What is it?"

"A written exchange between Gordon Belton and Mike Reynolds."

"Never heard of them."

"They're two current players on the Badgers' roster. Third-stringers, not exactly stars. I pulled that exchange off an online forum, one of those friend-sharing sites."

"You some kind of hacker?"

"Not at all; I just know the system. Amazing all the things you can become privy to if you know where to look. Snooping and cross-referencing—it's Journalism One-oh-one." She nodded at the sheet. "That's only part of their conversation, but I think you'll see why it caught my attention."

Cole unfolded the sheet and read:

—*doesn't matter. whole plan fukt-up from get-go.*

—*fukt-up? B.S. Did what we had 2 do 2 get District W.*

—*@ risk of jail?*

—*fuk jail. Going to district, baby!*

—*worth it?*

—*fuk yes. lose district, we're back at Brackenwall. Remember our last loss?*

—*don't write that shit!!!*

—*you remember or don't you?*

—*weekend of torture? not easy to 4get. fuk that.*

—*no shit fuk that. 2 many push-ups 2 count. 2 many sprints. Thought I would die.*

—wrists wrapped on meat hooks? booster dads slinging cow
  guts @ us? no thanx
—don't 4get the hose-down.
—Maybe U R right. Bridge prank well worth it.
—Fuk those J-rabs anyway.
—shouldn't b talkn' on it. our asses if caught.
—tru . . . All 4 now.

"A weekend of torture at the hands of their own booster club? Just for losing a game?" Cole folded up the sheet. "Jesus. And I thought we had it rough when your dad made us do forty-five minutes of calisthenics immediately following our loss to Lamar. They really are breeding monsters over there in Elmwood."

"Sure explains how Booker got the rest of the team to join in on his plans. Probably didn't take much convincing, given what happens when the team loses. Oh, and a final footnote: Guess who's the majority owner and general manager of the Brackenwall Meat Processing Company."

Cole looked at her. "I'm gonna go with Booker's old man."

"You got it. Floyd Martin Flamont. Elmwood Badgers defensive captain, nineteen seventy-one. Big shoes to fill."

"Still doesn't justify what those assholes did."

"No. It most certainly doesn't."

Cole nodded ahead. "This is it. Pull off onto the shoulder."

"Here? We're in the middle of nowhere."

"Yeah. Come on. We walk from here."

CHAPTER 21

SHALL I let you know when I start enjoying this?" Savannah asked.

"We're almost there. Here, hold this, it'll be easier." Cole handed over the flashlight and switched the gym bag into his good hand.

"The smell of that thing is going to make me puke."

"Just keep walking. It's not much farther."

They continued downward through the woods. The grade grew steeper the closer they got to the riverbank. The temperature was colder than it had been in town, probably below freezing. Slick mud shifted under their boots with each step.

Savannah shoved a tree limb away from her face. "If I'd known we were going to do this I would have brought my dad's machete."

"You know how to handle a machete?"

"That surprises you, Logan? For your information I know how to handle lots of—"

She slipped, her backside hitting the mud with a wet splat.

"You were saying?"

She shined the light into his eyes. "You gonna help me up or stand there and smirk."

He offered a hand and hoisted her up. "It's a damn shame, you know?"

She wiped the mud from her jeans. "What's a shame, Logan? Go ahead, rub it in."

"That's my favorite pair of jeans on you."

"Excuse me?"

"They're tighter, sit lower on your hips. With a figure like yours, I don't see why you'd want to wear any others. And sue me, but I'm also sort of intrigued by that little hole in the thigh."

The light hit his face again. It was a few seconds before she allowed herself to smile. "We better keep moving."

Cole extended a hand. "After you."

They went a few more paces before Savannah stopped and pointed the flashlight into the trees. "Please tell me that's not what I think it is."

Cole's eyes followed the beam as it broke out of the woods and fell onto the water. He chuckled. "Now there's something you don't see every day."

"That's why we came? To see Black Mona standing in the river? Naked?!"

"See why I was reluctant to explain anything to you beforehand?"

He moved past her, offered his hand, and helped her down onto the bank. Less than thirty hours had passed since he had been there, but things had been so confusing then that very little of the surroundings looked familiar.

They stood at the river's edge and watched in silence. Mona was waist deep in the water, about a third of the way across. Her long gray hair hung loosely over her bare chest, covering her breasts. The rest of her pale torso glowed white in the flashlight beam. She moved her arms in small circles, her hands gently skimming the surface of the water. Her eyes were closed and she appeared completely at peace, totally unaffected by the bitter temperature.

The water level had receded some and the river had calmed considerably since the night before, but the current still moved swiftly.

Savannah took Cole's hand, more out of fear than affection, he suspected. "What the hell have you gotten me into?"

He squeezed her hand but didn't answer.

Mona opened one eye. "You brought your friend."

"Yeah. I hope that's all right."

"Fine. The more the merrier."

"You mind telling us—"

"Shh! Just a minute," Mona said. "I'm getting a vibe."

"A vibe?" Savannah whispered.

Mona fell back into her trance for another minute before nodding with satisfaction and heading for shore. Her skin was sagged and pruned and looked almost translucent in the light. She stepped onto the sand and Cole saw that she was completely naked. He scanned the area and saw no clothing, or even a dry towel.

"Mona, how did you know where to come?" he asked. "I mean, you weren't even here last night, and yet this is the exact spot—"

"Felt it. I put in upstream, just below the bridge. Just drifted till I felt the vibe. Forty-odd dead boys put out a pretty strong signal, you know?"

"Can I offer you my jacket?" he asked. "*Please?*"

"Why?"

"Aren't you cold?"

"Hell no. I always work naked. Anyway, I don't want anything blocking the signals. You bring the smokes?"

Cole lit a Winston and handed it to her. He started to light one for himself but glanced at Savannah and decided against it.

"Got the skunk?"

He held up the gym bag. "We could only find an armadillo. I hope that's all right."

Mona rubbed at her jaw. "Should be. That armor might take a little longer to burn, delaying the signal, but it should be all right."

"Burn?"

"Yeah, you two go gather some wood. We'll need a fire."

"It's gonna be wet," Cole said.

"That's good, lot of smoke. Makes the signal stronger."

"Hold on," Savannah said. "I'm not going to gather any freaking firewood in the dark until someone tells me what this is all about. I'm cold. I'm tired. I'm wet. And I'm more than a little freaked-out. Naked old women in the river? Dead animals thrown into a fire? Is this like a cult thing or something? If you two are planning on sacrificing a virgin, I can assure you, you're too late."

Mona looked at Cole. "You didn't tell her?" He shrugged. "Don't worry about it, honey. You're gonna love it. Now just be a dove and go grab a shrub or two. We're almost ready."

Savannah glared daggers at Cole.

"Stay here," he said. "I'll get it."

He went back to the woods and gathered some stray limbs. Mona instructed Savannah to hand her a box she'd stashed behind one of the rocks in the sand. Savannah handed over a large red Tupperware container. Cole returned with an armload of kindling, which he dropped in a pile at his feet.

Mona took a can of lighter fluid from the box and emptied it over the brush. She held out her hand. "Lighter?"

In seconds they had a good flame going, the wet wood catching quicker than Cole would have thought. The smoke was suffocating, but the heat was a godsend. Cole and Savannah knelt, huddling close to the flames to warm their hands. The moment of comfort ended as soon as Mona tossed the dead armadillo onto the fire. A shower of sparks flew, and the stench sent them both scurrying away.

Mona dusted off her hands on her bare, wrinkled rump. "The riverbed drops off sharp midstream. I'd say the bottom's at least thirty feet down, so it could take a while for it to rise."

"Rise?" Savannah looked at Cole. "No. This is not happening.

Whatever is about to happen . . . it is *not* happening. I'm outta here."
She marched off.

Cole ran to head her off. "Wait."

"No, you wait. This is . . . what is this?"

"It may be nothing, but I've seen what she can do. *You've* seen it!
You saw what she did to my hand. You know it's real."

"Just what are you hoping to accomplish here?"

"Mona thinks she might be able to . . . to bring the bus up."

"Well, I don't believe it. And even if she could, I don't want to
stand here and look at a bus full of my dead classmates. It's sick,
Cole. Sick!"

"But that's the thing. She might be able to bring them back to
life."

She actually laughed at this. "Good-bye, Logan. It's been real."

"Savannah, wait. Damnit, stop!"

"What is it now?"

"Remember the cat we found in the woods yesterday, the one
with the blood all over it?"

"It was yesterday, idiot, of course I remember."

"Well, that same cat was killed with a hatchet on my front lawn
yesterday morning. I saw it myself, right before I was attacked.
Mona brought it back to life. I'm certain of it now."

"It's not possible."

"You're right. It's not. But it happened. You got nothing to lose
in just waiting. Will you please just wait and see what happens? I
need you here."

"I don't want to stand here and look at a bunch of dead football
players, Cole."

"No football player deserves to die in the service of his team,"
Mona said. She stood on the opposite side of the fire, every inch of
her naked body visible in the light. "I think we owe these boys
something for their sacrifice, don't you? Something better than sitting at the bottom of a river?" She peered at Savannah through the

rising flames. "Don't you think we owe it to them to save their poor souls?"

The light glistened in Savannah's eyes. Cole waited until she moved back to the fire, passing him without a glance. He followed.

Mona reached back into the Tupperware box and came out with a handful of chicken bones, which she dropped onto the flames. Cole went back into the trees for more brush and promptly fed the fire, stoking it with his boot.

"Savannah, honey, I need some hair," Mona said.

"Pardon?"

"Just a strand or two for the fire. I'd use mine, but it tends to work better with the fruits of youth."

Savanna rolled her eyes and tugged out a few strands. Mona motioned for her to toss them into the flames.

Next, Mona took from the box an old Pepto-Bismol bottle. The screw cap had been replaced with tinfoil and most of the label had been scratched away. She removed the foil and tipped the bottle. What trickled out looked like a stream of white rice.

"What's that?" Cole asked.

"Toenail clippings. Save 'em up for occasions like this."

"What, may I ask, is the purpose of all this?" Savannah huffed.

"Gotta feed the dead with life, honey."

Mona proceeded to empty the contents of the Tupperware box, adding to the fire a rooster's claw, a dead mouse, a live mouse, a Jack-rabbits souvenir game program, a toy pom-pom, a rattlesnake tail, a rabbit-foot keychain, a foam-rubber *We're #1* hand, and a jockstrap.

When the box was empty, she brought her eyes up to Cole. "Don't suppose you have to tinkle do you?"

"Come again?"

"Sometimes helps if someone pisses on the fire."

Cole shook his head. "Not at the moment, no."

Mona shifted her gaze to Savannah.

"Not on your life."

"Damn," Mona said. "Stupid me, I just went in the river. Screw it, we'll just have to hope for the best." She came around the fire and took Cole's and Savannah's hands, forming a circle. "Now I need you to repeat after me. Say exactly what I say, exactly as I say it. There are three phrases. At the end of each phrase I need you to kiss on the mouth."

Savannah folded her arms. "You're kidding, right?"

"We have no time to waste! Please, do exactly as I say. Now, repeat: Allaka . . . allaka . . . allaka."

They repeated the words and kissed.

"Mallaka . . . mallaka . . . mallaka."

Again, they complied.

"Kimbo . . . kimbo . . . gooooo Jackrabbits!"

By the third kiss, Cole was beginning to enjoy himself. He looked toward the water and whispered, "Is it working? What exactly did we just do?"

"Not a damn thing," Mona answered. "I just wanted to see if y'all would really fall for it. Now shall we begin?"

Cole winked at Savannah.

The gesture was not returned. "Can we just get on with this?"

"What time you got?" Mona asked.

Cole checked his watch. "Midnight. Straight up."

"Yes. It's time. Stand back, both of you."

They did as instructed, backing up to the trees.

"Do you have any idea how messed up this is?" Savannah whispered as Mona walked slow circles around the fire.

"We'll see."

Mona made two slow circles, then increased her pace. She broke into a sidestep—crouched at the knees, arms extended. Cole was impressed by her agility, given her age and the fact that she rarely drew a breath that didn't pass through a cigarette filter. She began to speak some sort of gibberish that sounded less like words than a bunch of jumbled consonants.

This went on for three or four minutes until the fire erupted, sending a ball of white flame into the air. Savannah screamed.

Cole started to speak, but Mona interrupted him.

"Stay back!"

"But, Mona—"

"Stay back! It's time. It's finally time!"

Another fireball shot toward the heavens. The smoldering campfire instantly became a roaring bonfire. Lightning flashed. Thunder hammered the sky as an ominous blanket of cloud crept in overhead.

Savannah huddled against Cole's chest.

"It's okay," he said, not quite believing his own words. He hollered for Mona to make it stop.

Mona shook her head. "It's okay. Stay back. The signal is strong. Oh, so strong!"

Another clap of thunder rocked the air.

"Mona, stop it now!" Cole cried.

"It's coming. I can feel it!"

"Goddamnit, I said stop!"

A purple mist rolled in on the wind, creeping low over the river's surface. It swirled in tight circles at midstream, like a whirlpool, and the water began to glow bright orange.

"Yes, yes! Rise!" Mona intoned. "Rise!"

She walked toward the water. The circle of light spread wider. Steam rose off the surface as it began to boil. Mona walked straight into it.

"Mona, don't!" Cole yelled.

"Please, no!" Savannah cried, peering between her fingers.

Mona stepped forward again, reciting over and over the same nonsensical chant. She was ankle deep, then knee deep. Soon she floated at midstream near the center of the bubbling swirl. Thunder boomed again. Lightning streaked through the clouds. Rain poured in sheets as the river boiled even higher.

"Can you see it?" Mona called. "It's so beautiful!"

Cole ran to the water's edge. "Jesus Christ, Mona, get out of there!"

There was a loud burp as the top of the bus broke the surface.

"Oh, my god!" Savannah ran to Cole's side and tried to pull him back, but his legs wouldn't move.

The bus rose higher. The windows appeared, then the lettering printed below them.

Mona swam for shore, then turned back and extended her arms. "Come, my darlings! Come! Come!" The bus yawed until its front end faced the shore. Mona waved her arms toward her chest. "Come! It is safe!"

The bus's engine fired up with a liquid roar. Water shot from the exhaust pipes. The headlights switched on, glowing like yellow eyes in the rain. The vehicle crept forward until its wheels met the sand. With one more monstrous rev of the engine, it was free of the river. It rolled thirty feet across the shore before creaking to a stop near the fire.

Cole pivoted back around and watched the orange hue of the water fade to a dull pink, then disappear completely. The bubbles died. The steam drifted away with the wind.

The rain stopped as though a faucet had been shut off.

The bus engine coughed twice, then went silent.

Then the sound of a heavy thud turned Cole again.

He found Mona lying prone on the sand, unmoving.

CHAPTER 22

C OLE rolled Mona onto her back and pressed two fingers to her neck. There was a pulse, but it was faint and slow. He wrapped his jacket around her and gently slid her closer to the fire.

Savannah stood in front of the bus, motionless and unblinking. Cole retrieved the flashlight and went to her side.

Streams of moss concealed all but scant patches of the vehicle's yellow paint. Grime covered what few windows remained intact. Through the open windows, Cole saw only blackness.

"You okay?" he whispered.

Savannah mustered a nod.

Cole aimed the flashlight at the windshield. Metal clanged from inside, causing Savannah to jump. A creak of bending steel followed. Then came a groan, so deep and resonant it hardly sounded human. More groans echoed the first. They were like yawns, only deeper, almost beastial.

Cole and Savannah stepped back together.

The noises intensified. Shadows moved through the murky glass. The bus began to shift on creaky axles.

Cole put a finger to his lips, then moved around to the side of the vehicle. Savannah followed. Raising his arm again, Cole shined the light into one of the open windows.

A head popped into the beam.

Cole cried out and fell backward off his feet, bringing Savannah down with him.

Instinct told him to grab Savannah's hand and run and not stop until their legs gave out. He was a breath away from doing it when Mona called out to him.

Her arm came up slowly, motioning Cole toward her. "Come here, boy. Come quickly."

He took Savannah with him. They fell to their knees at Mona's side.

"Take it easy," he whispered. "It's all right. Everything's going to be all right."

Mona shook her head. "No. It wasn't right. I can see that now. I can *feel* it. It . . . it didn't fully take."

Cole's gut sank. "What do you mean, it didn't take? Mona, what are you talking about?"

She coughed, strangled on her own breath. Cole saw the life draining out of her.

The bus was rocking violently now. The groans were getting louder.

Mona took hold of Cole's collar. "It's up to you now. My time has come. Now I must pay the price—my penance for getting what we wanted."

"What's that, Mona? What were we really hoping for here?"

"You know the answer to that, Cole." Her eyes widened. "*Revenge*. It was revenge we sought here more than anything. But our work has come at a great price. Those boys on that bus are not the boys you knew yesterday."

"What does that mean?"

"They're *damned*, Cole." The words came out in a whisper. "It was the only way I could bring them back. They are as damned as I am now."

Her eyes rolled back. The lids fluttered closed.

Cole took her by the shoulders. "What do you mean, *damned*? Mona, you have to tell me what that means!"

Her eyes opened. She held his face in her hands. "The forces at work here are dark, boy. There is much more at stake now than just winning a game . . . much more than just revenge. But you must hurry. There isn't much time before the change."

"What change? Mona, what the fuck are you talking about?"

"The *bad* change. Two days, Cole. You must hurry. Because after the change . . . it will be too late for them."

"Why?" Cole looked at the rocking bus. "What's going to happen to them?"

"Two days, Cole. You must lead your team to victory . . . because only victory can save their souls now . . ."

Her voice faded. Her eyes closed, and her arms fell to the sand.

Cole put his ear to her mouth. Nothing. "Mona! Goddamnit, don't do this!" He lifted her flaccid body off the sand and shook her again. "Mona, you can't do this!"

Savannah's hand fell on his shoulder.

"She's gone, Cole. She's gone."

An explosion of broken metal split the air behind them. Cole turned to see the bus's accordion door sailing through the night like a fluttering bat wing. It flew some fifty yards before splashing into the river.

Then the first muddy cleat stepped slowly down onto the sand.

They watched in silence as the players filed down the steps and proceeded to line up shoulder-to-shoulder alongside the bus.

When the last man was in place, Cole scanned the line of blood-smeared faces. He saw eyes that were sunken and hollow, and tongues hanging limply from bloodless lips. He saw shanks of steel embedded in pruned flesh, and mangled limbs contorted into positions that could be achieved only with pulverized bones.

O'Dell Lamar stood at the end of the row. Cole hardly recognized the boy who had clung so tightly to him in his final moments the night before.

Cole left Savannah's side and approached the tailback with timid steps. When he was within arm's reach, he stopped, steeled himself, then took the final step. O'Dell remained like stone, his clouded eyes showing no semblance of cognition.

There was no rise and fall to the man's chest, no puffs of vapor escaping his lips. Cole placed his fingers at O'Dell's neck. The skin felt like refrigerated meat.

There was no pulse.

Cole stepped away. He looked back at Savannah, who had moved nearer to the water's edge. She was shivering, her arms wrapped around her chest.

"It's okay," he said. "Don't be afraid."

Bringing his eyes back to the players, he swallowed hard and cleared his throat. "Do any of you remember what happened to you last night? Do any of you know how you got here?"

He got nothing but the same empty stares in response.

He walked up to Shane Butler. The wide receiver held a football in his hands—hands that had once seemingly been created by God Himself for the sole purpose of snagging catches from heights that other less gifted receivers could only dream of. Cole studied those hands now. The skin appeared slick and pale. The fingers were gnarled and twisted into grotesque angles at every knuckle. Shane offered no protest as Cole slipped the ball from the receiver's palms. The ball was waterlogged but had maintained its integrity. Cole stepped back, shifting it from hand to hand.

"I don't know if you guys can understand me. I don't even know if you remember who I am. But at the moment that doesn't matter." He spoke with the same tone he would use in a huddle with the game on the line. "What matters, men, is that we have a job to do . . . and not much time to do it. Truth is, not much has changed since last night. We still have a game to win, and we still have an opponent who will do anything in its power to keep us from winning it. If you'll follow me now, I can assure you we will win. If you don't . . ." He shared a glance with Savannah. "If you don't follow me, I can only say that we will have already lost. We will have lost more than you could ever know."

He spun the ball, setting the laces firmly at his fingers. As fast as he could, he fired a tight spiral at Shane Butler's numbers. Shane's hands came up. The ball slapped the receiver's palms with a blistering crack, only to be tucked away in robotic fashion at his side.

Cole made eye contact with each man. When he got to the end of the row, he pointed to the door of the bus. "Load up, men. We have work to do."

CHAPTER 23

Y OU sure you don't want to take a seat?"

Savannah looked into the back of the bus. "There aren't any seats. At least, none that are still bolted down. And if it's all the same, I'd rather not get any closer to your little friends back there than I have to."

She stood on the top step beside the open door as Cole struggled to steer the bus over the rough terrain. They had been driving parallel to the river for twenty minutes, but had made little progress. The topography seemed to grow more treacherous with each passing minute. They crept over another large rock and pitched sideways. Everything in the vehicle shifted. Savannah took hold of the stair rail to keep from falling out the door.

"I hope you know what you're doing, Logan."

"The river narrows and curves about three hundred yards ahead. The cliffs end just beyond. Been riding my bike around these parts my whole life. We should be able to cut through the woods and get onto FM Four just past the curve. At least it's paved."

The gears shrieked as he downshifted to get over a steep dip.

"I meant that I hope you know what you're doing about them."
She jabbed a thumb over her shoulder.

"Oh." Cole glanced into the mirror above his head. His team-mates looked like lost, comatose children scattered over the debris and the upended seats. "Well, I haven't gotten that far yet."

"I saw you feel O'Dell's neck for a pulse."

He nodded.

"And . . . what did you feel?"

"Nothing. No pulse."

"You mean . . ."

"They're corpses, Savannah. Dead as disco."

He leaned over the steering wheel, using all his weight to veer the bus around a fallen tree.

"So what's your plan now?"

"I'm going let them finish what they started, what we all started."

"Meaning?"

"We've still got a football season to complete."

He pulled the bus off the sandbar and steered into the woods. Savannah held on with both hands as he weaved the vehicle between trees, accelerating to keep the tires from settling. Behind them, the Jackrabbits bobbed up and down without complaint.

"Logan, just for a moment I'm going to suspend every vestige of common sense and practicality, and speak within the context that we are, in fact, driving a school bus full of the walking dead."

"Okay."

"Do you honestly think that we can just drive back to Killington and tell the entire town: 'Hey, just kidding. Your sons are not really dead . . . well, they're *dead*, but they're still standing upright, and hey, you can't have it all, right? So what say we challenge those Badgers to a game, show them once and for all that nobody messes with the Killington Jackrabbits and gets away with it'?"

"Sounds good to me." He slammed the gearshift forward and pressed the gas harder.

"Logan, I'm being serious. Did you look at those guys? Did you *smell* them, for godsake? They're banged up to hell . . ."

"Yeah, but they can't feel any pain . . ."

"But you don't even know if they can run, much less play football. And let's be honest, they're not exactly projecting a wealth of intellectual capacity. What makes you think they'll understand a single thing you try to tell them?"

"They got back on the bus when I told them to, didn't they? And did you see Butler catch that pass?"

"Could have just been a reflex."

"Shane Butler is fast, but not *that* fast. He sure never had reflexes like that in life, I can tell you. Anyway, you heard what Mona said."

"Just because I heard it doesn't mean I believe it. Also, it doesn't mean it made any sense."

Cole saw a streetlight through the trees ahead. He stopped the bus about fifty feet short of the road, and leaned toward Savannah. Lowering his voice to a whisper, he said, "Look, I can assure you I don't need you to tell me how fucked-up this whole situation is."

"That's putting it lightly. We just sent a naked woman to her watery grave at the bottom of a river, not to mention my father's assistant coaches and the bus driver we sent down behind her."

"I'm still trying to figure out why none of them came back around. Why would Mona's spell have only saved the players?"

"Do you really think I can answer that question, Logan?"

"Anyway, it's not my fault we had to send those bodies back into the river. You wouldn't let me bring 'em along."

"Well forgive me for not wanting to ride on a bus with a bunch of dead people."

"You're riding with thirty-nine of them right now!" He brought his voice back down. "Look, I know it wasn't right just rolling those people back into the water, but at the moment we didn't have much choice. We couldn't really bring them along, and I would've felt just as bad leaving them on the bank. I promise when this is over I'll see to it that they're found and receive a proper burial." He met her eyes. "Just two days, right?"

She said nothing.

"Savannah, for better or worse, I started this, and now I have to finish it. And there's only one way I can do that."

"What, win a football game? You really think that's going to fix this?"

"Mona said—"

"I heard what she said, Cole, but if you believe that winning some stupid game is going to save those boys' souls—"

He slammed a fist on the dashboard. "Goddamnit! Don't you get it? I'm partially responsible for what happened to these guys in the first place. They're my teammates, Savannah! If I had been up-front about the threats made not only against me but against them, too, then none of this would have happened. And as far as believing what Mona said, give me one reason why I shouldn't. So far everything she's said has been true; everything she's done has been real." He held up his three-fingered hand. "I owe it to her, Savannah. I owe it to all of them. If this doesn't work, I assure you, theirs aren't the only souls that are gonna need saving."

Savannah offered no retort. She stared at the empty, rain-slick road before them. "Two days? That's what we have?"

"That's what Mona said. Not a lot of time to explain how these guys survived, where they've been for thirty-six hours, and why they have to play—and beat—the Badgers by Monday night."

"Let's not forget that no one can know they're dead."

"I think we should keep the team together, and keep them away from their parents as much as possible."

"Agreed. So where do we start?"

"I was afraid you were going to ask that."

CHAPTER 24

IT took another forty-five minutes to make it back to Savannah's
car. The bus's stripped transmission, skewed axles, and wobbling
wheels had not made for an easy journey.

The question about where to go next was still unanswered.

Cole knew they couldn't just cruise the bus through the center
of town to announce the triumphant return of Killington's fallen
heroes.

Or could they? They were going to have to make the announcement sometime, and soon. Still, he felt they needed more time to
think things through before they made the big unveiling. That meant
they needed a place to hide both the team and the bus in the interim.

Savannah thought they should stay outside of town. Cole
agreed, but that still didn't solve the problem. The bus was more
than forty feet long. There weren't many places large enough to hide
it, inside or outside of town.

Savannah suggested that perhaps they could use a barn.

Cole considered it. He remembered that the father of Willard
Blunt, the Jackrabbits' strong safety, ran a small cattle ranch off
Route 6, south of town.

The problem was that Thedford Blunt wasn't exactly known for his warm country hospitality. He *was* known, however, as a man who drank rotgut whiskey for pleasure and fought men for sport. Cole had once seen him hack off a man's ear with a bottle cap at the pool hall.

Cole had also been to the Blunts' ranch once before and witnessed yet another example of the man's fury, which he elected not to share with Savannah at the moment.

He looked into the mirror above him. Willard Blunt sat against the rear door, staring into space through bloodied eyes. A deep laceration ran the length of his forehead. A front tooth poked through his bottom lip. Given what Cole knew about Willard's father, the Blunts' ranch was the last place they wanted to be caught trespassing . . . even if they *were* bringing back what remained of Thedford's only child.

But dawn was not far off. They needed to get the bus off the road before first light, and at the moment they didn't have a whole lot of options.

Cole decided they had to risk it. He told Savannah to follow him in her car and said that he'd signal out the window if there was any trouble.

It was clear that she was eager to get off the bus, but Cole also sensed her reluctance to leave him alone with the Jackrabbits. In truth, he was a little apprehensive about it himself. He resolved to push such thoughts away.

He started the engine again and pulled away from the shoulder, with Savannah following closely in the Honda.

With the seats ripped out, the players sat low enough so as not to be seen through the windows, but the wrecked vehicle was hardly inconspicuous. With the exception of a few curious looks from the drivers of passing cars, they made it to the ranch in half an hour without incident.

Cole pulled onto the shoulder along the property's southwest fence line. Some thirty head of cattle were grazing the flat, sparsely wooded pasture as the first light of a cloudy dawn rose behind them.

The barn was about two hundred yards inside the perimeter, favorably located across the property from the ranch house. But the only access onto the property was from the gravel drive that passed right by the house. Seeing no sign of life on the ranch, and no cars approaching on the road, Cole leaned out the window and instructed Savannah to leave her car and join him.

She reclaimed her position on the steps inside the bus. He gunned the engine and drove straight for the fence. The barbwire gave way with ease. He sped across the pasture and pulled up close to the barn's large double doors. Cattle snorted with curiosity, but Cole saw no indication that anyone had been alerted to the presence of the bus.

Savannah stepped out and tried the barn doors on the outside chance that they were unlocked. They weren't. Cole told her to step aside and revved the engine again.

"Hold on, you moron!" Savannah yelled.

"What is it?"

"Guys. Always gotta do things the hard way, don't you?"

He backed up a few feet as Savannah walked around to the side of the structure. She jumped up and took hold of a frayed end of rope. Cole followed the rope up with his eyes. It hung near a ventilation gap, about eighteen inches wide, just below the roof. Before he could protest, Savannah started climbing hand over hand. She was inside the barn in less than a minute. Twenty seconds later the double doors opened before him, revealing Savannah inside, extending a welcoming arm.

"Not bad," he said as he drove past.

She shrugged. "Brownies. Took the blue ribbon in the rope climb three years running."

Cole pulled forward until the back end was clear of the door, then he killed the motor. Savannah shut and relatched the doors.

"So what now?"

He peered out in both directions. Horse stalls flanked the bus on both sides. About half of them were occupied. Dusty shards of light shone through cracks all around them. The musty air smelled of wet straw and manure, and it felt no warmer inside the barn than it had outside.

Movement caught Cole's eye in the mirror. His teammates were coming slowly up and looking vacantly out the windows.

"I suppose we should let them stretch their legs a little, shouldn't we?"

Before Savannah could answer, Cole saw a shadow move across the wall behind her.

Then he heard a shotgun cock.

"Who the fuck are you two?"

CHAPTER 25

I T had been a sleepless night.

Nina Hernandez's humiliating rejection had left Booker feeling as sexually frustrated as he was pissed off. At dawn, after tossing and turning through the wee hours of the morning, he had finally said to hell with the written pledge his coach had made him sign about abstaining from personal gratification.

He was fast approaching the height of ecstasy—standing at the bathroom mirror, a Hooters calendar splayed across the counter before him—when the doorbell rang.

"Booker, can you get that!"

"I'm busy, Mom!"

"Busy doing what?"

"I'm . . . cleaning the garden hose!"

"Well, get the door. I'm not decent!"

"Neither am I!"

"Do what?"

"I said I'm not . . . ah, Christ!" His passion doused, Booker zipped up, shut his eyes, and imagined his geometry teacher naked. His erection quickly subsided to a less noticeable bulge in his shorts.

He was still shirtless when he flung open the front door to find two uniformed policemen standing before him.

"Booker Flamont?"

"Who wants to know?"

"My name is Sheriff Curtis Clark, Killington County. This is Deputy Taylor. We'd like you to come down to the station and answer a few questions."

"What's this pertaining about?"

"We'll discuss that at the station. Now, if you wouldn't mind getting dressed."

"Well, whatever it is, I didn't do nothin'. I was at Dougie Scagnetti's playing Xbox."

Coach Hickham had gone to bed long after midnight, but had passed the remainder of the night staring at the ceiling and replaying the incident at the river over and over in his mind.

It wasn't until the alarm sounded at six that he lurched back to the present. He shut off the alarm and came stiffly up from the mattress. Tired as he was, his mind was acutely alert. His thoughts went to Savannah. She hadn't come home by the time he'd gone to bed. Nor had she told him when she left or where she was going. Although they rarely spoke these days, this was unusual for her.

Since the day they had moved to Killington, she had never come home late, save for the odd occasion when time got away from her in the photo lab at school. Hickham had never found it necessary to impose a curfew. Last night, before retiring, he had tried her cell phone twice but was told by a recorded voice that the phone was out of the service area. That had been six hours ago.

He grabbed his bathrobe and went down the hall to Savannah's room. The door was closed. He knocked but got no answer. He opened the door and found her bed empty and made.

The phone rang, startling him. He rushed to the kitchen and fumbled for the receiver. "Savannah?"

"Coach?"

"Yeah, it's Hickham. Who is this?"

"Hey, Coach, it's Wyndle."

"Principal Hodges. Is this about my daughter?"

"Your daughter? No, this is about football."

"Savannah didn't come home last night."

"Well, you know teenagers. Listen, Jimmy, reason I'm calling is to see if you wouldn't mind saying a few words at the memorial gathering."

"What memorial gathering?"

"I just got off the horn with Farley Butler, head of the boosters. He's offered to host a little get-together at his place tonight, five o'clock. It's a closed party, just for the parents of the dead kids, maybe a couple kids on the student council or something. I think it'd be fittin' for you to say a few words. That is, if you're feeling up to it."

Hickham hung up on him, waited for a tone, then dialed Savannah's cell.

CHAPTER 26

I SAID, who the fuck are you two?"

Thedford Blunt stumbled into Cole's view. The rancher held the shotgun at waist level, the twin barrels pointed at Savannah's back. Savannah didn't turn toward him, but kept her eyes on Cole.

Cole took his hands off the steering wheel and raised them high just as music began to play from somewhere inside the barn.

"Fuck's that racket?" Thedford spat.

"Ring tone," Savannah answered, her voice trembling. "My cell phone."

Cole looked at the square bulge in the front pocket of her jeans. They listened to the tinny melody until it stopped, only to start again seconds later.

"Turn that shit off!" Thedford took another step toward Savannah.

"I have to answer it."

Cole shook his head, but she ignored his warning and took the phone out of her pocket.

Thedford came forward again, bringing the shotgun to within inches of Savannah's back.

She flipped open the phone and brought it to her ear with a shaky hand. "Hello? . . . Dad, calm down. Everything's fine . . ."

Coach Hickham sounded anything but calm. Cole could hear his panicked voice through the speaker.

"Dad, don't be ridiculous. I'm fine. Everything's fine." The tremble in Savannah's voice had disappeared. Given that there was a shotgun at her back, she sounded not only composed but almost blasé. "What? . . . And this is tonight? All right, then, if I don't see you beforehand, I'll see you there."

She closed the phone, returned it to her pocket, and brought her eyes back to Cole.

Thedford said, "I'm 'onna ask one more time what in the blue fuck this is all about 'fore I start shootin'."

Cole had no doubt that he meant it. He guessed that Thedford had probably drunk himself into a stupor overnight and passed out in the barn. The man looked like hell warmed over. There was a whiskey stain on the breast of his thermal-underwear top. His ball cap rested low and crooked on cauliflower ears. Another stain darkened the crotch of his overalls where he'd pissed himself.

He was clearly still drunk—certainly drunk enough to pull the trigger, whether by accident or with the intention of actually killing someone.

Thedford set the gun at his shoulder and brought a jittery finger to the trigger.

Cole talked fast. "Mr. Blunt, it's me, Cole Logan. The Jackrabbits' quarterback."

"Logan?" Thedford blinked a few times, then squinted like he'd forgotten to put on his glasses. "Fuck you doin' here, boy?"

"If you put the gun down, I'll tell you."

"Tell me first!"

"Mr. Blunt, now you know I'm not an intruder. I was a friend of your boy's—"

"My boy's dead!"

"That's what we're here to talk to you about."

"Who the fuck's this?" Thedford nudged Savannah's back with the gun barrels.

Savannah shut her eyes and bit down on a quivering lip.

"This is Savannah Hickham. The coach's daughter. Now, will you drop the gun?"

Thedford studied Cole skeptically before lowering the weapon. He still kept it clutched firmly at his side, finger on the trigger.

Cole dropped his hands, slid out from under the steering wheel, and came down the steps. Savannah turned so that she stood beside him just outside the door.

"We have something to tell you," Cole said. "It's about Willard."

"Williard's dead!"

"No, sir. See . . . things didn't happen the way everyone thinks they did."

"I tole you, my boy's dead!" The gun came back up, the barrels trained at Cole's head. "I'm rid of him now, don't you know? Now let me be."

"But I'm trying to—"

Thedford's jaw fell open. A rope of spittle stretched from his lower lip. "Christ on His throne, who's that?"

Cole looked over his shoulder. Rubin Varney, holder on extra points, was standing on the top step behind him. Rubin's eyes were deeply recessed, the pupils like drops of black dye. His skin was ashen. An armrest jutted from the skin near his collarbone, leaving his shoulder pads sitting slightly askew.

A nearby horse stomped his hooves anxiously and began turning nervous circles in place.

"Mother of Christ, Logan, who is that?"

"Rube Varney," Cole answered. "That's what we're trying to tell you, Mr. Blunt. Things didn't happen the way everyone thinks they did." Over his shoulder he said, "It's okay, guys, you can come down now."

Cole and Savannah separated to clear a path. The rest of the players followed Rubin down the steps in the same lumbering manner they had displayed on the riverbank. They fanned out across the barn floor, cleats raking through strewn hay at their feet.

Drool still hung from Thedford's mouth in a silvery strand. He didn't speak until his son appeared toward the end of the line.

"Willard? Jesus H, is that you, boy?"

Willard's right shoulder was grossly dislocated, and there was a clipboard handle embedded in his left thigh. At first he seemed to move toward the sound of his father's voice. For a moment Cole thought that some sort of familial connection had been made. But in the next moment, he realized it wasn't so. Willard moved past his father without so much as a look, drag-stepping toward the other side of the barn.

The gun slipped from Thedford's hand. "Willard, it's me. It's your pa." His face soured. "You answer me when I'm talkin' to you, boy!"

Willard didn't answer. He didn't even turn.

All of the horses were stomping in their stalls now, snorting fitfully, and jerking their heads around.

"Willard!"

Cole jumped.

"Goddamnit, I'm talking to you, boy!" Thedford made a move toward his son, but Cole grabbed his arm, stopping him. "You get your hand off me, Logan."

Cole tightened his grip. "Mr. Blunt, there's something you have to know about your son. About all of these guys . . ."

Thedford shrugged free of Cole's grasp, retrieved the shotgun at his feet, and marched after Willard.

"Goddamnit, I'm talkin' to you, boy, and I expect an answer." He spun Willard around like a limp doll, then slammed the shotgun against his son's chest, pinning his back against a stall. "Where the fuck you been, boy? You's supposed to be dead!" When he got no answer, Thedford slapped Willard hard across the cheek.

Savannah screamed.

"Mr. Blunt, don't!" Cole rushed toward him.

"Answer me, boy, or I'll beat you good!" Another slap. Willard's head jerked from one side to the other.

Thedford raised the gun barrels to his son's nose. "You were supposed to be dead, you sonofa—"

Before Thedford finished the statement, Cole drove a fist into the back of Thedford's neck, knocking him out cold.

"You okay?"

Savannah nodded. She sat with her back against the side of the barn, looking out across the pasture.

Cole came down beside her. "Got kind of crazy in there, huh?"

The gravity of all that had happened in the last forty-eight hours had finally come crashing down on her about the time Cole delivered the blow to Thedford's neck. She had rushed out of the barn the second he'd hit the floor.

"Is he all right?" she asked. "Not that I really care."

"When he wakes up I'll ask him. I tied him up in one of the empty stalls. He shouldn't bother us anymore until we're out of here."

She brushed a tear from her face. "It was almost like he wanted his son to be dead, Cole. How could anyone be that . . . God, I can't even think of a word for it."

"There are two words for it: drunk and mean." He looked into the distance. "You know, last year the booster club actually let that asshole host the Fall Kickoff Barbecue here. They held it right out there—picnic tables, balloons, the works. What a scene that turned out to be."

"Why, what happened?"

"I'm guessing Thedford had been drinking more than just the lemonade because something set him off good just as the party hit full swing. He started stumbling around, cussing a blue streak, up-

ending tables. Brisket, beans, and potato salad flew everywhere."
Cole chuckled at the memory, then his face turned serious again. "I
can still remember the look on Willard's face as he watched his father fly off the handle."

"Was he angry?"

"No. He was embarrassed."

"Did you know Willard well?"

Cole shook his head. "Seemed like a good guy, though. He was a
damn reliable defenseman in the backfield, I can tell you that." He
paused. "I'll never forget one conversation we had, though."

"What about?"

He picked up a twig and began to trace circles through the dirt.
"Sophomore year. Late in the fourth quarter, final game of the season . . . Willard made a rare mistake, missing a coverage assignment
that gave the other team a game-winning touchdown. No one put
up much of a fuss over it; we were far below five hundred on the
season anyway. The playoffs were a pipe dream. Anyway, the next
morning Willard came to school with a purple shiner on his left eye.
He claimed that he got it slipping down the stairs. I knew that was
bullshit and told him so. To this day, I don't know why I said it."

"And?"

He tossed the twig away. "Well, all I can say is that at least *my*
dad was a lazy drunk who pretty much left me the hell alone. I think
Willard's old man is the other kind."

"Drunk and mean?"

He nodded. "Let's just say I don't feel too bad about knocking
him out, even if it *was* from behind."

"I gotta admit I'm glad you did it."

Cole's eyes fell to the ground. "After the pep rally Friday, Willard
was there for me. He was there in the parking lot with O'Dell and
they both tried to help me, to talk sense into me . . . and I didn't listen.
I blew them off. Just like I'd blown them off for the past four years."

"It's in the past now, Cole. You can't change it."

"Yeah . . . well. I guess I wish now that I had gotten to know Willard better. Hell, I wish I'd gotten to know them all better."

A horse cried a shrill whinny inside the barn. Savannah felt hooves stomping through the wall.

"We have to get those guys out of there soon," she said. "If for no other reason than for the sake of those poor horses. They're terrified."

"They're horses. They'll survive."

"Well, I also don't want to be around when that bastard wakes up." She stood, dusted off her hands. "I think I know how we're going to reintroduce those guys to the town, Logan."

"Yeah?" He came to his feet. "I'm open to suggestions."

She told him about the memorial gathering at the Butlers' house, which she had learned about while on the phone with her father. "Dad said the Butlers were holding it in their backyard. Mr. Hodges has asked my dad to say a few words to everyone."

"Everyone? Did your dad say who all would be there?"

"No, he only said that *he* would be there. I didn't have a chance to get all the details, seeing as there was a gun at my back. But I assume there will be a pretty good turnout, don't you? It will be as good a time as any to drop our big bomb."

"I guess you're right."

"Any idea as to how we're going to explain what happened to those guys?"

"I'm for not divulging that they're dead."

"No shit, genius, but we're still going to have to explain why they look like something out of a bad horror movie. We're also going to have to come up with a story as to how they survived and where they've been for the past two days."

"That won't be too hard. We'll just make some shit up."

"They sent divers down to the bottom of that river, Cole. They saw the bus and they saw the dead boys in it. How are we going to convince them otherwise?"

"Well, what if they didn't?"

"Didn't what?" she asked.

"What if we told them it wasn't the real players they saw? What if it was, like, dummies or something? That's it! We fill the bus with mannequins, send it back down into the river!"

"Logan, that's the lamest idea I've ever heard."

"Why?"

"Well, as it happens, we don't have forty mannequins at our disposal, but may I also remind you that my dad was on that bus, too? I think he could attest that it wasn't mannequins he'd been riding with. Any other brilliant ideas?"

"Well, hell, I don't know. I'm too damn tired to think straight anymore!" He chunked a rock across the field in frustration. "This is all a waste of breath anyway. Why waste our time thinking up magic tricks? The fact is those guys are dead, and they're gonna stay dead no matter what we do. Their lives are a lost cause; it's their *souls* we're trying to save. Our primary focus should be on making sure they get to play ball."

"I agree. But you still haven't answered my question."

"All right look, I figure everyone will be so glad to see the Jackrabbits back, they're not even gonna care about the hows and whys. At least at first."

"That's a bit of a stretch for me to believe, but I'm not from around here, so for the moment I'll give you the benefit of the doubt."

"Trust me, I know this town. All we have to do is avoid the hard questions for a couple days. And how do we do that? With a diversion. And there could be no better diversion than the suggestion of a grudge match against Elmwood Heights."

Savanna considered it. "Okay, I'll go along. But we still have to convince everyone that the boys aren't dead."

"Why would anyone think they're dead? They're up and walking. Thedford Blunt didn't think Willard was dead, and Willard's his own son."

"Thedford Blunt was stumble-down drunk. He wouldn't think King Tut was dead. But did you get a good look at those guys, Logan?"

"So they're a little pale . . . no one's gonna expect them to look tan and rested."

"Pale? Cole, one of those boys had a cleat poking out of his kidney. They don't look pale, they look *dead*."

"Well then, we'll fix 'em up a little. What time does this memorial thing start?"

"Five p.m."

"Perfect. It'll be getting dark by then, make it harder for people to get a good look at the guys. Plus that gives us plenty of time to clean them up."

"Clean them up? I'm not going anywhere near those things."

"Look, this isn't a big deal. We'll line them up and hose them down, for godsake. You can work the hose and I'll pull out whatever's poking out of 'em. They won't feel a thing. Hell, they *can't* feel a thing." He clapped his hands together. "This is perfect! It'll work. I know it'll work."

Savannah didn't see how it possibly could. She was about to tell him so when she realized that he was smiling at her.

He started to laugh. He was actually taking pleasure from her distress, which only served to turn her distress into anger.

"What the hell is so funny, Logan?"

"You."

She blew a strand of hair out of her eyes. "Look, asshole, I'm glad you find this amusi . . ."

His mouth pressed hard against hers. She was less shocked that he had the audacity to kiss her than by the fact that she put up absolutely no resistance. In fact, as his lips parted hers and their tongues met, she surrendered to him completely. His hands slid inside her jacket and moved slowly over her ribs, then downward until the tips of his fingers had crept into the waistband of her jeans. He pulled her toward him until her waist was pressed firmly to his groin, her breast against his torso.

The kiss stretched on for some time before he broke it.

"Why did you do that?" she asked, breathless.

"Because it needed doing." His hands remained where they were. "Why did you take that phone call?"

"What?"

"There was a gun at your back. Thedford ordered you to switch off the phone, but you didn't. You answered it. Why?"

"I knew it would be my dad calling to see if I was all right. I knew that if I didn't answer, he would . . . well, it would only complicate what we were trying to do."

"We? So you believe in what we're doing? You believe we can pull it off?"

She reached back, removed his hands, and stepped away. "No, Logan. I don't believe that playing some stupid football game is going to save those boys' souls."

"Winning some stupid football game. So if you don't think it can be done, then why are you here?"

"Because I believe in your reasons for trying."

"Is that all?"

"No. But it's all I'm going to say right now. Look, we'd better get to work."

She moved past him and stepped back into the barn. It took a few seconds for her eyes to readjust to the darkness. When they did, she saw with sickening horror that Cole had already been wrong about one thing: the horses were not going to survive.

CHAPTER 27

CURTIS stepped into the interrogation room with a manila file folder tucked under his arm, a fresh cup of coffee in his hand. "Sorry to have kept you waiting, Mr. Flamont."

"It's been three damn hours," Booker said. "What's this all about, anyway? Nobody's telling me shit."

The sheriff took a seat at the small metal table, across from Booker. "I thought you'd like to know that your folks are outside. You'll be able to see them shortly."

"My old man's here?"

"Is that a problem?"

"No." Booker shifted uncomfortably. "No, it's . . . no problem."

"I also want to inform you that it's your right to have an attorney present at this time. In fact, I recommend it."

"Why would I need a lawyer when I didn't do anything?"

"So you are electing not to have an attorney present?"

"Damn straight. You know who needs lawyers?"

"Who?"

"Criminals. Go ahead, fire away."

"Before we begin, can I get you anything to eat or drink?"

"Yeah, get my ass some nachos."

"I'm afraid we're limited to whatever's left in the vending machine."

"Figures. Just ask what you got to ask. I got things to do." Booker leaned his chair back and planted a foot on the table. "You don't mind if I get comfortable, do you?"

Curtis shrugged. "Go right ahead. Nice sneakers, by the way."

"Yeah, thanks."

"Shame they got so muddy."

Booker peered down at his Nikes. His brow creased. He brought his foot down to the floor. "It's all this damn rain, you know?"

Curtis nodded. "Tell me about it. Mind if I ask what's wrong with your face?"

Booker touched his swollen cheek. "Bee sting. Got me in the tool shed."

"Looks to me like it got you on the face." The joke fell by the wayside. Curtis continued. "Would you mind telling me where you were between the hours of seven p.m. Friday evening and six a.m. on Saturday?"

Booker tapped a finger on his lips. "Let's see, Friday night . . ." He snapped. "Oh, I was at my friend's house. Dougie Scagnetti. We all were."

"All?"

"Yeah, the football team. The Badgers. I'm one of the captains, you know? Gotta keep my boys in line, make sure they're not out causing trouble during the season." He leaned back, clasped his hands behind his head. "Yeah, we were all over at Dougie's playing Nintendo. Ice Hockey, I think it was. We ordered pizza and kept a receipt."

"You always keep a receipt when you order pizza?"

"Sure. You know, taxes and whatnot."

"Of course." Curtis opened the file folder and thumbed through a few sheets for effect. "Are you aware of the bus accident Friday night involving the Killington High Jackrabbits?"

"Yep. Saw it in the paper. Damn shame what happened to those boys. So young, so innocent. What's this world coming to when a bus driver is allowed to drive like a damn maniac with young people in his care?"

"And I assume you are also aware of the attack on Cole Logan at his residence on Friday morning? It's been in the papers as well."

Booker rubbed at his temples. "Logan ... Logan ..." He snapped his fingers again. "Oh, sure, quarterback, right? Didn't I hear something about his fingers being cut off with a Boy Scout hatchet? Damn, it's a violent world we live in. I'll tell you what they should—"

"Hatchet?"

"Huh?"

"You said his fingers were cut with a hatchet. A *Boy Scout* hatchet."

"Well, weren't they? I mean, that's what I heard."

"Interesting. I didn't know we had officially released the means by which Mr. Logan's fingers were severed."

"Say again?"

"The hatchet, Mr. Flamont. I didn't know the suspected weapon used in Mr. Logan's assault had been released to the public."

Booker swallowed hard enough for Curtis to hear it. He pointed across the table. "You know, I ain't dumb. Don't think that gettin' all *NYPD Blue* on me is gonna make me fuck up my story."

"Is that what it is, a story?"

"All's I know is that's what I heard."

Curtis twisted a chewed matchstick between his fingers. He let Booker sweat for a full minute, then said, "You're full of crap, aren't you, son?"

"Do what?"

"Mr. Flamont, so far this morning we've questioned fourteen of your thirty-seven teammates as to their whereabouts Friday night. To a man we discovered that they all had muddy sneakers just like yours. They also all claimed to have been at the Scagnetti residence playing video games, eating pizza . . . and keeping a *receipt*."

"Right. So there you have it. That receipt's our alimony."

"I think you mean alibi."

"Whatever the fuck. We were at Dougie's all night, just like we told you. How could we have had anything to do with that bus falling off that damn bridge?"

"Who's accusing you of having anything to do with that?"

"Huh?"

"What makes you think this interrogation is about the bus accident?"

"Isn't that . . . I mean . . . you just said a minute ago . . ."

"I asked if you *knew* about the bus accident. I didn't say that's what we brought you in here for."

Booker stood. "Look, I know exactly what you're trying to do, so you can just cut the—"

"Sit down." Curtis said coolly.

"Kiss my ass!"

"I said sit down . . . before I get the dogs." It was an empty threat, of course, but it succeeded in getting Booker back in the chair. Curtis took a minicassette recorder out of his shirt pocket and placed it on the table between them. "Mr. Flamont, it strikes me as a little strange that you could have been at the Scagnetti house all night, given what's on this tape, which was delivered to us yesterday afternoon by a Miss Savannah Hickham."

Booker's eyes narrowed at the player. "What the fuck's that?"

"You *are* acquainted with Miss Hickham, are you not?"

"The hell I am. Never heard of her."

"I'm sure this tape will jog your memory."

"Hey, what is this shit? I think I want a lawyer here after all."

Curtis hit play. Booker listened to ten seconds of the incriminating dialogue before pounding his fists on the table. "That bitch!"

"Watch your mouth, son."

"That tape don't prove shit. I was at Dougie's playing Xbox all damn night."

"I thought it was Nintendo."

"Whatever. Anyone who says different can kiss my ass."

"You were there all night you say?"

"Damn right."

"I see." Curtis's eyes went to the file folder again. "Mr. Flamont, are you an acquaintance of one Nina Hernandez?"

"What's she got to do with any of this?"

"Two of my deputies spoke with her this morning. She claims you were with *her* between the hours of twelve midnight and three a.m. Saturday."

"That bitch!"

"And according to the transcript . . ." Curtis slipped on his reading glasses and read from the sheet in his hand. "Miss Hernandez didn't go anywhere near your balls."

CHAPTER 28

URTIS scanned the crowd as he mouthed the last lines of the national anthem, his Stetson pressed against his heart. The stands on both sides of the basketball court were filled to capacity with parents, school faculty, students, city officials, and members of the local media. All were on their feet, most of them staring through glistening eyes at the Stars and Stripes above the scoreboard.

It took seeing them all together for Curtis to realize just how many people he had personally dealt with in some way or another over the years. He saw grown men he used to discipline as children. Some he had helped. Others he had arrested. Many he had just let slide, like the young man he spotted in the student section who had simply been too embarrassed to pay for his skin mag at the 7-Eleven last month. He saw two college-age girls he'd recently booked for shoplifting pantyhose from Eckerd. He also spotted a familiar middle-age woman at midcourt. Just last week he'd let her off the hook for doing forty-one in a twenty when she'd told him she had a roast burning in the oven. Cashiers and cowboys, pastors and plumbers. Every walk of life was in attendance, all of them linked by the town's single common denominator: the Killington Jackrabbits.

The anthem finished and the crowd took their seats. Principal Hodges emerged from the locker room and made his way to the podium, which stood under the south backboard, enclosed by a ring of plastic poinsettias. As the principal shuffled through a stack of note cards, Curtis set his Stetson back on his head and took his seat a few feet away.

Mr. Hodges tilted the microphone down. "First of all, I want to say that, as principal of this great institution, my heart goes out to the families of all of our beloved players. And that goes for the families of the assistant coaching staff and of Mr. Jim Tom Grady, our esteemed bus driver, as well. Secondly, I want to say to the student body that in the face of adversity, Killington High School has always been a frontrunner in—"

"Cut the shit!"

"Yeah, we want answers! Who the hell did this?"

Curtis cringed as shouting heads popped up across the bleachers. The assembly was only three minutes old, and already his worst fears were coming true.

"Word around town is this weren't no accident!" shouted a man in the fourth row.

"Are the Badgers really responsible?" hollered another. "'Cause they're gonna burn if they are!"

Principal Hodges gestured for quiet. "Please, folks. There's no reason why we can't do this in an orderly manner."

"Put a cork in it, Hodges. We want to hear from the sheriff!"

Mr. Hodges crumpled the note cards with one fist, covered the mike with the other, and peered down at the sheriff. "Perhaps I'll let you take it from here, Curtis." Before yielding the floor, he added, "Oh, let me just take this opportunity to announce that Mr. Farley Butler, the head of our booster club, has generously offered to host a memorial gathering at his house for the players' parents and loved ones. It will begin at five o'clock this evening. We hope you will all attend, so that we can begin this difficult healing process together."

Curtis took the principal's place at the podium. "Uh, thank you, Mr. Hodges . . . ladies and gentlemen . . ." He remembered the matchstick wedged between his lips and stuck it into his hatband. "Well . . . from the law enforcement standpoint, I can tell you that my office is working tirelessly to ensure that our investigation of the bus incident is carried out with the utmost adherence to proper procedure. But it *is* slow, meticulous work and it *is* going to take time. What I can tell you now is that, while nothing has been proven at this time, we do have reason to suspect foul play."

"No shit!" came a voice to Curtis's right.

"The Badgers, weren't it?" said another to his left. "Damn them all to hell!"

Principal Hodges's hand came out of nowhere to slap the podium. "Order! Order!"

But the crowd was already too far gone. Heads were still popping up in every direction, shouting invectives.

Curtis made no attempt to compete with either the vocal outbursts or Mr. Hodges's continuous pounding.

A moment later one voice rang out above all the others. Coot Taylor, the deputy fire chief, whose deceased son, Elmont, had been a second-string defensive end, shouted, "Sheriff, I only got two questions: Who're are you bringin' in and when are you doin' it? I wanna start seein' people fry for this!"

Coming into the assembly, Curtis had had no intention of revealing anything more than what he had already said in his opening remarks. Now, standing under the glare of the hostile crowd, he still considered that to be the wisest course of action. But against his better judgment, he wondered if maybe he should give them something more. His silence might lead some people to take the law into their own hands. The crowd already had the makings of a lynch mob.

He waited two full minutes for quiet, then continued. "Before I say anything else . . . if any of you have notions of settling any scores yourselves, I would strongly advise against it. This is a police matter and it should and *will* be handled by the proper authorities. Is that understood?" There were nods all around. "All right then, here it is." He swallowed and returned the matchstick to his lips—all business now. "This morning, myself and various members of my force brought into custody and questioned a number of men about the bus incident. And it does appear that some, if not all of them, took some part in sabotaging the vehicle."

"Well, who was it?" Coot Taylor hollered. "Spit it out!"

Curtis gripped the edge of the podium and peered up from under his hat. Then he told the crowd who had killed their team.

CHAPTER 29

A T 5:27 p.m., with dusk falling, Cole pulled the Jackrabbits' bus around to the back of the boarded-up Taco Mayo located across James Bowie Boulevard from the Butlers' street. Parked cars already lined both sides of the tree-lined cul-de-sac, and a few had spilled over to the adjacent street.

Cole killed the motor. "Looks like we'll have a pretty good turnout. That's good. The more people in attendance, the sooner the word will get around, don't you think?"

When his question went unanswered, he turned to Savannah, who stood at his side, her hand covering her nose to stifle the stench of the players piled in behind them. She was still wearing the scowl she'd had all afternoon.

Cole sighed. "You gonna keep this silent treatment up all night? What's your problem?"

"Logan, what we're doing is so morally and spiritually messed up that I can't even begin to answer that question."

"Savannah, you have to let it go. It wasn't that big a deal."

"How can you say that?"

"It was a horse! One horse! A sway-backed, soft-mouth nag. It's not like a *person* died or anything!"

"Cole, they mutilated it."

"So it was a quick death."

"Then they ate it!"

"Well, at least it didn't die for nothing. What are you, one of those vegans?"

Her face trembled. "You are unbelievable!"

"Look, I'm sorry, but I'm not exactly treading on charted territory here. They're dead. How the hell could I have known they were hungry?"

"You couldn't. That's my point. Those things back there are *dead*!"

"Didn't I just say that?"

"And they're *eating*! Dead things aren't supposed to eat."

"Hell, I'm encouraged by it," he said. "If they can still eat, then maybe they can still play football. I mean, it's pretty much the only two things they ever did in life."

"Logan, we're meddling with things we have no business meddling with. And now you want to get the whole town involved."

"What happened to all that talk about believing in me, in what we were doing? Did all that die with the damn horse?"

She opened her mouth to retort, but stopped and took a deep, calming breath instead. "Logan, listen. We're already felons about six times over . . ."

"To my knowledge there's no law against raising the dead."

"How about breaking and entering? What about trespassing on a man's private property, knocking him cold . . . *repeatedly*, and leaving him tied up in his own barn?"

Twice during their long hours spent in the Blunts' barn, Thedford Blunt had started to come around, only to be sent back into unconsciousness by Cole. A swiftly swung feedbag to the back of the head was all it had taken.

"I left Thedford's whiskey bottle within reach for when he wakes up. Probably be the best wake-up he's had in years. If it makes you feel any better, I also left him with two crab apples and a bucket of oats. Trust me, he'll survive."

"That's what you said about the horses."

Cole held his tongue and gave her a moment to simmer down. "Look, I know you're scared. I'm scared, too. But it's not like we have a whole lot of choices at this point. We're not just gonna send those guys back into the river. And I'm much more scared of what will happen if we don't see this through than if we do. You heard what Mona said. We don't do this, these guys are gonna . . ."

"Change. Yeah, I remember. The *bad change* is the expression she used. Well, Logan, I think we saw stage one of the bad change back there in that barn. In bright red Technicolor!"

"You're right. They have changed. But it's not all bad." He looked back at his teammates, then lowered his voice. "Don't tell me you haven't noticed it, too. Since they ate that horse, they look . . . I don't know, healthier. Stronger. Almost like they've healed a little. Their movement is better. They seem more alert, more . . ."

"Mean. They look meaner, Cole. *Scarier.*"

He had to concede her point. Much as he didn't want to admit it, he had begun to think the same thing over the course of the day.

He and Savannah had carried through his "makeover" plan after they'd reentered the barn . . . even after they discovered the gruesome fate of Thedford's horse. When the Jackrabbits had gotten their fill of the dead animal, Cole had assigned Savannah the task of spraying off the blood and entrails with a garden hose they'd found in one of the stalls. Meanwhile, Cole had gone about the dirty work of removing the various objects embedded in his teammates' bodies. The work had been slow going, and the hours had stretched out interminably. He had been forced to pull out everything from metal screws and glass shards to steel shanks and football spikes.

There had also been a few even less desirable procedures. A

number of limbs had to be forcibly shoved back into joints. Some players had body parts that were so damaged they had to be removed completely. Cole had had to snip off Deke Watley's dangling left ear with a bailing wire clamp. Clemont Nutley's thumb and Jaimie LeBrane's pinky toe had met a similar fate. The most challenging procedure had been to push Fenmore Pewley's spleen back into his midsection. Cole had crudely stitched the wound closed with a leather saddle lace.

Their work had succeeded in making the players more presentable. But it was the consumption of the horse that had done the most to improve the Jackrabbits' appearance.

Minutes into the feast, the color began to return to their skin. A sense of focus replaced the vacancy in their eyes. And Savannah was right: along with the improved physicality came a noticeable change in the players' demeanor. They seemed less lethargic and more reactive, even agitated. In truth, Cole thought they looked pissed off, but he didn't share that opinion with Savannah.

He swiveled the driver's seat around and took her hands. "Look, I can see that they've changed, too. And I'll admit that while they appear healthier than they did, they still seem . . . not quite right."

"It's like they don't look dead anymore," she whispered. "But then, they don't look alive, either. There's something almost evil about them, Cole. It scares me."

"I know. But looking evil is a good thing for a football team, right? Let's not forget the monsters we're gonna be going up against if we can make this game happen." He squeezed her hands. "I can't do this alone, Savannah. I think we're both in it too deep to turn back now. But I have to know that you're still with me."

She brought her eyes back slowly and nodded.

The bus rocked under an anxious shift of the players' weight.

It was time for the Jackrabbits' entrance.

"Okay, Savannah . . . you're on."

CHAPTER 30

As Savannah had expected, the atmosphere in the Butlers' backyard was somber. The funereal gloom, however, was in strange contrast to the scene that greeted her when she stepped onto the back patio. If not for the sagging pool cover and the winter coats people were wearing, the gathering could have passed for a Labor Day picnic that had pushed on into the evening.

The wooden patio extended some twenty feet from the house before opening onto the cool-deck of a kidney-shaped swimming pool. Beyond the pool was a quarter acre of thick manicured grass, all contained inside an eight-foot privacy fence. It was quite a spread for Killington, Texas.

Given the reason for the occasion, Savannah was mortified to find ice chests scattered around, all brimming with cold beer and Dr Pepper. Card tables were strewn with bowls of Fritos and Ruffles and plastic tubs of guacamole, pimento cheese, potato salad, and Ranch Style Beans. As of yet, the food appeared to be untouched. A number of flaming tiki torches bathed the scene in a soft warm glow, and a few electric space heaters had been strategically placed throughout the yard to counter the chilly air.

Savannah's entrance had so far gone unnoticed. The guests, whom she estimated to number about a hundred, were spread evenly around the pool. From his perch at the end of the diving board, Principal Hodges was holding the rapt attention of every moist eye, droning ruefully into the microphone of a portable karaoke player. Most of the guests appeared to be parents of the players. There were a few faculty members in attendance, maybe a handful of Killington students. Savannah saw no sign of her father, and didn't know whether to be grateful or concerned.

Knowing how restless the Jackrabbits had been getting on the bus, she knew she had no time to waste. Steeling herself, she raised her hand and interrupted the principal midsentence. "I have something to say!"

All eyes turned to her. Murmurs spread through the throng of people.

Savannah shared a look with the principal.

Then Mr. Hodges cut his eyes to Coach Hickham, who had suddenly emerged from behind the pool slide. Before her father could instruct her otherwise, Savannah pressed her way through the crowd and stepped onto the diving board.

"May I please make an announcement?"

Mr. Hodges fidgeted with his tie. "Gee, young lady, I didn't know you were—"

"Savannah, what's going on?"

She looked down at her father. "I'm about to tell you . . . all of you."

The coach eyed her with suspicion. Mr. Hodges scratched his head.

Savannah had considered several variations of what she had to say, but given the time constraints, she opted for the one that went right to the point: "I'm here to tell you that the Jackrabbits are alive."

The long silence that followed was split by the sound of the swinging gate at the back end of the property.

. . .

Cole's eyes found Savannah's immediately. He nodded and stepped forward into the yard, the rest of the Jackrabbits trailing in single file behind him.

The crowd began to back up slowly, stunned by the ghostly silhouettes approaching across the dimly lit yard. The guests converged in a tight cluster on the side of the pool opposite the team.

One by one the Jackrabbits stepped onto the pristine pool deck, then fanned out in both directions.

When all were in position, Cole went forward and took Savannah's place on the diving board. "Ladies and gentlemen," he said with no fanfare, "allow me to present your Killington Jackrabbits."

O'Dell Lamar's mother was the first to break the extended silence. "My baby! He's alive!" She rushed around the pool's perimeter, shoving past everyone standing in her path, until she had taken O'Dell into her arms.

Other parents followed her lead. Within seconds the team was surrounded. Some people shook the players' hands. Others embraced them. Many just touched them as if to ensure that they were real. Cole hissed with disgust when Marvin Bumbgardner's girlfriend kissed him hard on the mouth.

Although Cole had prepared himself for this moment, he was still on edge, having no choice but to let the team out of his control, at least for a while.

From a few feet behind him he heard Mr. Hodges mumbling "Jesus, Mary, and Joseph" over and over.

To his right, he heard a shaken Coach Hickham say, "My God, Savannah. What the hell is going on here?"

"It's okay, Dad," she answered quietly. "It's okay."

There wasn't much conviction in her tone.

Cole waited as long as he thought appropriate, but felt that he needed to start talking fast. The clock was ticking. Declining Savannah's offer of the microphone, he called out, "Ladies and gentlemen, I hate to interrupt . . . but if I can have your attention, there are just a few things I'd like to say." The commotion began to settle as heads once again turned his way. He swallowed to wet his nervous throat. "Thank you. Now, as you might have noticed, the guys are still a little shaken up . . . so I think that the best thing we can do is just give them a little space." The comment was met with a number of puzzled looks.

"Please, ladies and gentlemen," he continued. "I know you're all eager to comfort your sons, but as their captain and quarterback, I think that what they really need right now is a little room to—"

"Where's Jim Tom?" a female voice called out.

A frail woman in her late sixties broke from the crowd and approached the diving board. She looked familiar, but Cole couldn't quite place her. Her brow was creased with worry. A streak of mascara ran down her left cheek.

"Where's Jim Tom?" she said again. "Where's my husband? He was with them! He was driving the bus . . . but I don't see him now."

Cole recognized the woman now as the wife of Jim Tom Grady, the retired Marine who had volunteered his service as the Jackrabbits' bus driver for as long as Cole could remember.

This part Cole hadn't had the chance to prepare for. He couldn't very well tell the woman the truth, which was that her husband—as well as the entire assistant coaching staff—hadn't come back as the players had. He certainly couldn't tell her that he had sent their bodies back down to the bottom of the river.

Pained by every word, he looked the woman in the eyes and lied. "I'm afraid I haven't seen your husband, ma'am. I can't comment on that. I'm sorry to say that goes for the assistant coaching staff, too. I cannot speak for their whereabouts."

The can of worms had been opened, and the barrage of questions began.

"Where'd you find 'em, Logan?"

"Did you actually *find* them, or did they come to you?"

"What saved 'em, some kind of underwater air pocket or something?"

"They've been through a lot," Cole said, sidestepping the inquiries. "There'll be plenty of time to answer the questions that are on everyone's mind."

He needed a diversion, and fast. He looked at Savannah, who could only spur him on with a roll of her hands.

"As, uh . . . as the quarterback of this team, I think our primary focus should be on the well-being of these guys here. Which is why I think we should immediately get them back to doing what they do best . . . and that's playing football."

A hush swept over the crowd.

Cole felt the stab of every eye on him. "What's more, I'd say it's also time we got back at the ones that did this to us. And I'm here to tell you right now . . . it was the Elmwood Badgers."

"No shit," a voice called from the crowd. "Tell us something we don't know."

Cole cut his eyes back to Savannah. Her thrown expression matched his own. They were unaware that this news had been made public.

Cole swallowed audibly. "Right. Of course. My point is . . . I mean, we *all* know that it was the Elmwood Badgers that did this. Which, uh . . . which is why I think it's time we tell the Badgers that they're going to have to try a whole lot harder to get rid of the Killington Jackrabbits. Unlike them, we settle our scores on the field." He came up straight and rolled his shoulders back with confidence. "So I say we tell them that tomorrow night . . . seven o' clock . . . Jackrabbit Stadium . . . we'll be waiting. If the Badgers have the guts to show up, me and these guys here would love to show them all who the real district champio—"

The applause drowned his words before he could even finish the statement.

"Amen to that!" their host, Farley Butler said, stepping onto the board, microphone in hand. "I think our quarterback here has hit the nail right on the head. What say we bring those Badgers on over here so our boys can claim that district title once and for all! Now, who's with me?"

It looked like Farley had the support of the majority, but Cole still spotted concern on some faces. Yielding the floor, he came down and moved to Savannah's side.

Mr. Hodges stepped up next to Farley and raised a hand for quiet. "Order, ladies and gentleman, order. Now, we all know that by virtue of our forfeiture Friday night, Stanton High was awarded the remaining spot in the district championship."

Farley Butler said, "Stanton High doesn't deserve to carry our boys' jocks, Mr. Hodges, and everyone knows it! I say we force those Badgers to play the game they were too chicken to play in the first place!"

Mr. Hodges peered down the line of players. "Well . . . now, let's just all hold on for a minute. As principal, I have to ensure the safety of my students. It's perfectly clear that these boys have been through a lot. Like Logan said, they're a bit shook up. Are we sure they're up to playing?"

"Up to it?" Farley chuckled. "Hell yeah, they're up to it. Aren't you boys?"

Cole saw no glimmer of comprehension from his teammates, who had remained like statues throughout all the commotion.

"Listen, people," Farley continued. "Someone strikes at us, we're gonna strike back even harder. It's the goddamn American way! Now, we gonna tuck tail, or are we gonna fight the good fight?"

"Here here!" a voice shouted.

"It does warrant some consideration, I suppose." Mr. Hodges said.

Farley waved this off. "Consideration? Hell, sounds to me like it's settled. Come on y'all, let's eat!"

Cole had almost allowed himself to breathe again when Savannah took hold of his arm. She indicated her father, who was retreating slowly across the grass, head down, hands buried in his pockets.

From his position on the diving board, Farley Butler had noticed the coach's subtle exit as well. The head of the boosters flipped on the microphone again. "Where do you think you're going, Coach?" The crowd chatter faded abruptly. Farley pointed an accusatory finger. "You got a game to coach, Hickham. What say you do your job?"

Hickham continued on his path toward the back gate, seemingly oblivious.

"What if your daughter had been on that bus, Coach?"

The coach stopped and turned, his face devoid of expression.

Farley said, "You can't bench us all, Hickham! You already did it to Cole Logan. The boy loses two of his fingers, yet still wants to give his all for this team . . . and you turned your back on him. Benched him. Now you gonna do it to the rest of the team? You owe these boys, Coach. You owe us all!"

Cole turned to catch Hickham's response, but the coach had already disappeared through the open gate.

CHAPTER 31

Y OU got a visitor," said the cell-block guard through a mouthful of Butterfinger.

Booker stopped doing push-ups.

Manny looked up from his game of solitaire.

Elray farted in his sleep.

"Is it my lawyer?" Booker asked.

"Says he's a friend of y'alls'. Name of Stubby."

Booker looked at Manny, who shrugged. "Yeah, we'll see him. He's a douche bag, but we'll see him."

"You got five minutes." The guard sauntered off.

Cecil "Stubby" McGraw replaced him at the bars. He wore a Gumby sweatshirt and a pair of pajama bottoms with images of fishing lures on them. His complexion was beet red. He was out of breath, as though he'd been running. Stubby was the Elmwood Badgers' equipment manager. Booker hadn't spoken to the freshman since he'd hung Stubby on a towel hook by the waistband of his shorts a few weeks back. It was retaliation for a sideline mishap in which Stubby had mistakenly wiped the sweat from Booker's eyes with a towel coated in jock-itch ointment. The error had robbed

Booker of three crucial minutes of playing time in the game against Claremont High.

"What the fuck you doin' here, Stubby?" Booker asked.

"I heard about all you guys getting pinched this morning and I—"

"*All* of us?"

"Yeah, the Badgers. I've been on the horn all day. The cops are rounding up the entire team, questioning them about what y'all did to the Jackrabbits' bus."

"We didn't do shit to the Jackrabbits' bus, fuckface."

"Right. Of course. I meant to say what they *suspect* y'all did to the Jackrabbits' bus."

Booker looked at the empty cells on either side of him. "If they're bringin' in the rest of the guys, then where the hell are they?"

Stubby pointed. "I think there's another cell block through that door. You know cops. Makes sense that they'd separate you—you know, to mess with your heads and stuff. Anyway, I ran over here to tell you that something terrible has happened to the Jackrabbits."

"I think we've established that, fuckstick. They're in the damn river."

Stubby shook his head. "That's what I'm trying to tell you. They ain't."

"Ain't what?"

"Ain't dead."

"If you're talking about Cole Logan, we already know *he's* alive," Manny said.

"I'm not talking about Logan." He held up his BlackBerry. "I'm talking about the text messages that have been spreading like a plague for the past twenty minutes. I came as fast as I could when they started coming in. Seems the Jackrabbits just showed up at some kind of memorial party at some dude's house. I'll be damned if the team didn't walk right in on their own feet. Full pads and all."

"The whole team?" Manny asked.

"Every swingin' dick."

"Stubby, if this is some kind of joke, I'm gonna rip your face off and skull fuck you."

"I'm telling you, Booker, this news is coming from too many sources to be false. The whole Jackrabbits roster is topside again, alive and well. It's terrible!"

Booker slammed a fist into the bars. "How fuckin' hard can it be to get rid of these guys?"

Stubby said, "Seems Cole Logan is the one that found them . . . or at least, he's the one that delivered them back to their folks."

"Logan?" Booker squeezed the bars hard enough to make his bones creak.

"But there's more. Logan didn't just bring the guys back. He challenged us to a game. Tomorrow night. At Jackrabbit Stadium. Actually, the whole town sort of issued the challenge. They sure seem worked up over this whole bus incident."

"What do you mean they *challenged* us?"

"I mean they challenged you guys. The Badgers. They think they deserve to be the district champs."

Booker looked at Manny. "They're pissing in our faces."

"Hell yeah, they are."

"Fuckin' Jackrabbits!" Booker slammed the bars again. "They want a game, we'll give 'em a damn game."

"I kinda thought you'd say that." Stubby's face turned serious. "But I gotta warn you fellas, I think those Jackrabbits are really out for blood."

Booker asked what he meant.

"From what I read, they're a little worse for wear . . . but they're also plenty pissed off. I'm talking red-assed with a capital *R*. Now that I think about it, one of the texts said the players weren't just red, they were *purple*. It said their faces were like stone. I'd say they're looking for some serious payback for what you guys did to them."

Booker reached through the bars, squeezed Stubby's neck, and lifted him off the floor. "I thought I told you we didn't do shit to those Jackrabbits!"

"Sure," Subby wheezed. "Whatever, dude. I didn't mean nothin' by it."

Booker let him go.

Stubby hit the ground and stumbled away. He raised his hands defensively. "Look, dude, I'm just the messenger. I came here for two reasons: First, I figure I owe you for smearing jock cream in your eyes. Second, I'm hoping you'll agree to never give me one of those power wedgies again. Can we call it a deal?"

"Not yet. What else you got?"

"Couple things. I should tell you there's a strong possibility this game will never happen, no matter how many people are in favor of it."

"How come?"

"For starters our whole team is in the slammer. Then there's the issue of the sheriff. I just saw him upstairs, heading out the door. He's been up there ranting and raving over the news of this game, saying there ain't no way he's gonna let it happen."

"I ain't worried about no cops," Booker said. "This is Killington and Elmwood we're talking 'bout. This rivalry goes far and above johnny law."

"I hope you're right." Stubby stepped back up to the bars. "So listen . . . if this game *does* happen, I think I got just the thing to keep your blood flowing in here until kickoff time tomorrow."

Booker's face lit up. "Porn?"

"Better."

"Beer?" Manny asked.

Stubby shook his head. "Even better." He reached into the front of his pants and brought out a ziplock bag. "Thought a little Hombre Muchacho might be just the thing to cheer you fellas up. Considering what I've read about the Jackrabbits' level of fury, I think y'all are gonna need it."

Booker reached through the bars and swiped the bag from Stubby's hand.

"My underwear's full of the stuff," Stubby said. "Gonna slip that guard another Butterfinger so he'll let me see the rest of the guys. I'll make sure they get their share, too."

"How the hell did you get ahold of this much Hombre Muchacho?" Manny asked, a tinge of jealousy in his voice.

"Sorry, dude. I had to go through one of your competitors. No offense, but he knocked a little off the price because I bought in bulk . . . pardon the pun. Get it? *Bulk?* Anyway, I've been building up my own personal stash for a while now."

"What the hell for?" Manny asked.

"Gonna try out for varsity next year. Thought I might need a little something extra to make the cut, play with the likes of you fellas."

"Let's get it on, baby!" Booker held the bag up to the light and gazed at it with reverence.

"Just go easy," Stubby warned. "I had to mix up several different batches, so the concentration might be a little different than usual."

"You mixed up the batches?" Manny paled with horror. "No shit it'll be different! You're never supposed to mix the batches." He turned to Booker. "Bro, you can't take that stuff. It's like poison."

Booker didn't hear him. He was already transfixed by the two syringes and accompanying bottles printed with Spanish labels.

CHAPTER 32

THE cookout was in full swing.

Cleatus Musgrove gazed out over the picnic tables where the Jackrabbits had been devouring their food like pigs at a slop trough for the past half hour. He whistled with admiration. "Boy, Farley, they sure are hungry. Wyatt just polished off his fourth burger and is about to dig in on number five."

"Good," said Farley Butler with a skillful twirl of the spatula. "Your boy's gonna need his energy against Elmwood Heights. They all will."

"That ain't no lie. That is, if we can get the coach turned around."

"Hickham'll come around, I can guarantee you that."

"What makes you so sure?"

Farley winked and nudged Cleatus in the ribs. "'Cause he knows that if he don't, I ain't gonna continue to pad that fat salary of his."

The men shared a chuckle and clacked beer cans. Then concern crept into Cleatus's features. "You know, Farley, it's the damnest thing . . ."

"What's that, Cleatus?"

"My boy always took his burgers with the works—lettuce, to-mato, pickle, and onion. Now he ain't goin' for nothing but the meat."

"He's a ball player, Cleatus; he's going for the protein. Fuck the vegetables. Here, have another cool one." Farley handed Cleatus a Keystone, cracked open another for himself, and tossed more patties onto the flaming grill. "Eat up, boys! There's more where that came from!"

"Tell me something, Farley."

"What's that, Cleatus?"

"Are you concerned about the boys', uh, condition?"

Farley stifled a belch. "I was a little concerned at first. But I think what the Logan kid said was spot-on. They're just shook up is all, might need a little space before they start acting themselves again."

"So you think Logan's right?"

"'Course he's right, he's their quarterback! Led 'em to the best record this school has ever known. I figure he ought to know what's going on in those boys' heads better'n anyone."

"You have a point. But, hell, they ain't even talkin'. I hadn't got a single word outta Wyatt yet."

"He's just focused is all."

"I'd like to agree with you. But heck, Farley, look at 'em. They're just staring off into space. And that stench . . ."

"Let me ask you somethin', Cleatus. Has your boy done much talking to you lately . . . I mean even before the crash?"

Cleatus thought about it, then shook his head. "Not unless he needs money."

"See? It's the same with my boy. They're teenagers, Cleatus. They don't want to talk to *us*. Let me ask you somethin' else: What does Wyatt do most times around the dinner table?"

Cleatus shrugged. "I suppose he just sort of . . . stares off into space, eats."

"So there you go. Wyatt's right as rain." Farley gave Cleatus a healthy slap on the shoulder. "Those boys have been through a lot, Cleatus. Best thing we can do now is just steer clear, let 'em eat, and let 'em reacclimatize to society. Did you try the dip?"

Cole watched Cleatus Musgrove move away from Farley Butler. Cole had overheard most of their conversation from his seat at the table a few feet away. With the exception of Coach Hickham's inexplicable exit—which had left Cole feeling more angry than worried—he felt confident about the way things were going. The Jackrabbits seemed calm and content, and so far the parents had taken his advice and were keeping their distance. Most of them were mingling around the swimming pool, smoking, eating, marveling over their sons' return, and talking about football.

Cole returned his focus to the team. Cleatus Musgrove had been right about one thing—the boys were ravenous. Clearly, Thedford Blunt's horse hadn't done much to quell their appetites. The Jack-rabbits were devouring burgers like desert scavengers with a fresh kill. Their chewing, slurping, and groaning had put Cole off his own meal. He pushed his burger away and sat back in his chair, wondering what the hell was wrong with Coach Hickham and wishing he could smoke.

"Oh, my god . . ."

He turned. Savannah was standing behind him, a hand over her mouth.

"That's the grossest thing I've ever seen," she said.

"Where the hell did you go?"

She stepped back, picking up the hostility in his tone. "I went to the bathroom, if you must know."

"I'd hoped that maybe you'd gone to talk some sense into your father."

"No, Logan. I didn't. I'm not sure I'm the one who should—"

"What the hell's the matter with him?" he snapped. "How the fuck could he just turn his back on us?"

She folded her arms across her chest. "I can't answer that question, Logan, but I'd appreciate it if you'd take your anger out on him and not me. Anyway, can we talk about this later?" She indicated the team. "I think we've got more pressing matters at hand right now."

Farley Butler stepped in to drop another plate of patties onto each table. "Come and get it, boys!" he said, wiping greasy hands on an apron that read *Who pissed in the gravy?*

The Jackrabbits dug in with abandon.

As Farley started to turn away, he did a double take at Savannah. "Oh. Uh, I don't believe we've been formally introdu—"

"No. I don't believe we have." Her tone was tepid.

Farley read it loud and clear. "Well, listen . . . uh, about what I said to your daddy back there . . . it wasn't personal, you know? I just want what's best for the team and all."

She nodded and looked past him dismissively. "Of course."

"Great. Okay, then. I'll leave y'all to it. Shout if you need anything." He made a hasty retreat.

Savannah said, "I'm sorry, Logan, but if I stand here and watch this any longer, I'm going to hurl. I'm gonna go get a Coke or something. Feel free to join me if you want."

Cole shook his head. "I gotta keep an eye on these guys." She shrugged and started to go, but he reached out to stop her. "Look, I'm sorry. Didn't mean to be a dick a minute ago. It's just that . . ."

"I know, Logan. It's cool." She squeezed his hand. "I won't be long."

Savannah went elbow deep into an ice chest and came up with a can of Dr Pepper. Eager to distance herself from the barbaric feast and avoid the possibility of having to answer any questions from the other guests, she stepped away from the party and strolled casually toward the back of the yard. As she neared the back fence and took her first sip of Dr Pepper, a voice spoke from the shadows, startling her.

"We need to talk, young lady."

She spun around.

Curtis stepped into the glow of a nearby tiki torch, a formidable scowl visible beneath his Stetson. Before Savannah could even get a word out, the sheriff took her by the elbow and ushered her into a small fenced enclosure at the back of the yard.

When they were out of sight, she pulled her arm free of his grasp and backed up against the pool pump behind her. "Good to see you, too, Sheriff. Is something wrong? You seem a little tense."

"You're damn right, I'm tense!" He paused, peered over her shoulder for prying eyes, then brought his voice back down. "I just got notification at the station that thirty-nine men I'd thought were dead are not only alive and well but are planning to play in some damn-fool football game at the high school tomorrow!"

"Sheriff—"

"I'm also told that whatever's going on, you and Logan are responsible for it. You have a lot of explaining to do, missy."

"Sheriff, calm down. Wait here. I'll go get Cole."

"I'm talkin' to you right now, missy . . . because I happen to believe that, unlike Cole Logan, you might actually have a lick of sense in your skull."

"I appreciate that."

"So is it true? Did Logan challenge the Badgers to some harebrained grudge match? 'Cause I can tell you right now it'll happen over my dead body."

She and Cole had anticipated such a reaction from the sheriff. That still didn't make it any easier for Savannah to hear.

"All right . . ." he said. "Let's have it, young lady. Where'd you find them?"

"You mean the Jackrabbits?"

"No, the Toledo Mud Hens. Yes, the Jackrabbits! Was this some kind of joke all along?"

"Joke? Sheriff, you don't understand—"

"You're damn right I don't!" He took the matchstick from his mouth and jabbed it in her face. "I don't understand how three frogmen could have seen that team at the bottom of the river, and then two nights later here they are wolfin' down cheeseburgers."

"Incredible, isn't it?" Savannah said levelly, then quickly shifted the direction of the conversation. "What amazes me even more is that after all those boys have been through, they still want to play football. It's a great thing, if you ask me."

"Oh hell, not you, too—"

"After all, they've got so much to play for. School pride, solidarity—"

"Solidarity, my foot. It's about revenge, plain and simple."

"And is that such a bad thing?" she asked. "Don't the Badgers have a little revenge coming their way?"

"Justice will be served, I can assure you. *My* way. May I remind you that you were the one who brought me that tape of Booker Flamont in the first place?"

"I know that, Sheriff." It was a noble deed that Savannah had come to regret. It was certainly something that she dreaded telling Cole about. "So I take it you've put the tape to use?"

"Hell yes, I put it to use! I got every damn one of the Badgers in my custody. They fell like dominoes. But my point is that *you're* the one that made it happen. I figured you'd be happier than anyone to see those Badgers kept under lock and key."

Savannah quickly glanced around the corner. Cole still sat where she had left him, but he was scanning the crowd, looking worried. She came back and said, "Just let them play, Sheriff. Please."

"Not a chance. Even if I wanted to, it's not as simple as you'd think."

"What's complicated? Bus the Badgers to the field, let them play, and bus them back to jail. You could keep rifles trained on the field for all anyone would care, just let them out long enough to play the game."

His eyes narrowed. "What's it to you, anyway?"

"What do you mean?"

"I never saw you anywhere near that football team . . . your own father's team. That's no secret in this town, Savannah. Why the sudden interest now?"

"Booker Flamont and his friends tried to kill my father, Sheriff. Isn't that reason enough for wanting to see my dad's team get back at the Badgers . . . in a way that would hurt them the most?"

He studied her for a few beats. "No. I ain't buying it. You and Logan are still hiding something. And I can promise you I'm gonna find out what it is."

"Well, he's sitting right over there, Sheriff. Why aren't you speaking to him?"

Curtis replaced the matchstick in his mouth and shook his head. "No. Not here. Not now. I got enough on my plate back at the jailhouse. But you tell Logan that I ain't done with the both of you."

"Fine. But have you made your decision?"

"'Bout what?"

"About the game!"

"Young lady, hell will freeze over before I let that game happen." He tugged the brim of his Stetson down low. "You can tell Logan I said that, too."

"Curtis?" Cole sat up on the bench. "He's here?"

"*Was*," Savannah said. "He just slipped out through the back gate . . . same way he came in, I think." She glanced at Cole's teammates. "I see your friends have still not gotten their fill."

"Well, tell me! What did Curtis say?"

"I think you're going to have to kill him, Logan."

"Why?"

"'Cause he said the game would only happen over his dead body."

"Shit."

"Did you expect anything different?"

"Honestly, no."

"I tried everything to convice him to let them play. He's hearing none of it."

"I'll have to talk to him myself."

"I wouldn't recommend it. He's pretty hot. Only reason he didn't collar you here is that he couldn't afford to make a scene. His opinions wouldn't exactly go over well with this crowd. Plus, he's got his hands full at the . . ." She stopped and drew in a sharp breath.

"At the what?"

"At the, uh . . . *jail.*"

"The jail? What are you talking about?"

"Promise you won't get mad?"

"Hell, Savannah, what is it?"

"It's just that . . . yesterday I gave the sheriff a tape that . . . well, let's just say that he's heard every word Booker said at the Circle K."

"You what? Jesus, Savannah, that's gonna fuck up everything! When exactly were you going to tell me about this?"

"I'm sorry, but we've been a little preoccupied, you know. And keep your voice down; people are looking."

Cole gritted his teeth. "How the hell can I make this game happen if our opponents are in jail?"

"You tell me, Logan. You're the one with all the brilliant ideas. After all, our situation has improved *so* much since we crashed the party here." She made no attempt to mask her sarcasm. "Here we are with only twenty-four hours left and your opponents are in jail, your coach is not interested, and may I remind you that you still have a man shackled up in his own barn?"

Cole had no grounds for argument. He stomped a foot in frustration. "Shit, we have to get to your dad. It's the only way. If we can convince him to get behind this game, maybe *he* can convince Curtis. You think he went home from here?"

"My guess would be the school. He's more comfortable in his office than at home."

"We have to get over there."

"Okay. But do you really want to let these guys out of your sight?"

"What choice do I have? I can't kidnap them. At some point their parents are gonna have to take them away. At least they seem calm. Quiet, but calm. Hopefully their parents will just send them straight to bed. We'll have to pray they don't act weird."

"I wouldn't count on that, Logan."

"Why do you say that?"

"Well, for one thing your tailback is shoveling fistfuls of meat into his mouth."

"Yeah? So? They're all doing that."

Her eyes came up. "Cole, he's eating it blood raw."

Cole spun around. O'Dell Lamar's face was caked with red juice, his jaws working hard on a mouthful of uncooked ground meat. The players on either side of him were digging fistfuls of crimson mush out of a plastic tube, clawing for their share. O'Dell was fending them off with angry grunts and elbow jabs.

"Shit!" Cole looked around in panic. The parents were still by the pool, and Farley Butler was hidden behind a cloud of smoke at the grill. Cole ripped the tube of meat from O'Dell's hands and gave the tailback a hard whack on the head. "What the hell's the matter with you?"

O'Dell just looked at him, grunted, and went back to eating the cooked burgers.

"I think it's time to get them away from the food," Savannah said.

"There's that hotshot QB!"

Cole turned. Cleatus Musgrove stepped up to him, lit a Merit, and stuck out his hand.

Cole shook it. "Mr. Musgrove."

"How goes it, son?" Cleatus pointed to the mess in Cole's hands. "Gonna toss another couple patties on the fire there, eh?"

"Uh, yes, sir. Thought I would." Cole introduced Savannah.

"Oh, I know who this little lady is. Say, we gonna get your daddy's head turned around on this Elmwood Heights deal or what?"

Before Savannah could answer, Cole indicated the football tucked under Cleatus's arm. "Where'd you get that, sir?"

"Huh? Oh, I was just inside the house, shaking the dew off the vine; saw this ball in the game room there and thought I'd bring it out for the boys. Thought maybe if we cranked up the flood lights, the boys could shake out the cobwebs with a little pickup game."

Savannah gripped Cole's arm hard. "Maybe it *would* be a good time to take a break from the meal, wouldn't you say, Logan?"

Picking up on her meaning, Cole looked back at the players. Dale Kelsey, tight end, had licked his plate clean and was now gnawing on one of his shoes. Two seats down, Shane Butler was biting into a plastic pepper shaker. "Uh, yeah. Maybe a little football is just what they need. May I, Mr. Musgrove?"

Cleatus handed over the ball. "Be my guest."

Cole held it high overhead. "Hey, fellas . . ." The players' heads came up at the sound of their master's voice. "Fumble!"

The Jackrabbits peered at the ball with fiery eyes. Cole stepped back and heaved it through the air. It sailed some thirty yards over the pool area before landing in the middle of the leaf-strewn lawn beyond.

The Jackrabbits pounced immediately.

Chairs and tables flew in the mad stampede. The crowd parted to make way as several players tried to run across the pool cover, only to find themselves churning through frigid, shoulder-deep water to get to the other side. Food tables were trampled in an explosion of chips and spreads. Beans rained down like hailstones on the pool deck. Snapped tiki torches sent sparks flying.

It wasn't clear who fell on the ball first, given the darkness and how quickly the bodies stacked on top of it, but the impressive display was met with rousing applause from the crowd.

Cleatus Musgrove wrapped an arm around Cole's shoulder. "Looks like we've got our boys back, Logan. I'd say they're gonna be just fine."

CHAPTER 33

Go ahead and say it."

"Say what, Logan?"

"That you have a problem with what we just did."

Savannah started the car and headed up the Blunts' driveway toward the property exit. "I don't have a problem with it. It just seems a little . . . *inhumane*."

"Inhumane?" Cole waved her off. "Don't worry. Long as Willard doesn't wander off, he'll be fine."

"Cole, he's your teammate. You just left him propped up on a porch swing in the cold."

"Well, the view's nice."

"You think this is funny?"

"No, I think you're being oversensitive. He's dead, Savannah. You gotta keep reminding yourself of that. He's incapable of feeling cold or lonely or afraid or anything else. Hell, he wouldn't feel a cattle prod rammed up his ass. I tried the front door, but it was locked, and I didn't think it was a good idea to break any windows. Willard will be just fine where he is. His dad will let him inside later."

"Right . . . whenever his dad wakes up. Or should I say *if* he wakes up."

"Don't worry. Thedford will come around. He's not exactly a rookie when it comes to being drunk and unconscious."

They had been quick in volunteering to drive Willard home from the Butlers' house. They had told Farley Butler that they'd be happy to do it, seeing as how Willard was the only Jackrabbit there without a parent. Of course, they had failed to mention that they were also holding Willard's father captive.

When they got back to the barn, they'd found Thedford in much the same condition as they had left him—securely tied up and snoring like a buzz saw. The only difference was that the whiskey bottle Cole had left within arm's reach was empty. Thedford had clearly awoken during their absence, realized he was restrained, and decided to drink some more.

After removing the tack gear from the rancher's wrists and ankles, Cole had simply left the man where he lay, a saddle blanket draped over his body. They'd then dropped Willard off back at the house, figuring that when the old man came around, he'd head up to the house to find his son waiting.

Savannah steered the Honda off the property and headed back toward town. Cole could see that she was still unsettled.

"Look," he said. "I don't want you to think that I'm comfortable with any of this, because I'm not. Whatever control I had over this thing is gone. It's completely out of my hands until tomorrow. I couldn't very well take Willard home with me. And I certainly couldn't have stayed with him. You and I both know that Thedford wouldn't think twice about shooting me if given a second chance."

"But who's to say he won't kill his son? This morning he certainly looked capable of it."

Cole looked at her.

"Right," she said. "Okay, I got it, he's already dead. But that still doesn't make me feel any better."

"Let's just focus on what we *can* control."

"Fine. So where to now?"

"To the school. To see if your father's there."

"You think . . ." She stopped.

"What?"

"You think you'll be able to get him on our side?"

"Well, you're his daughter. I would hope so."

"So what are you going to say to him?"

"You sound like I'll be the only one talking. You're coming in with me, aren't you?"

She didn't answer.

"Well, *aren't* you?"

"Cole, I'll help you as much as I can to fix this thing. But this one you're going to have to do on your own."

"What the hell for?"

"Please don't ask me that."

"Savannah, you're his daughter for godsake. What's the matter, are you afraid of him?"

"Cole, please . . ."

"What is it with you two? Why doesn't anybody know this story?"

"Because it's nobody's business!"

"At the moment it sure as hell is *my* business!"

"Look, you want me to drive you, or not?"

Cole blew out an exasperated breath. "Yeah. Sure. Whatever."

They didn't speak until she pulled onto the high school grounds fifteen minutes later. Hickham's truck was parked under the lights in its usual spot outside the clubhouse, adjacent to the gym. Savannah pulled in a few spaces away.

"I'll wait for you if you want," she said as Cole got out of the car.

"Do whatever you want." He shut the door and stepped away.

Savannah lowered the passenger window. "Hey, Logan."

"Yeah, what is it?"

"Make sure you tell him how good the team looked at the Butlers', how well they were playing."

"Yeah. No kidding. That's sort of the plan, you know."

"And one other thing . . . make sure to tell him that none of them were hurt."

"Why? What's that got to do with anything?"

"Just do it. Just make sure he knows that none of them got hurt while they were playing, despite all their injuries. Will you remember that?"

"Sure. What's it to you?"

"It's nothing to me. But my dad will want to know."

Cole turned and headed inside.

"Ow! Fuck, Manny!"

"Hold still!"

"It hurts!"

"It don't hurt, you big nancy. You want me to do this, or don't you?" Manny depressed the plunger. When the full contents of the syringe had entered Booker's left buttock, he yanked out the needle.

"Ow!" Booker whacked Manny in the head with the heel of his palm. "Why'd you have to be so rough?"

"Bro, chill. I think you're raging."

"Damn straight I'm raging . . . and it's about time, too." Booker started punching the air like a prizefighter, his eyes red with hate.

Manny signaled for Elray to stay clear of him, then said, "Booker, I think Stubby really fucked-up good on this one."

"Are you kidding? That douche bag is a genius! Just look at me."

"Yeah, that's my point. Stubby said he mixed the batches. You never mix the batches. I can already tell this shit is stronger than normal."

Booker ignored him and continued to jab the air like a wild man.

Manny had observed this kind of behavior in Booker before, but never to such an alarming degree. Stubby McGraw had smuggled in a week's supply of Hombre Muchacho—at least, it would have lasted that long if they had adhered to the prescribed dosage. To make up for missed injections, Booker had insisted on exhausting the entire stash in under two hours. He had just forced Manny to inject the sixth and final dose into a blood stream already processing six cups of coffee and fourteen minipackets of Domino sugar.

Booker hit the floor and began doing push-ups, clapping his hands at the top of each repetition.

"Come on, bro, go easy," Manny said. "I think you might have OD'd."

"Are you spelling out your words again?"

"No, you dumb shit, I'm trying to tell you that you've overdosed. Bro, you gotta remember, this Hombre Muchacho shit is not your lab-tested, high-end Barry Bonds stuff. It's Mexican. And except for tacos and hookers, nothing good ever came out of Mexico. You gotta remember, too, that El Toro Grande is not a highly reputed dealer when it comes to quality control. You can never be too sure what you're getting from this guy."

"Well, whatever it is, I feel locked, loaded, and ready to kick ass." Booker came up off the floor and marched over to Elray. "Hey, Elray, hit me in the face."

Elray shrugged, then punched him in the nose.

Booker smiled, his face euphoric. "Yeah, man! Sweet pain, baby. Sweet pain!"

Manny placed a hesitant hand on Booker's shoulder. "Bro, what say you lie down for a while, sleep it off?"

"Fuck that!"

"But you're scaring me."

"Good. Means I'm right where I need to be. Let's just hope

Stubby got some Hombre Muchacho smuggled in to the rest of the guys, too."

"God help us if he did."

"No, Manny. God help the Jackrabbits. Considering what we got in store for 'em, they're gonna need His ass. Now shut the hell up and let me rage. I got a game to win."

CHAPTER 34

WHY won't you just answer my question?"

"I'll answer your question when you answer mine, Logan."

"I already told you, Coach, they just showed up at my house this afternoon. I stepped outside to get some air, and there they were. Trust me, I was as surprised to see them as everyone else."

"You think I'm stupid, Logan?"

"No, I think you're scared to coach your team, and I want to know why. How could you turn your back on us now? I hand you back your team, all but gift wrapped, and then you just walked out on us."

"How'd they do it, Logan?"

"How'd they do what?"

"Don't play dumb with me, son, you saw that bus go down in that river, and I was *on* it when it went down. How did they get out?"

"I couldn't tell you."

"Couldn't? Or *won't*? Where have they been since Friday night?"

"Coach, your guess is as good as mine. All I know is what I know, which is exactly what everyone else knows."

"So they just showed up on your front lawn, like the morning dew?"

"That's pretty much it."

"In the team bus?"

"The bus?" Cole's mind raced. "Well, the bus was actually parked out by the—"

"It's crap, Logan! I'm not buying a word of it." Hickham came out of his chair. "I'll tell you what I think. I think the whole thing was some sort of prank from the beginning. And if I find out that you brought my daughter into it, there's gonna be hell to pay."

"This look like a prank to you?" Cole held up his three-fingered hand. "'Cause the whole thing began with this, Coach. It began with the Badgers. They're the pranksters. They're the ones that sent our bus off that bridge. The joke was not done *by* us; it was done *to* us."

"Well, it's funny that the only ones who know what happened after that bus sank are the ones who went down with it. And they aren't talking. Now, why is that, Logan? Doesn't that strike you as a little odd? Hell, doesn't it strike their parents as odd? And where the hell are my assistant coaches? Where's Jim Tom Grady?"

Cole shook his head and crossed away. "I don't know the answer to those questions. And as for the silence of the team . . . I guess they're still just a little dazed."

"You're damn right they're *dazed*! Most of them look like they've passed through a wood chipper and they're not even showing any signs of pain. And this is the team you expect me to field?"

"They can do it, Coach."

"Logan, those boys were so punch-drunk they couldn't write their names, much less play an organized football game in less than twenty-four hours."

"What if I told you they could? What if I told you that your team just played a scrimmage in the Butlers' backyard? Not some little pickup game, Coach; I'm talking about an organized scrimmage, using our plays and squad rotations . . . *your* plays, Coach."

"I'd tell you that you were full of it."

"Well, it's true. Ask around. A lot of people stuck around at the Butlers' place to see it. The players' own parents sure saw it. And I can promise you *they* didn't have a problem seeing the guys back on the field."

Hickham took off his ball cap, ran his fingers through his hair. "You're telling me that those boys, who were standing on that pool deck an hour and a half ago, were playing organized football?"

"Yes," Cole answered truthfully. "I'm also telling you they've never played better. Or faster. Or smarter."

"That's impossible."

"I would have thought so, too, if I hadn't been there to see it. I've never seen them play the way they were playing tonight, Coach. They were playing with a purpose that goes beyond trophies or championships. They were playing for revenge. They were playing to get back at the Badgers for what they did to us. They don't want to do it with fists or knives or guns. They want to do it the right way . . . *your* way. On the field. How can you see anything wrong with that?"

"Where should I begin?"

"We can't do it alone, Coach. We need you. We just need you to do your job. One more game."

Hickham turned away. He stood staring at the shelves beside his desk. Before him were awards, honors, and pictures from years past. The trophies were dusty and tarnished, the photos yellowed.

"Look at that stuff, Coach. That's your history there, all your successes from other places. Everyone in town knows about 'em. We know what you're capable of."

"My history is not as successful as everyone might think."

"Well, it's good enough for the people of Killington, Texas. It's why we felt so lucky to get you here. Coach, you know damn well that the Badgers are too good for us to beat without you. And you also know that the sheriff won't even consider letting this thing happen if you're not behind it."

"I can't do it, Logan."

"Why not?"

"I just can't." He turned back. "I can't field a team in that condition. The safety of those boys has to come first."

"Coach, if you'd only seen them tonight. They weren't hurting. They were hitting harder than I've ever seen them hit, and I can assure you they weren't in any pain. And if you care for them so much, then you owe them this game. If you want to walk away after the final whistle blows tomorrow night, fine. But I'm asking you for this one favor. Christ, I'm *begging* you. Remember, this is my last shot, too. I guarantee that with your help, we'll all go out a winner."

"There are no guarantees, Logan."

"This time there are."

"And how's that?"

"Because losing is not an option with this one, Coach. You just have to trust me on that."

Hickham exhaled slowly. The silence stretched out between them. "You know, Cole . . . I never did thank you."

"For what?"

"For what you did in that river the other night."

"I'm not here for thanks, Coach. I didn't save anyone. All I did Friday night was skip the bus and turn my back on this team when they needed me. I'm just asking you not to make the same mistake. I know that when you benched me Friday night you were just looking out for the safety of one of your boys. I can see that now. And I know that today you're only trying to do the same for the rest of the guys. But right now I'm asking you to take the same risk that everyone else is willing to take. I mean, that's football, right? Knowing when to take your chances? Well, we're at fourth and inches, Coach, and it's your call. Are we going to punt . . . or are we gonna go for it?"

CHAPTER 35

D ON Paul Klevin lit a Salem. "I'll tell y'all right now what this whole football deal boils down to . . ."

"Hold that thought," Kip said. "Let's finish ordering. I'm so hungry I could eat a horse."

Bernice asked Don Paul how he wanted his patty melt.

"Bloody, with pepper jack."

"Sides?"

"Tater tots, okra, and limas. Dollop of honey on the roll."

"Comin' up."

"Got any T-bones?" Kip asked.

"One left."

"Char it. Don't hold back on the A1. Beans, collards, and slaw. You can skip the honey. Matter of fact, skip the roll, substitute a sweet potato."

"Bring me his roll," Don Paul said. "And a root beer."

"And coffee," the men said in unison.

Bernice stabbed her pencil through her hair bun. "Don't say anything till I get back." She disappeared into the kitchen.

A clap of thunder rolled overhead as the jukebox faded out on a Tex Ritter and moved on to a Faron Young.

Kip lit a Winston. "They're saying rain."

"I heard a norther."

"Hmm."

They listened to the music and smoked until Bernice returned with the coffee. She took a seat on the stool opposite the booth.

"So what were you were saying, D.P.?"

"I's sayin' a front's coming through. Amarillo is already under three feet of—"

"Not that. You were talking about this football game."

"Oh, right. I was sayin' that the sheriff would be crazy not to let those schools play this game."

"You're just saying that because you're a die-hard football fan."

"Maybe. But I'm also sayin' it 'cause if those boys don't settle their score on the field, all hell's gonna break loose off it."

"You really think?"

"Go ahead, Kip, tell her."

Kip blew the steam off his coffee and took a sip. "Well, all I know is that the stage is set for something explosive to happen, one way or the other."

"How so?"

"Little while back, around eight thirty, I had to drive over to Elmwood to pick up a new fan belt for the truck. Let's just say there's no question the folks over there have heard Cole Logan's challenge loud and clear. Every house window in town has messages written in shoe polish, wishing the Badgers good luck against the Jackrabbits, that kind of thing."

"Didn't take long, did it?" Don Paul muttered.

"I can't believe it," Bernice said. "Word really spread that quick?"

"It's all over the radio, too," said Don Paul.

"Out of curiosity, I made a pass by Elmwood Heights," Kip continued. "The marquee outside the schoolhouse already has a printed message meant for us Jackrabbits fans, which I won't bother to re-peat in your company, Bernice."

"I think I get the idea."

"And when I circled around to the Elmwood ball field, I saw a full-scale rally going on there. They had a bonfire blazin' right on the fifty-yard line, kids standing all around it, carrying on, holding up signs that said *Free our Badgers!* and *Let Them Play!* One of them even said, *Kill Killington . . . Drown the Fuckers Again!*"

"And tell her about the scarecrow."

"Oh, yeah. There was a scarecrow-looking figure hanging by a noose from one of the goalposts. They'd dressed it in a Jackrabbits jersey and novelty bunny ears. 'Bout thirty kids were beating the hell out of it with baseball bats while the band, the cheerleaders, and near enough the whole student body cheered on."

"Bastards, everyone of them," said Don Paul.

"Oh, stop now, D. P. . . ."

"Well, it's true, Bernice. I for one hope to hell this game does happen tomorrow night. Teach those Elmwood sumbitches that our Jackrabbits won't be treated like the redheaded stepchildren of this district anymore. Hell, I'd break those Badgers out of the slammer myself if I could."

"But what about our boys?" Bernice asked. "Weren't they re-ported to be in pretty bad shape?"

"Like death warmed over is what I've heard." Kip took a thoughtful drag off his cigarette. "I don't know where the hell Sa-vannah and the Logan kid found that team, but rumor is they look like they've come straight out of the morgue."

"Well, where *did* they find them?" Bernice asked. "I sat right here yesterday morning, listening to y'all's tale about how they found that bus at the bottom of that river Friday night . . . *with* the boys still on it. So what gives?"

"It's a good question," Kip said. "And one I'd like answered, too."

"Christ, *I* don't care how the boys came back," Don Paul said.

"Long as they're back. If I had to guess, I'd say it was some kind of prank all along. Maybe someone had sunk a bus just like the Jack-rabbits' bus beforehand, filled it with dummies or something to throw off the rescue workers. Hell, could have been some kind of magic voodoo that brought 'em back for all we know."

Bernice laughed. "Yeah. Right. Remind me to ask Black Mona 'bout that next time she comes in. She's the expert, after all."

Don Paul shrugged. "My point is, who gives a damn how the team got back. All that matters now is beating the Badgers tomorrow night. That and getting my patty melt. How 'bout it, Bernice?"

"All right, all right, it's coming." Bernice started for the kitchen but turned back. "There's one other thing that doesn't make sense to me. How come Savannah was sittin' here Friday morning talking so ugly about the Logan kid, and now y'all're telling me that the two of 'em are in cahoots. How can that be?"

"Why don't you ask them yourself?" Kip nodded toward the door.

Cole felt their stares immediately.

Savannah said a curt hello to the waitress and the two men at the booth, calling each of them by name. The waitress was the same woman who had offered Cole her cigarettes the day before.

"Evenin', Savannah." Looking at Cole, the waitress said, "It's good to have you back again so soon. Y'all just sit anywhere."

Curious eyes followed them as Savannah led him to a booth at the back of the restaurant.

"How do you know those people?"

"*Those people,* as you call them, are my friends," she said. "I come here a lot before school. Bernice runs the place. The other two are here all the time. They're three of your biggest fans, you know."

"Swell. So seeing as how you two are so chummy, how about calling the waitress over. I wanna order."

"I haven't looked at the menu."

"Jesus, I thought you came here all the time."

"Logan, are you aware that you're being an asshole, or should I call you out on it?"

"Look, you offered me a ride. I told you to take me home. I didn't tell you to bring me here."

"Gee, sorry. It's almost ten p.m. and I was hungry and I thought you might be, too. But if you want, we can go."

"Good. Let's get the hell out of here."

"Look, Logan, I'm sorry my dad turned you down. But take it out on him, not me."

"You could have helped me back there."

"I couldn't have done a thing for you back there."

"Well, you could have tried, damnit!" His fist hit the table, rattling the silverware.

"Y'all decided yet?"

Cole's eyes drifted up to Bernice, who looked less impressed by his presence than she had been a moment before.

"Hand slipped," he murmured

"It happens," she said coolly. "Lot on your plate right now, I know. So I'll just get y'all's order and leave you be."

Savannah thanked her. "And you might tell Don Paul to stop craning his neck our way. He's liable to strain it."

Bernice winked. "Not to worry. I'll keep those boys occupied. Now what'll it be?"

Savannah ordered French toast. Cole, steak and eggs.

When Bernice walked away, Cole lit a Winston and stared off. Savannah asked if he'd care to share what he was thinking about.

"You know what I'm thinking about. And until you're ready to tell me what I need to know, I'm just gonna keep on thinking in silence."

Now it was she who pounded the table. "Okay, Logan. You want to hear the Hickham family sob story? You want to know why my dad won't coach your stupid game? Fine. He's still blaming himself for an accident that happened two years ago. You happy now?"

Cole blew a stream of smoke from the corner of his mouth. "Not yet."

Their eyes met. "All right. I'll tell you." She jabbed a fork across the table. "But this stays right here, you got it? Not a word leaves this booth."

"You really think I got anyone to tell?"

She looked off and took a deep breath. "My father won three state championships in four years at my former high school in South Carolina."

"No shit. Everyone knows that—"

"You want to hear this, or not?"

He flicked an ash into the tray and motioned for her to continue.

"It was a big school. Very affluent. More than three thousand students. Almost bigger than the whole town of Killington. Dad was well on his way to becoming the winningest coach in state history."

"And?"

"And then someone died."

"Who?"

She didn't answer.

He said, "Are you talking about your mother?"

"No. My mother had died two years before."

"So who was it?"

"He was one of my dad's star players. A sophomore. A defensive standout named Tommy Beck."

Cole crushed out the cigarette. "What happened?"

Her eyes fell to the tabletop. "Tommy had some kind of heart defect, although no one knew about it until afterwards. The autopsy said it was congenital, something he was born with. They said it was like a time bomb, could have gone off at any moment from infancy to old age. Whatever it was, his heart stopped one afternoon on the practice field, four days after Tommy's seventeenth birthday. He was dead before he hit the turf."

Cole let her words settle on him. "And your father blames himself for this?"

"Dad was really driving Tommy hard the day he died. Actually, he was *punishing* him, making him run sprints for a missed tackle or something. It was August, second practice of the day, temperature over a hundred degrees. You have to understand that however stern a coach my father is now, it's nothing compared to the tyrant he once was. You should have seen him back then. He'd have made Bobby Knight look like a teddy bear."

Cole found this hard to believe. He had always compared Hickham's coaching style to that of the much more taciturn Tom Landry—firm but disciplined, achieving the respect of his players through rigidly high expectations, rather than instilling absolute terror in them.

He said, "I can't think of a single successful coach that *doesn't* put his players through the ringer every August, from the Pee-Wee League to the NFL. Two-a-days in scorching temperatures, wind sprints, punishment for poor performance. It sort of goes with the territory. I mean, you said the autopsy showed that the kid had a congenital defect. So what was the problem? Did someone blame your dad for the kid's death? Did he get fired or sued or something?"

She shook her head. "He was far too successful a coach for that. And that's what bothered my dad more than anything. While everyone genuinely mourned Tommy's death, his loss was viewed by most as *unfortunate* collateral damage—the price a team has to pay to achieve ultimate victory. My father didn't see it that way. When he wasn't fired, he quit on his own accord. It wasn't because someone told him to, or even wanted him to. He just did it."

"And then?"

"In the six months following the funeral, my dad hardly left the house. He drank a lot. He didn't go anywhere near a football field.

Didn't watch football on TV. He didn't even attempt to pull himself together until Farley Butler tracked him down, called him up out of the blue, and offered him the position here, coaching an unheralded team in a dying town for a huge cut in salary."

"Why'd he take it?"

"No offense, but I think it's what Dad felt he deserved. I think coming here was just another way of punishing himself. Believe me, the Jackrabbits' success this season has been as much a surprise to him as it is to everyone else."

Cole let this sink in. "I suppose I can see why he blames himself for the kid's death. But I get the idea that you blame him, too."

"You're right. Well, I *did,* anyway."

"Tommy Beck wasn't just another player was he?"

She brought her eyes up and shook her head. "We had been dating for about a year when he died."

"Makes sense why your dad would have felt so terrible about it, then."

"Actually, he didn't know we were seeing each other. Not until after Tommy died. No one knew. We just thought there would be too many complications. I guess I'd be lying if I said Tommy and I didn't get a kick out of the secrecy."

Bernice returned with their order. She placed the plates on the table and moved off without a word.

Savannah paid no mind to the food. "So there it is. Guess you can see why I don't get too involved in football anymore."

"You loved him," Cole said—more as a statement than a question.

"What?"

"Tommy. You loved this guy, didn't you?"

She shifted in her seat. "I'd never felt that way about someone before, if that answers your question."

It did. But it also explained a lot more to Cole.

"So that's why your father was so adamant about my not suiting up Friday night. Given what all had happened to me, I guess he didn't want another Tommy Beck on his hands."

"It's also why he doesn't want to field that team tomorrow night, Cole. He doesn't want *forty* Tommy Becks on his hands. He thought he'd lost them once. Now that they're back, he's not going to want to lose them again."

"They're already lost, Savannah."

"He doesn't know that . . ."

"Maybe he needs to. Maybe *you* need to tell him."

"I can't."

"Why not? Why can't you talk to him? You said you don't blame him anymore for what happened. So why all the distance between you two now? Why are you like strangers?"

"We were like strangers even before Tommy's death. I was fourteen when my mom passed away from cancer. After that, Dad and I just didn't relate to each other anymore. Dad found solace in football, or at least tried to. He threw himself into the game. It was all he did, all he thought about. It was like he used it to tamp down all his pain. Then when Tommy died, the gulf between us only grew. When Dad decided to come here . . . he just came. He didn't ask me if I wanted to move; he just did it. Took me away from my home, my school, my friends. Right before my senior year. It wasn't an easy move."

Cole pushed his plate away untouched. "This game tomorrow night could help him as much as anyone, Savannah. Whatever faith or hope or *nerve* your father lost could be found with a win tomorrow night. Can't you see that?"

"Yes. It's the only reason I agreed to go along with you in the first place."

"So go further. You have to talk to him."

"My father is still the least of our problems, Logan. We've sent thirty-nine dead boys home with their parents. And we've got at least that many to bust out of jail in less than twenty-four hours."

"It's not enough just to get the teams on the field, Savannah. The Jackrabbits also have to win the game. I can't coach them myself. The Badgers are too good to beat without your father's help. So let me worry about the players, you worry about your dad. I think it's time the two of you had a little talk."

CHAPTER 36

SAVANNAH pulled the Honda up to the front of Cole's trailer under a heavy rain.

"Try him again right quick," Cole said.

She dialed her father's cell for the third time. Still no answer. She also tried his office number at the school to no avail. "Can't reach him."

"That unusual?"

"Unusual, but not unheard of. But it's after eleven. Should I be worried?"

"Ah, he couldn't have gone far." Cole reached for the door handle. "Just go home and wait for him. Call me as soon as you've talked to him."

"What are you going to do?"

"I'm gonna wait for your call . . . and think of a way to break those shitheads out of jail tomorrow."

"Oh."

"Why?"

"Just asking."

"Did you want to come in or something?"

"I . . . no. I mean, is anyone here?"

Cole peered through streaming water. "I don't think so. Does it matter?"

"I should probably go."

"Suit yourself."

"I mean, I could come in for a minute, I guess. I can keep trying my dad from here, then head home as soon as I reach him."

Cole shrugged. "Up to you."

Leaving their boots on the doormat outside, they entered the trailer and shook the rain off their wet clothes. Cole had Savannah wait by the door as he made a quick pass through the living area, picking up empty cans, newspapers, and ashtrays. He set a stack of dirty breakfast dishes in the sink, then disappeared down the hall and returned with a bath towel. Savannah used it to dry the rain from her face, then took a seat on the sofa.

"Want something to drink?"

"No. Thanks."

"There's Doctor Pepper in the fridge if you change your mind." He indicated the stains on his skin and clothing, which he'd gotten during the football scrimmage. "I'm just gonna wash this stuff off and change. I won't be long."

He switched on the television and adjusted the antennae, but the picture remained snowy and the sound muffled. He went to the window unit across the room and turned on the heater. The blast of warm air was a godsend for Savannah, despite the fact that it accentuated the smell of stale smoke.

"Better?"

She nodded. "Much. Thank you."

"You should keep trying your dad."

He headed down the hall, pulling his shirt over his head as he stepped into the shadows. A moment later Savannah heard the bathroom door close and the shower turn on.

She crossed to the television and shifted the rabbit ears again.

The signal didn't improve, so she turned it off. Her eyes went to the framed pictures hanging above the TV. One was a faded color photo of a young man wearing a cap and gown, the number 73 hanging from the mortarboard's tassel. The man's complexion was darker than Cole's, his eyes a little closer together, but the resemblance was obvious. Another frame held a black-and-white photo of the same man in full military dress. The contrast between the two pictures was dramatic. Comparing the dates, she realized that they were taken just a few years—and a tour of duty—apart.

A picture of Cole wearing a Dallas Cowboys tank top hung between the two portraits. One of his front teeth was missing. He was holding a cane pole, a tiny perch dangling from the line. Cole's father beamed proudly behind him, shirtless, in a pair of cutoffs. Seeing as how the man was a drunk who'd skipped out on his family, Savannah was surprised by how much of a presence he still held in the house.

She took her cell phone out of her pocket. She was halfway through dialing her dad's number when her curiosity got the best of her. She closed the phone and headed down the hallway.

The trailer shifted with every step across the creaky floor. She moved past the bathroom door on her right and peered into the darkened room to her left. She couldn't make out much more than a carpeted floor strewn with skirts, wadded tops, hose, bras, panties, and shoes. The room smelled of cheap perfume and aerosol hairspray.

She moved on to the closed door at the end of the hall, turned the knob, and stepped inside. Something squished beneath her sock. She was standing on Cole's wet Levi's, the waistband still stiffly upright where he had stepped out of them moments before. A shudder passed through her. She stepped over them and moved farther into the cramped room.

Gym socks, jeans, T-shirts, Fruit of the Loom briefs, magazines, and dumbbells cluttered the floor. Every inch of wall space was covered. To her right, posters of Axl Rose and Eddie Vedder hung on either side of Pamela Anderson in a ski suit unzipped to the navel. A life-size cutout of Brett Favre hung on the opposite wall, a football tucked under one arm, the Vince Lombardi Trophy under the other. The edge of a creased *Playboy* curled from under the mattress on the floor.

None of what she saw surprised her much. What *did* surprise her was that she felt fascinated rather than repelled by it all.

She blinked back to attention. The shower was still running. She made a move for the door, but stopped when she heard something click behind her. She turned and listened. There were more clicks, followed by a scratching sound.

The noise was coming from outside the window. She moved to the narrow space between the dresser and the foot of the mattress. The sound stopped as soon as she got there. After a quick glance over her shoulder, she moved the curtain aside.

There was only blackness beyond the rain-streaked glass.

Then lightning flashed.

The beast on the ledge outside the window quivered with rabid fury. Its fur was matted with blood, its teeth flecked with gore. The animal's undercarriage was swollen to capacity.

Thunder clapped, and the world outside went dark again.

Savannah covered her mouth with a shaking hand, her heart like a piston in her chest.

Seconds passed.

Then, through the heavy patter of rain she heard another sound outside the glass—meowing. The sound was as desperate as it was disarming. Each wounded call was fraught with pain and fright.

Savannah listened for a few moments until the cries faded off.

She moved closer to the glass.

"Coodles?" She inched her face up to the window and tapped gently on the glass. "Coodles? Are you th—."

A feral hiss split the silence as the beast sprang out of the blackness and slammed into the glass. The window shattered into a white web of jagged cracks, a smear of red at its center where the animal's jaws had struck the pane.

Savannah jerked back. As she spun away her side rammed into the corner of the dresser. Her breath rushed out of her, robbing her of the ability to scream. The pain was searing. Her extremities went numb. Her vision became a field of dots, swimming over a spinning room.

Then all bent black.

She never felt the impact of the fall.

CHAPTER 37

SHERIFF'S Deputy Hubie Polk set down his copy of *Maxim* magazine and pressed the flickering button on the switchboard.

"Sheriff's office." He propped his feet up on the dispatch desk. "What seems to be the trouble?"

"This is Marvin Meekin."

"Who?"

"Philip Meekin's daddy."

"Who?"

"Blind-side middle linebacker, number seventy-seven."

"Oh, right. Seventy-seven. Hell of a player. I'm glad he's not dead."

"Thanks. Reason I'm calling is he's missing."

"Missing?"

"Yeah, got his mama worked into quite a lather."

Hubie yawned, then took a bite out of his Arby's melt. "Well, you know teenagers."

"I thought I knew Phil, but he's been actin' strange all evening. Ever since he showed back up."

"Showed back up?"

"Yeah. You know, after . . ."

"Yeah, yeah, that bus deal."

"Right. Anyway, the boy hasn't said a damn word all night. Seems like all he wants to do is eat. Just about ate us out of house and home. Ribs. Pork chops. Bolonga. *Spam.* You name it. What do you make of that?"

"Of what? A teenager that don't talk to his folks and eats everything in sight? Sounds like a healthy American kid to me." Hubie turned the page of his magazine, gazed at a redhead vacuuming her dorm room in a thong.

"Normally I'd agree with you," Mr. Meekin said, "but Philip's just not hisself. He's been drooling like a faucet. His skin's gone pasty, and he stinks something fierce."

"You don't say."

"And a few hours back, he went to smashing his head into the garage door over and over. Coming right out of a four-point stance—you know, like he does on the ball field."

"Well, your boy's been through a lot. He's probably still just a little dazed."

"You really think that's it?"

"Sure. If it makes you feel any better, I got a whole jailhouse over here full of boys smashing their heads against the bars."

"You mean them Badgers?"

"Yep. They're smashing up everything in sight, including each other. But I'm not too worried . . . 'boys will be boys' and all."

"I suppose. My wife wanted to take Philip to the hospital, but I suggested we just put him to bed, let him sleep it off."

"Sounds rational."

"Trouble is I got up to take a leak a few minutes ago, decided I'd check in on him, and saw that he was missing."

"Just up and gone, huh?"

"Hmm. So what can you do about it?"

"Me?"

"Yes, you. Christ, am I talking to the Sheriff's Office or the Dairy Queen? It's almost two in the morning and my boy's AWOL."

Hubie swallowed a bite of roast beef. "Well, it's department policy not to consider a kid *missing* until we feel he's had time to sober up. These missing kids always have a way of turning up, you know?"

"Yeah? That what they told Lindbergh?"

"Who the hell is Lindbergh?"

"How 'bout you just put me on to the sheriff."

"Would if I could. He's at home grabbing a few winks. Look, the way I see it, your boy is probably out with Marvin Bumbgardner, Kevin O'Flannery, and Shane Butler."

"What makes you say that?"

"'Cause their folks have all called here in the last half hour to report them missing, too."

"That so?"

"Sure enough. So you see, you got nothing to worry about."

"I suppose. Hope the old lady'll see it that way."

"I'd bet my eyeteeth those boys are down at the Sonic having a corn dog or something. Tell you what, why don't you give it another few hours? If your boy ain't back by dawn, call back, we'll send the morning shift out right away."

"But—"

Hubie hung up, wiped spicy mustard from his chin, and took the next call.

"KSO . . . what seems to be the trouble?"

"This is Teddy Smoot's mother."

"Teddy who?"

"Smoot. Second string QB. Number sixteen."

"Oh. Right."

"He's gone missing."

"Well, you know teenagers."

CHAPTER 38

A BIRD'S piercing chirp yanked Thedford Blunt from the depths of a dreamless sleep.

He glanced bleary-eyed at the cuckoo clock above the television. Its spring-loaded inhabitant merrily announced the five o'clock hour from its perch between a pair of bat-wing doors. If there had been a gun within reach of the La-Z-Boy, he'd have shot the thing. It was something he'd been meaning to do for years anyway, ever since Loretta had packed up and moved off to live with her sister in Odessa.

At last the cuckoo took its leave for another hour. Thedford rubbed crusted eyes and tried to bring the TV into focus. A clap of thunder brought his attention to the window, where he saw that it was still dark out and raining heavily.

He still felt a little drunk, which meant that his hangover hadn't kicked in yet, thankfully. He yawned and shifted stiffly in the chair. The dull throb at the back of his neck was an instant reminder of the blow he'd received the previous morning. Just the thought of what that quarterback punk had done to him stirred him with rage. One thing Thedford knew for certain—the little bastard was going to pay for it. *Teenage shit-ass.* Hell, they were all shit-asses these days. And none more so than his own son, who wasn't worth a piss hole in the snow. Especially at times when Thedford needed him the most, like yesterday.

When he'd finally awoken in the barn just after 8 p.m., he'd been relieved to find that at some time during his drunken slumber, he had been freed from his restraints. The walk back to the house—uphill and across a dark, rain-swept pasture—had proven a difficult struggle in his delicate condition. His foul mood hadn't improved any when he reached the house only to discover Willard perched comfortably on the porch swing, watching the storm roll in over the pasture as if he had not a care in the world. Not even for his father, who'd spent the entire day a captive in his own goddamn barn.

When confronted, Willard had shown no interest in his father's suffering. When asked why he hadn't come down to offer his help, Willard had refused to answer. In fact he'd looked straight through Thedford as though he weren't even there. Even a few good licks across the chest from Thedford's belt hadn't managed to get Willard's attention. If anything, the boy had acted only more spiteful, looking back at his father with an expression of flagrant indifference.

What's more, Thedford had discovered that one of his horses was missing, and Willard didn't have an answer for that, either.

Thedford seethed as the episode replayed in his mind. Even now, hours after he'd locked Willard in his room, it still made his blood boil to think about it.

He cursed. Here he'd been awake for only ninety seconds, and he was pissed off all over again.

He was also hungry and craved eggs.

He clicked off the TV and set the remote on the floor next to Waylon, the pit bull snoring at his feet. He felt light-headed when he stood, but at least his head wasn't spinning. In fact, he felt pretty grounded.

Thedford went to the refrigerator and found only a liter bottle of RC Cola and a furry block of Velveeta.

"Willard!" he shouted down the hall. "Did you eat all the goddamn eggs?"

Willard didn't answer.

"I'm talking to you, boy!" He marched down the hall to his son's door. Remembering that he had locked it, he took a step back and kicked. The knob clattered to the floor, and the door wobbled open. "Wake up, goddamnit, I'm starvi . . ."

A blast of cold air hit him in the face. The room was empty. Willard was gone. The window beside the dresser had been smashed. The curtains fluttered over the room like white ghosts as rain blew in through the broken glass

Thedford turned hot with anger. "Sonofabitch!"

He marched back through the house, went out the front door, and looked across the driveway. The pickup was still where he had last parked it. Across the pasture, he saw a light glowing in the barn.

"Little bastard!"

He stumbled down the porch steps and climbed into the truck. He started it up, jammed the gear down, and floored the pedal. The tires screamed, spinning in the mud. Already soaked to the bone, he resigned himself to continue on foot. Before striking out, he checked to ensure that he was still wearing his belt, which he had every intention of using on Willard's insolent ass.

Rain pricked his face as he tramped across the pasture, his path lit only by the occasional flutter of lightning. "What the hell are you doing down here, boy?" he called minutes later when he reached the corral outside the barn. "Goddamnit, Willard, I'm gonna strap you good for th—"

The first thing Thedford saw when he stepped into the barn was the crimson lake that obscured the planked flooring. His eyes darted around the room. The images hit him like a series of snapshots: Equine limbs. Bones. Innards. Hair. Hooves. And the forty young men feeding on it all.

Thedford's cry brought silence to the guttural feast.

Every eye turned to him.

The boys were dispersed into every corner of the barn. Their faces were ashen masks with clouded marble eyes. Their muscles swelled beneath blood-splattered uniforms. Ropelike veins bulged beneath their skin.

One by one, they dropped what they were eating and came slowly to their feet.

Thedford swallowed the bile rising in his throat. His eyes found Willard standing with a queer casualness in one of the stalls to his left. Splayed at Willard's feet were the gory remains of a black gelding.

"W-what's happening here, Willard? What's all this about, boy?"

Willard approached his father, his cleats creating tiny ripples in the red pool at his feet.

The other players followed Willard's lead, converging at the center of the barn. Their movement was deliberate, calculated. Within seconds they had narrowed the radius around Thedford to just a few feet.

Thedford ran from the barn at a full sprint. His boots felt like cement blocks in the mud. He went a hundred yards before risking a glance behind him. As soon as he did, something tripped him up, toppling him to the ground. He rolled onto his back. Lightning flashed and he realized that he lay in a mound of entrails. The dead cow that enveloped him had been ripped apart. The animal's tongue was torn away, its eyes plucked from their sockets. The smell of the fresh kill stung Thedford's nose.

He struggled to his feet and ran on. Lightning flashed again, offering a glimpse of other mutilated cattle scattered across the pasture.

When he reached the house, he slammed the door behind him

and slid the dead bolt closed. He ran into his bedroom and took down the Winchester from the rack above the bed. Ensuring that the rifle was loaded and cocked, he ran back through the house. He made it as far as the kitchen before his terror took a paralyzing hold. He crouched at the base of the refrigerator, biting down on a shaky fist clutched tightly around the rifle barrel.

Minutes passed. The only sounds were the storm raging outside and the stammer of his breath.

Waylon began to bark. The sound came from down the hall, in the direction of Willard's room. It was not the dog's usual bark; it sounded more defensive than threatening. There was fear in it.

The barking ceased with a painful yelp.

Thedford came to his feet and aimed the Winchester into the darkened hallway.

Waylon sailed out of the blackness as though launched from a catapult, missing Thedford's head by inches. The dog slammed into the refrigerator door beside Thedford, then slid to the floor in a flaccid heap. Its entire snout and lower jaw had been ripped away. The gaping hole that remained oozed a thick gray goop.

Thedford's bladder betrayed him in a gush.

He looked back into the hallway and out of the blackness came a pair of eyes—gray, pupil-less orbs that appeared to float in midair. The floor creaked, and a figure emerged. It was Willard. Thedford watched his son's sluglike tongue lick a dollop of Waylon's brain from his chin.

Thedford squeezed the trigger with no hesitation. The rifle fired. The bullet hit its target with precision.

The smoking wound in Willard's stomach did nothing to slow his progress. His lips parted in a vulpine grin and he continued his slow pursuit.

The Winchester fell from Thedford's hands.

One of Willard's teammates appeared behind Willard and fell into step at his heels.

Thedford screamed until his voice failed. Cornered now at the junction of the refrigerator and the counter, his feet shuffled backward on the blood-smeared linoleum.

Splintered wood cracked in the den, just off the kitchen. The front door tumbled into the room and another figure lumbered into the house on muddy cleats. Two more came in behind it. Through the living room window, Thedford saw more of them closing in across the rain-speckled yard.

The window above the kitchen sink exploded in a cascade of shattered glass. A pair of Spalding lineman gloves reached inside and clawed at the air.

Thedford rifled through the drawers on either side of him, flinging in all directions whatever he could get his hands on—silverware, keys, batteries, cassette tapes, spare bulbs, a cheese grater.

By the time the drawers were clear and his endurance spent, his attackers were upon him.

Both flanks of men entered the kitchen at the same time.

Willard was the first to take hold, yanking his father's left arm from its socket with a single tug. Before Thedford could even register the pain, his son bit into the severed appendage with a snarl.

More clambering arms took hold. Thedford heard a wet squish and looked down to find an arm buried to the elbow in his abdomen. A clawing hand took hold of his spine and yanked. His body buckled to the floor, writhing wildly. Adolescent teeth, chock-full of cavity fillings and wire braces, tore into him from all sides.

The last thing Thedford Blunt heard was the sound of his own neck snapping between a set of hungry teenage jaws.

CHAPTER 39

N^{o!"}
Savannah's voice jolted Cole awake.

He felt her shoot upright beside him on the mattress.

The sudden outburst left him lucid and aware, but Savannah was clearly disoriented, having awoken to the sound of her own scream. Her eyes darted frantically around the room.

Cole spoke her name and she jumped. "Cole!"

"Yeah, it's—"

"Cole—"

"It's me, Savannah! I'm right here."

She scanned the room, lit only by the gray slivers of dawn that were visible around the edge of the curtain.

"It's okay," he said. "You must have had a bad dream." He placed a hand on her back and felt cold sweat on her shirt. Her heart was racing.

"Cole, where . . . what time is it?"

He glanced at the clock. "It's early. Just after six."

"In the morning?"

"It's okay," he said. "You just fell asleep, remember? While I was in the shower?" Her eyes were still wide with alarm. "Must have been some dream."

"A dream?" Her eyes shifted to the curtain above the mattress. She stood and in a single swift motion slid the curtain away from the window.

Cole took in the broken glass with the smear of blood at its center. "Jesus, what the hell is that?"

"It wasn't a dream, Cole." Her voice was shaking. "It was real."

Cole took her hand and led her back down to the edge of the mattress beside him. "Savannah, tell me what happened. *When* did it happen?"

She told him what she had seen out the window the night before, describing Coodles's horrifying transformation in vivid detail. He listened patiently until she had finished, then he took a moment to consider what she had described. As hard as he tried, he couldn't imagine that a housecat—even an undead housecat—could be capable of such ferocity.

"Savannah, don't take this the wrong way, but are you sure you're not making this out to be more than it really was?"

She pulled her hand away. "Are you saying you don't believe me?"

"I just think that—"

"I know what I saw, Cole."

"Think about it. We're talking about a cat whose owner hasn't been home in two days. He hasn't been fed. He probably can't get inside Mona's trailer, and he's stuck in a rainstorm. If he was trembling, he was probably just cold and scared. You know, skittish."

"Skittish? Sure. And those corpses we pulled out of that river are just a little *dazed*, right? Logan, let me explain this again as plainly as I can. Coodles has turned into a beast from hell. His stomach was swollen up like a balloon. His teeth had all sorts of meat stuck in them. *Red* meat, Logan, not something spooned out of a can of Friskies. Did you get a good look at that window? Coodles did that with his face, trying to get to me. It scared the crap out of me! Hell, I spun away so fast I rammed into the dresser and knocked myself out cold."

"I thought you had just fallen asleep."

"No, you idiot, I had passed out. The fact that the mattress broke my fall was just luck."

"Actually, you only made it halfway onto the mattress. I moved you the rest of the way, made sure you were comfortable, and—"

"And then felt that it was appropriate to join me?"

The abrupt shift in conversation took him aback. "Come again?"

"Where do you get off thinking it's all right to just climb into bed with me?"

His jaw tightened. "Hey listen, sweetheart, in *my* room I sleep on *my* bed. Anyway, relax. You're still fully clothed, aren't you? And I didn't lay an unnecessary hand on you all night."

"Is that the truth?"

"Ah hell." He flung his arms in the air. "I should have just tossed you onto the goddamn beanbag chair."

"And while we're on the subject, how come you're not wearing a shirt?"

"I never sleep in a shirt. You're lucky I bothered to throw on jeans."

Her eyes drifted down to his Levi's, which were only partially buttoned at the fly.

Her eyes shot back up. She cleared her throat. "We're drifting off topic."

Silence fell between them as both their tempers simmered down.

Cole relaxed his shoulders and softened his stern expression.

Savannah hugged her arms across her chest and shuddered against the chill in the room. The distress on her face was palpable. Cole could no longer assume that what she'd seen was anything less than a grim reality.

Another minute passed. "Listen," he said. "I believe you, all right? And I'm sorry for doubting you. It won't happen again."

She moved her hair away from her eyes and faced him. "I'm scared, Cole. I'm really scared now."

He raised her chin with his thumb. "I'm not going to let anything happen to you, Savannah. No matter what happens with the team, I'm not going to let anything harm you. I promise."

Before allowing himself to consider how she might react, he kissed her.

She instantly backed away. Her hands came up defensively against his chest.

But then, just as quickly, the hands softened.

She returned the kiss, and he felt the tightness in her lips vanish. The kiss intensified as he pulled her closer. Savanna's fingers drifted down his stomach, tracing the narrow strip of hair below his navel.

Cole kissed his way down her chin and over her neck. He opened two snaps on her shirt, allowing his tongue the freedom to traverse the freckled skin between her breasts. His mouth crept over the fabric of her bra until his lips discovered the stiffness of her nipple.

Savannah leaned her head back, surrendering. She opened another button at his fly and moved her hand inside. She took hold of him and stroked him slowly. Growing harder with her every thrust, Cole brought her down onto the mattress and parted her legs with his own. Kneeling above her, he took his time unfastening the buttons of her jeans. The denim parted to reveal the yellow lace band of her panties. As he moved up to kiss her again, Savannah raised her hips and slid her jeans farther down. She expelled a quiet moan as Cole pressed himself firmly against the rise between her legs.

Then they heard a knock at the front door.

Cole shot to his feet.

Savannah launched upward from the mattress. The movement brought a stabbing pain to her ribs where she had struck the dresser the night before. The pain stole her breath as she hurriedly closed the snaps of her shirt.

The knock at the door became a pounding fist.

Savannah started to speak, but Cole placed a finger to his lips and motioned for her to stay in the room. He buttoned his jeans, threw on a sweatshirt, and rushed out, closing the door behind him.

Savannah stood and finished dressing, her head spinning. She rubbed old mascara out of her eyes and fought to shake the tingles that had seized her entire body moments before.

The pounding on the front door ceased.

Her curiosity was luring her toward the door, but she forced herself to follow Cole's instruction and wait.

Her eyes moved back to the window. Rain had washed away most of the blood, but not all of it. She stepped over and peered between the cracks in the glass. There was no sign of Coodles in the yard, but what she did see was no less alarming—Curtis's squad car parked behind the Honda.

No sooner had she seen it than the sheriff's raised voice brought her back around. Curiosity took over. She moved to the door, opened it slowly, and crept into the hallway. She heard Curtis stomp a boot on the wooden deck outside.

"No more crap, Logan! I need to know what you know!"

"I'm telling you, Curtis, I don't know shit. I've been asleep all night. I only woke up when I heard you knocking."

"So yesterday evening you make the whole team appear like some damn rabbit from a hat, but today you don't even know where a one of 'em is?"

"Hold on. Are you saying that one of the Jackrabbits is missing?" Cole asked.

"No, I'm sayin' that every damn one of them is missing! We've been getting calls from frantic parents all morning."

The implications of what Savannah had just heard left her numb. The idea that the Jackrabbits were missing was enough to scare her. The possibility that they were missing *and* experiencing the same metamorphosis that had befallen Coodles racked her with terror.

She moved in closer but stopped when the trailer shifted under her weight. Cole clearly felt it, too. His arm waved her back from behind the door.

"I don't know what to tell you, Curtis," he said. "If there was a team meeting scheduled somewhere, then I didn't get the memo. Last time I saw any of the guys was at the Butlers' house last night."

"You expect me to believe that?"

"It's the truth."

"I seriously doubt that. This whole Jackrabbits thing stinks, Logan, like a wet fart in Oklahoma. But we'll deal with that in a minute. Right now I need to see Savannah."

"Savannah?"

"Yeah, Savannah. You know, your coach's daughter, whose car is parked in your driveway here? Coach Hickham called me a half hour ago, hot as hell. You better just thank your lucky stars I talked him out of coming over here hisself. Now go on and get her."

Savannah pressed her back to the wall, frozen.

"She's not here," Cole said.

"Logan, I'm not playing games. Go get her or I'll go in there myself and get her."

"She's not in here, Curtis. She let me borrow her car yesterday because my bike's still flooded."

"How 'bout I just speak to your mother, then."

"She's not here, either. Didn't come in all night, far as I know."

Savannah stuck her head into Cole's mother's room. It was empty, the bed untouched.

As Curtis lit back into Cole, Savannah returned to Cole's room, not knowing what to do. She considered just showing herself to the sheriff. She needed to speak with her father anyway. Maybe she could convince Curtis to drive her home. That would leave her car with Cole, so he could go searching for the Jackrabbits.

But she decided against the idea. She knew Curtis would never let Cole out from under his thumb. Not again. If Cole was going to get away from the sheriff now, she was going to have to take him away.

She went back to the window. She had to slide the pane open carefully to prevent the shattered glass from falling away. When she had opened it wide enough to climb through, she used a dresser drawer as a foothold and hoisted herself up. She was already halfway out when another thought struck her. She slipped back into the room and searched the floor for the jeans Cole had been wearing the night before. When she found what she was looking for, she dashed back to the window and climbed outside.

"For the last time, Curtis, she's not here. And even if she was, is there a law against that?" Cole's eyes subtly fell to Savannah's boots standing upright next to his own. They were only inches from Curtis's feet.

"Look, Logan, I'm not gonna jerk around with you about the coach's daughter. I figure Jimmy Hickham will nail you on that one harder than I ever could. But I am gonna need you to come with me right now."

"Where are we going?"

"Down to the station. You're gonna answer my questions about this football team once and for all."

"I've already told you everything I know."

"Fine. I guess you can just join your Badger buddies in my jail-house until something else jogs your memory."

"You're gonna throw me in jail? On what charge?"

"Obstruction of justice, interfering with the peace of the community . . . getting under my skin."

Cole knew it wasn't an empty threat. He also knew there was no way Curtis was going to leave without him. He wondered if he should just surrender and take his chances at the sheriff's office. After all, he still had to bust the Badgers out of jail by nightfall. Perhaps it would be a task more easily accomplished from the inside.

But he knew he couldn't surrender with the Jackrabbits at large. If all of them were missing, then something had clearly gone seriously wrong. All he knew for certain was that he had to do something, and quick. Something drastic.

As though Curtis had read his mind, the sheriff moved a foot across the threshold, preventing Cole the option of slamming the door.

Movement in the background drew Cole's attention. In his periphery he saw Savannah tiptoeing around the cars. A shock of adrenaline shot through him. He didn't know what she was doing, but he hoped he could stall Curtis long enough to find out.

"Curtis, if the whole team is missing, why are you here and not out looking for them? Why are you wasting your time with me when I've already told you I don't know anything." He saw Savannah move past the Honda, creep behind the squad car, then disappear from sight.

"Don't tell me how to do my job, Logan. Just get your shoes; you're coming with me right now. Whether you come in handcuffs or not is up to you."

"Well . . . all right. I guess I'll . . . I guess I'll get my shoes." Cole was desperate now. He feigned a move toward his bedroom, then came back. "Say, do you know if it's supposed to rain all day?"

"Rain? Logan, just get your damn shoes!"

Savannah was visible again. She was behind her own car and slowly opening the driver's door.

Cole stalled some more. "It's just that if it's going to rain, I'll need my boots. But if it's not going to rain, I can just wear my sneakers . . . or maybe even some loafers."

"Logan, I don't care if you put on your damn bunny slippers. Let's just get going before I sta—"

The Honda's engine revved to life.

Curtis spun around.

"Boots it is, then." In one fluid motion, Cole reached down, grabbed both pairs of boots, and dove headfirst off the porch steps. As he hit the mud, he tucked his head, somersaulted, and used his momentum to roll back up to his feet. It was a move he had done countless times, dive-rolling over the heads of blitzing defensemen to get into the end zone.

Savannah kicked the passenger door open and Cole was inside the car before Curtis could grumble his first curse.

Cole told Savannah to gun it.

The tires flung mud before taking hold and launching them forward.

Cole pulled his door closed and looked out the rear window. Curtis was already scrambling toward the squad car. "You're gonna have to stomp it. He's got a lot more under the hood than we do."

"He's not going anywhere." Savannah slammed the stick into second and peeled off the property.

"Well, he's sure as hell not gonna let us go!"

"He won't have a choice." She held up Cole's switchblade. "Unless he can catch us with slashed tires."

Cole was impressed. "Don't suppose you cut the wire on his radio, too?"

"What do you take me for, a rookie? Also cut your phone line, hope you don't mind."

"Would you mind if I kissed you again?"

"I never kiss on the first run from the law."

"Nobody likes a prude."

"You bet your ass prude. You tell anyone what happened in your room back there, I'll kill you."

"Unfinished business as far as I'm concerned."

Their eyes met in the rearview mirror.

Savannah smiled, then peeled through a tight corner as the dirt road switched to slick asphalt.

"So you heard what Curtis said back there, right?" Cole asked.

"Yeah. I heard. You *do* realize what's happening to them, don't you?"

"Yeah. *The change.*"

"Mona said two days, Logan. Our two days are almost up. And believe me, this change thing is pretty damn dramatic." Her meaning was clear.

"Coodles was really that fucked-up, huh?"

Minutes later Savannah stopped the car at a red light on Jenkins Avenue. The football stadium loomed just ahead. Cole heard distant sirens screaming in every direction. Savannah had done well to cut the lines, but Cole knew that that wouldn't buy them much time. Curtis had probably already reached a phone and had his men out looking for the Honda.

Savannah said, "Logan, if your teammates are going through the same transformation as that cat, they may already be too far gone to control."

Cole refused to let the idea enter his head. He gazed through the rain at the empty road ahead. "They're not in town anymore. Forty guys reported missing can't just wander the streets without being seen."

Savannah nodded. "And if they're all missing, then something *drew* them out. They can't communicate verbally. It's not like they called one another on a phone chain. So there had to have been some force *pulling* them out. Something pretty damn strong."

They looked at each other and said the word in unison: "*Hunger.*"

"So what do we do now, start combing the burger joints?"

Cole shook his head. "They're animals, Savannah. Pack hunters, which always flock to places familiar to them, places where they know they can hunt. Where they can *feast*."

Savannah thought about it, then went pale. "Oh, God. We really have to go back to that monster's ranch?"

Flashing lights glinted in the rearview mirror. A squad car crested the hill about three quarters of a mile behind them.

"Better step on it," Cole said. "Looks like the Jackrabbits aren't the only ones on the hunt."

CHAPTER 40

DISPATCH desk, go ahead."

"Who's this, Freddy?"

"It's Hubie. Freddy's in the crapper."

"When's he back?"

"Oh, I'd say about two Marlboros and an *Archie* comic from now. Who's this?"

"It's Smitty, down in the cell block. We have a situation down here, thought the sheriff oughtta come down and have a look."

"He ain't here."

"Better get him on the horn, then."

"Would if I could. Sheriff's radio's on the blink."

"Well, Christ, send anyone you can down here."

"Wera mit bort shaf at the mumnt."

"Say again? I couldn't make that out."

"Mmm. Sorry." Hubie swallowed. "Just trying to get this Whopper down. I said we're a bit short staffed at the moment. Got the whole force out looking for missin' ball players. The lines have been lightin' up like a damn Christmas tree all night. What's the trouble down there?"

"I think there's somethin' the matter with these Elmwood boys."

"How so?"

"Well, first off, they ain't lookin' so hot. Their eyes are bloodshot. Their bodies are all swole up. Couple of the fellas look like they've yanked half their hair out. And the smell of 'em. *Kee-rist,* you wouldn't believe it!"

"Maybe they just need breakfast."

"Had it. I fed 'em a full square about a half hour ago. Most of them ate so fast they forgot to chew."

"Think there's a bug going around or something?"

"You want my opinion, I'd say they're on drugs."

"Hadn't seen much of that in a while. Think it's the nose candy?"

"Don't matter what it is. Question is, how could they have gotten drugs into the jailhouse?"

"Up their butts, probably. You know kids these days. Want me to call for a medic?"

"How 'bout a zookeeper. I'm telling you, these kids are acting like caged animals."

"Hang on, lemme click my screen over to the security cam."

"Don't bother. 'Bout ten minutes ago one of 'em ripped it off the wall and crushed it under his armpit. Actually, the cameras are out in both blocks."

"No lie?"

"That ain't the half of it. You know the big one in Block A, got the fucked-up face? What's his name, Flamont something?"

"Yeah, Booker Flamont. Senior. Strong-side middle linebacker."

"Well, he's been doing one-arm chin-ups off the plumbing pipe for twenty minutes. I can't get a word out of him other than 'Fuck you, copper, more bacon.' The boys over in Block B aren't much better off. They've got a football game goin' on in the damn cell. Full tackle and everything."

"Where'd they get a football?"

"They're using the commode. Ripped the damn thing right out of the floor. I'm sixteen years on the block, Hubie, and I gotta tell you, for the first time in my career I'm a little jumpy."

"Ah, it ain't no big thing. Listen, I got a plan. Soon as Freddy gets back from the john, I'll send him on down there to take a look. Meantime, sit tight and I'll keep trying the sheriff on the horn. And just remember, they're only kids. We're still the law around here."

"Hope you're right. Get Freddy down here quick!"

CHAPTER 41

I THINK we're a little late, Logan."

Through the windshield Cole looked at what remained of Thedford Blunt's cattle herd. The skeletal mounds were chalk white, picked clean of all meat. Cole estimated there to be at least forty of them scattered across the horizon.

He told Savannah to drive onto the property.

She looked at him reluctantly. "Really?"

"It's all right. They're not here."

"How do you know?"

"'Cause there's nothing left to eat. Come on, we don't have much time. Head for the barn."

They drove onto the pasture, rolling over the same section of fence they had plowed through the day before. The Honda jounced across the muddy field until they reached the corral adjacent to the barn. The barn doors were partially open, but Cole couldn't make out anything inside.

"Wait here."

"Logan, you just said they're not here. Let's just go." She covered her nose with the neck of her sweatshirt. "That smell is killing me."

"I have to look."

"Why?"

"Because I left a man chained up in there yesterday."

He got out, shut the door, and ran through the rain until he was close enough to get a clear view inside the barn. He was back inside the car seconds later.

"Well?" she asked. "What's the story?"

"He wasn't in there."

"So that's a good thing, right?"

He didn't answer.

"Cole, you're white as a ghost. What *was* in there?"

"Huh?"

"What about the horses? Please, don't tell me . . ."

"They're fine." He lied. "The horses are fine."

There were footprints leading away from the barn, a large group of them—cleat marks. They led up the pasture toward the house. Cole told her to follow them.

Dodging cattle bones, they crossed the pasture and parked in front of the house.

"Doesn't look promising," Savannah intoned.

The front door had been ripped from its hinges, leaving the entry wide open. The trail of footprints led inside. Other prints fanned around to the back of the house.

Cole got out of the car and stood in the open door. The smell coming out of the house was strong enough to activate his gag reflex.

"Mr. Blunt?" he called. "Thedford Blunt, are you in there? It's Cole Logan."

Cole didn't know whether to expect a cry for help or the crack of gunfire. He got neither.

"Cole, I don't like this. Let's just go."

"I can't. I have to look. Just stay here. Turn the car around, roll down the window, and keep the motor running. If you hear me yell, drive on and don't look back."

"I'm not going to—"

"Just do it! Please."

After some hesitation she did as instructed, turning the front of the car away from the house.

Cole approached the front steps. There were holes in the treads where footfalls had broken through the wood. He moved up the stairs with careful steps. A cloud of flies greeted him when he reached the doorway.

"Mr. Blunt, are you in here?" he said, swatting madly at the air.

He stepped inside. The living room was ransacked. Muddy footprints clotted the carpet. Fist-size holes pocked the walls. Matt Lauer's face fluttered in static on the overturned television. An antler had been stripped from the trophy elk above the fireplace. One of its points now poked out of the backrest of the La-Z-Boy. A smashed cuckoo clock hung on one wall. The cuckoo itself dangled limply from a warped spring. Kitchen utensils and appliances littered the area.

Cole followed the trail of footprints toward the kitchen. Cheetos crunched under his boots with every tentative step.

He saw blood before he even rounded the corner—five narrow streaks of it raked in parallel lines across a lower cabinet. Finger trails. The window above the kitchen sink was shattered. More utensils were strewn across the floor and countertop.

He whispered Thedford's name again.

Getting no response, he took a breath and willed himself to take the final step around the corner.

There was movement in the side mirror. Savannah turned.

Cole tumbled down the stairs.

He rolled when he hit the ground and made it to the side of the car in a mad crawl. He came up on his knees next to her open window, his eyes wild with terror.

"Go!"

"Cole, what's wrong—"

"Just go!"

"Logan, just slow down, what's the matter?" There was a rifle in his hand. The barrel glistened red. "Where'd you get that gun? Is . . . is that your blood?"

He shook his head, struggling for breath. "Thedford Blunt is dead." He buried his face in the crook of his arm. He tried to be sick, but could only manage a few dry heaves.

"What do you mean he's . . . how?"

"Same way as the cows. Same way as the *horses!*"

"But you said—"

"They're dead, Savannah! All of them. The Jackrabbits killed them and they ate them." He wiped spittle from his lips and brought his head back up. Rage had replaced the terror in his eyes. Before she could question him further, he slammed a palm against the car door. "Goddamn it! The hell with all of this!"

"Cole, calm down . . ."

"Don't tell me to calm down! I'm walking away. Right fucking now! It's over!"

"You can't do that . . ."

"Why not? Why should I stick around? So I can see a few more people die on my watch? I mean seriously, why do I need any of this shit? Tell me, please! What the fuck is keeping me from getting on my bike, heading out of town, and never looking back . . ."

"You mean like your father did?"

He glared at her, his lips pressed white. She braced for a violent reaction, but to her surprise the comment seemed to deflate him. His shoulders slumped. His chin dropped to his chest.

"You know why you can't leave, Cole, so I'm not going to waste time telling you. What I will say is that your fate—and the fate of this town—is in your hands. And that fate is going to be decided in a matter of hours, so we don't have another minute to lose. What's done is done. All we can do is focus on what happens next."

He nodded. "I still need you to go," he said. "Get out of here as fast as you can."

"I'm not leaving without you."

"You have to. I have to find the team, and I don't want you anywhere around when I do."

"So what are you going to do? Hunt them down . . . shoot them?"

"That won't do any good. You heard what Mona said. There's only one way to end this. The Jackrabbits have to play and we have to *win*. Don't you see? She made sure that it could only end that way. It was her dying wish. And if it's not granted . . ." He shook his head. "It has to end now. We've already waited too long."

"Okay," she said. "What do you want me to do?"

"Go to your father. Tell him everything . . . from the beginning. Tell him about Mona, Coodles, my hand, all of it. Tell him we gotta have him with us and don't take no for an answer."

"Then what?"

"Do whatever you can to have that stadium filled by seven o'clock. Get the word out. Make sure everyone in town knows those teams are going to be on that field to play ball."

"Never thought the fans meant that much to you."

"I don't need fans; I need *chaos*. The more people we have there, the less control the sheriff's office will have. We need to create a situation where the authorities won't have any choice but to let the game proceed."

"You want me to divulge to the public that one of those teams is comprised of dead cannibals?"

A weak grin parted his lips. He shook his head. "They're still just a little dazed, right?"

She mirrored the smile. "Okay, Logan. I'll take care of it." She took his hand. "Where are you going to start looking?"

Cole gazed into the distance. "There are a lot of pastures around here. I'll hotwire the pickup over there, see what I see. To be honest, I'm not worried so much about the livestock anymore."

"Why not?"

"Now that they've had a taste of human flesh . . ."

"Right. Okay, I got it." She leaned her head out the window and kissed him. "Be careful out there, Cole Logan."

He squeezed her hand. "I will. Promise."

Her eyes moved to the gun. "I gather from the blood on that thing that it didn't do Thedford Blunt much good."

Cole stood and cocked the weapon. "Yeah, well, after what I just saw in that kitchen . . . if this goes bad and they turn on me, I might not be using the last shell on one of *them*."

CHAPTER 42

Y OU expect me to believe a word of that story?"

"No, Dad, I don't. God knows *I* wouldn't." Savannah folded her hands on the dining table. "But you have to believe it. Lives depend on you believing it. Not to mention quite a few souls."

Hickham knocked back the last of his coffee and fixed her with a cold glare. "Young lady, are you on drugs?"

"What? No, Dad, I'm not on—"

"'Cause let me just make sure that I'm understanding you correctly. You're telling me that some old lady used a magic spell to bring my football team back from the dead . . ."

"I know it sounds—"

"And now my team is damned to walk the earth for eternity, subsisting on horses and cattle, unless I can save their souls by helping them defeat the Elmwood Badgers for the district title?"

"That's pretty much it, Dad. Only, Cole thinks they've probably gone off livestock now that they've gotten a taste for human flesh."

"Pardon?"

"That's another thing. You know Willard Blunt, your starting free safety? Well, last night the Jackrabbits ate his father."

Through clenched teeth Hickham said, "Where the hell is Cole Logan?"

"He's out looking for the Jackrabbits."

"Looking for them? Where are they?"

"Well, if he knew that, he wouldn't be looking for them."

"Damnit, Savannah, this isn't funny!"

"Dad, believe me, I know that. I'm not trying to make jokes. If I seem glib, it's because I don't have time to talk my way around this stuff. Crazy as it sounds, everything I've told you is the truth."

"How about the *truth* as to where you were all night?"

"I was in Cole Logan's bed." On his look, she raised calming hands. "Don't worry, he . . . he was the perfect gentleman. Our falling asleep was just an accident. We were so tired—"

"I don't care if you were knocked unconscious. We have rules in this house!"

"Dad, this is beside the point! You want to ground me for staying out all night, fine. Send me to my room until June for all I care, but right now I need to know if you're going to help us!"

"Ah, hell, Savannah!" He stood and planted his hands on his hips. "All this you're telling me . . . it can't be true."

"Can't it? Think about it, Dad. Everyone in this godforsaken town is so brainwashed over this football team that they either can't or just *won't* see what's really going on. They're so hung up on wins and losses, victory and revenge, that they haven't even questioned how those guys could have possibly survived that crash. But you're not from here, which makes you one of the few sensible people around."

"Those boys walked into that picnic on their own two feet, Savannah. Why would their parents question the players' survival?"

"*They* wouldn't. And Cole and I knew they wouldn't. But you're not one of them, Dad. You can't tell me *you* haven't questioned it. You were on that bus Friday night. You saw what happened to your team, and you know they couldn't have lived through it."

"I thought you said they didn't live through it."

"That's right. They didn't. They're dead." She paused. "They're as dead as your assistant coaching staff." He turned from the window, and she nodded. "Yes. For whatever reason, Mona only brought back the players. I'm sorry for the loss of your colleagues, Dad. But if it's any help, I'd say your assistants got the better deal. At least they've gone on to a better place. The Jackrabbits are stuck in Killington, looking for food and stinking up the place even more."

The kitchen fell silent. Savannah gave him a moment to absorb what she'd said.

"I suppose you're going to tell me this Mona is also the one who healed Logan's hand?"

"Yes. Surely you had suspicions about that, too, right? There's no way that hand could have healed as quickly as it did, not without some kind of miracle . . . some kind of *magic*."

Hickham returned his gaze to the window. "So where is she now? This . . . Black Mona?"

Savannah told him about Mona's death at the riverside, finishing with the old lady's dying words. "The last thing she said was that victory over the Badgers was the only thing that could save the Jackrabbits' souls. Otherwise, I guess they'll just remain in limbo. From what I saw at the Blunts' ranch, it's not going to be a very pleasant eternity, not to mention a particularly safe one for the rest of society."

"So what you're telling me is that this crazy old woman sold my players' souls . . . and her own, for victory?"

"She's a Jackrabbits fan, Dad. It's what they do."

He returned to the table and gazed up through glassy eyes. "And what exactly do you want me to do?"

Her hand fell on his arm. "First, I want you to tell me that you're all right. That *we're* all right."

"Aren't we?"

"Not as long as you keep trying to outrun your mistakes. Dad, what happened to Tommy back home was an accident."

"Didn't you just call it one of my mistakes?"

"Stop it. I won't hear that talk anymore. It wasn't your fault. I knew it. Everyone knew it. The only one blaming you for Tommy dying is *you*." She came around the table and knelt at his side. "Dad, God rest Tommy's soul, but it's over. It's behind us. He's in a better place. What matters now is *now*. And right now you've got a game to coach—a game that only you can win. I stayed with the team last night at the Butlers' house. I've seen what they can still do. *Your* team, Dad. They played better than I've ever seen them. You must have pounded those plays in well, because they remember them even in death."

He shook his head. "It's crazy."

"Of course it's crazy. This whole place is crazy. So what's holding you back?"

"Fear."

"Of what?"

"Of seeing more boys hurt on my watch."

"Dad, it's football. It's a contact sport."

"Basketball is a contact sport. Football is a *hitting* sport."

"They're dead, Dad, they can't feel pain."

"Who's to say they won't try and eat me the way they did Thedford Blunt?"

"Well, they seem to listen to Cole. They've shown no sign of hostility toward him yet. Seeing as how you're the only other surviving member of the team, I don't see why they wouldn't extend you the same courtesy. It's a risk we'll just have to take."

"Who's to say they won't eat their opponents?"

"All the more reason they need a good coach, Dad—some firm discipline."

"I'm not kidding, Savannah."

"Neither am I."

"Why does all this mean so much to you?"

"Because I know it means so much to *you*. If you want to pack up and leave the game for good, that's fine. In fact, you'd have my blessing. But finish what you started here. You owe it to yourself. You owe it to those boys' parents. Remember, at the end of all this, they've still lost their sons. The players deserve to taste victory, Dad, district-level victory, one time . . . if only for a few moments. And you're the only one who can give it to them. So what do you think, Coach?"

He gnawed the inside of his cheek, his eyes staring intently at the table before him. Minutes passed before he finally looked up. "Well, I don't think we'll get a yard on the Badgers unless we put the squeeze on their front men and spread out their secondary."

Savannah smiled. She came to her feet and kissed her father on the forehead. "I love you, Dad."

"I love you, too. Now how the hell do we make this thing happen?"

CHAPTER 43

C OLE had been scouring the maze of back roads for almost an hour, but his efforts had yielded no sign of his teammates. For a while he had been able to follow a trail of slaughtered cattle, which had extended north onto properties miles beyond the Blunts' fence line. The trail had long since gone cold.

Twice he'd passed cattlemen sitting on horseback in the rain, peering under low hat brims at the mutilated remains of their livelihood. Cole imagined the horror on their faces. The bewilderment. As much as he felt obliged to stop and explain, he had driven past without a look, taking care to keep the Winchester low across his lap and out of view.

He checked his watch again. Midday was fast approaching. He cursed under his breath and increased his speed over the rutted dirt. More miles ticked away before he saw a locked gate and cattle guard blocking his path a short distance ahead. Dead end. He screeched to a stop and jammed the truck into reverse.

Something moved on the horizon behind him. A human figure. A second look in the rearview mirror showed a group of figures. He rolled down the window and stuck his head into the rain. A half mile back a line of silhouettes crested a rise in the rolling terrain, some three hundred yards inside a property fence.

Cole's foot tromped on the pedal. He weaved backward until the road widened. Jerking the steering wheel hard, he spun the truck around and continued forward. The truck's grille snapped through the fence posts seconds later.

His progress then slowed to a near halt. The field he had driven onto was not grazing pasture but fallow cropland. Parallel rows of plowed dirt stretched the width of the property. Gullies two feet deep brimmed with rainwater.

Cole gripped the wheel hard as the ruts pitched him across the cab. The bed of the truck bounced behind him with a life of its own.

Through sprays of water he saw his teammates looming in the distance, facing him now, unmoving.

Ahead and to his right he spotted a small house. Sprawling willows swayed in the wind on either side of it. Two figures were huddled under an umbrella about a hundred yards away from the front door—a man and a woman. Cole saw their faces shifting between his truck and the strange gathering of men on their property.

The Jackrabbits clearly saw them, too. They began to move en masse toward the couple.

Panic seized Cole. There were no mutilated cows or horses in sight, nothing to alert the couple that they were in danger. He dropped gears and pressed the gas harder. He slammed the horn but heard only a dull click. He flashed the truck's headlights repeatedly. Sticking his head out the window, he called out to the couple, but the howling wind muffled his warnings.

Someone else emerged from the house. A young girl, no older than five or six. She wore a pink raincoat and rubber boots. Blond curls spilled from under a matching bucket hat. She splashed whimsically through the puddles in a playful dash from the house. She ran past her parents unheeded, and continued on, heading straight for the Jackrabbits.

The truck pitched hard and slammed into another rut. Cole pumped the accelerator. The tires hummed without traction. He was stuck, still some seventy-five yards away. He toppled out of the truck. "Grab the girl!" he screamed. "Get her back in the house now!"

A lone figure stepped forward from the cluster of players, his helmet clutched at his side. It was Philip Meekin.

The linebacker's thick arms came up as he moved to meet the approaching child. The rest of the players circled in behind him.

"Goddamnit!" Cole reached back into the truck and grabbed the Winchester. He planted the rifle's barrel in the fork of the open door and sited his target.

A scream rang out. The girl was close enough now to clearly see the monsters before her. She tried to move back but lost her footing and fell to the ground. Philip dove for her and took hold of her ankle.

Cole fired at Philip's head.

The shot missed, his aim altered by the wind.

Fuck! Cole ejected the shell and took aim again, but the rest of the Jackrabbits, who were now moving in pursuit of the parents, obstructed his view.

Cole stumbled six feet to his right until his view was clear again.

Still screaming, the young girl kicked her legs furiously, some-how landing a square blow to Philip's nose. Even brain-dead, Philip had clearly been stunned. He brought a hand to his face, releasing his hold on the girl. She made it to her feet, but in her panic, she ran in the opposite direction from her parents. The entire team now separated the family.

Philip came to his feet and ran after the girl.

Cole knelt, shouldered the rifle, and took aim at his teammate once again, knowing that another miss would certainly mean the girl's end.

Philip closed in quickly. Moving at a level trajectory across the horizon, Philip was right on the girl's heels, his hands clawing the air just behind her blond ringlets.

Cole's aiming eye narrowed as the gun barrel followed Philip's head.

Philip lunged.

Cole fired.

Bone cracked as Philip's head recoiled in a spray of red. The linebacker hit the ground like a sack of cement, his arms extended stiffly skyward, the girl's pink rain hat clenched in his fist.

The child fell away, unharmed. She scurried backward on hands and feet, her cries ringing out through the wind.

As soon as the shot was fired, the rest of the Jackrabbits halted their pursuit and turned toward Cole.

Cole's eyes remained fixed on the tip of the smoking barrel until the girl's parents reached her. Her father took her in his arms, and the three of them rushed back into the house. The door slammed shut.

Phil Meekin's arms finally fell to the ground. He rolled over and came to his feet on unsteady legs. Steam rose from the gaping hole in his head. He stumbled around like a lost child, rubbing forcibly at the wound as though he were scratching an itch. In time he ambled back and rejoined his huddled teammates.

The rifle fell from Cole's trembling hands. He doubled over at the waist, struggling to slow his racing heart.

A horn blared, startling him. He jerked upright and turned back toward the road.

The Jackrabbits' bus was idling on the weedy shoulder just outside the busted fence.

Behind the wheel sat Coach Hickham.

"How'd you find me, anyway?

"Heard the shot," Hickham said. "Just luck, really, that I was so close. I've been driving around in circles for twenty minutes."

"Savannah sent you out here?"

"She thought maybe you could use some help . . . not to mention transport. Looks like she was right."

"Did she tell you . . ."

"She told me everything, Logan."

Cole looked at him. "Listen, Coach, I want you to understand—"

"I understand it all, Cole. I don't quite *believe* it, but I do understand it. And in case you're wondering, you and I are square as far as I'm concerned. Right now I just want to finish this thing." His eyes moved to his players. "If such a thing is even possible."

It had taken them fifteen minutes to get the Jackrabbits off the field, and another five to get them lined up alongside the bus. They'd burned up more time than Cole could afford, but he was relieved to see that the players still followed his orders with no visible hostility.

So far, such deference had extended to the coach as well.

Cole stepped up to Hickham's side. They stood before the team, both with their arms folded across their chests. Mud and gore caked the players' faces beyond recognition. Cole no longer doubted Savannah's description of Coodles, following the so-called change. If the cat had looked a fraction as horrific as the Jackrabbits did now, it was no wonder she had been scared out of her wits.

"Think maybe you oughtta say a few words?" Cole said.

Hickham answered out of the side of his mouth. "Logan, you really believe these things will understand a damn thing I tell them?"

"You're one of them, Coach, one of the boys from the bus. They'll understand. They may not know much, but I think they understand two things really well—food and football."

"Under different circumstances, I'd call it the ideal team."

"Just say what you gotta say. They'll understand it all right."

"What the hell happened to Meekin?" Hickham indicated the linebacker with a nod. Philip no longer had the left third of his skull. Bits of steaming brain matter still clung to his cheek.

"Oh, I shot him in the head." Cole shrugged at the coach's look. "That was the shot you heard. What'd you think, that I was hunting pheasants?"

"But, how could you . . ."

"He was about to eat a little girl."

Hickham paled.

Cole just rolled his shoulders again. "Don't worry, the girl's safe. And don't worry about Phil, either. He didn't feel a thing. None of them can feel any pain at all . . . watch." Cole shouldered the rifle and took aim at Chili Blaylock, tight end. Hickham pushed the gun barrel down before it fired.

"All right, all right, I got it!" He shook his head. "Jesus, I gotta get out of this town."

He turned away in a huff, hitched up his pants, and paced the length of the line. General Patton would have envied the intensity of his scowl. "All right, men, let's get to it. Logan here tells me that even though there's not a pulse among you, you understand what it is we've got to do today. Basically, it all boils down to this: You wanna spend the rest of your miserable deaths scrounging around town, looking for somebody to eat, then you go right ahead. But if you wanna go up and sit with your maker the way He intended, then you'll do exactly as I say. You cross me, I'll run your asses from here to Shreveport. You try to *eat* me and I'll plug you with that Winchester until it *does* hurt. That goes for eating anyone else, too . . . including your opponents. We're gonna settle this score one way and that's *my* way . . . on the field, regulation rules, no exceptions. Is that clear?"

Cole saw no glimmer of comprehension. Hickham continued.

"All right, then." He cocked his cap back. "Having said all that, if you *do* listen to me, I can promise that you'll exit this world as the East Texas Two-A champions of Region Six, District Four . . . which isn't a hell of a bad way to go out."

He clasped his hands behind his back. His features softened

some as he made another scan down the line of lost faces. "Gentlemen, if you've understood anything I've just said, then I hope you'll
understand this, too: It's been an honor to coach you this year. You
gave me everything you had and then some. And I'm damn sorry
for what's happened. My prayers will be with you and your families
until the day I join you on the other side . . . and that's a promise."
He looked at Cole through misty eyes. The two of them shared a
nod. Then the coach cleared his throat and blew his whistle. "Now
get your dead asses on that bus. We've got a game to win."

CHAPTER 44

H ELLO."

"What are you wearing?"

"Cole! Thank God!"

"Your dad let me use his cell."

"So he found you?"

"He found me; I found the Jackrabbits."

"So is everything okay?"

"That depends on your definition of—"

"Is anyone else dead, moron?"

"No . . . at least, not that I know of."

"Where are y'all?"

"Your dad's on the bus, heading for the locker room with the team, taking the long way around town to avoid the sheriff's patrol cars."

"You left him alone with them!"

"Only when I felt confident that everything was cool. Don't worry. The guys knew who he was and did as he said . . . same as they did with me. If it helps any, your dad's also got the rifle . . . just in case."

"Oh, I feel so much better. So where are you?"

"I just crossed the city line, heading back into town. The pickup got stuck, so I had to steal a car. Long story. I'll tell you later. Are you still at home?"

"No, I'm at the Buttered Bean. I didn't think it was a good idea to stay home with the sheriff out looking for me."

"Good call."

"I ditched my car a mile from here. Don't worry, nobody knows where I am. Anyway, listen, I've made calls to every news organization in the county, telling them to head over to Jackrabbits Stadium if they want to catch the biggest story in town. It's already all over the TV and radio. I also started a few email and text-messaging chains, which are passing through the Killington High student body as we speak. Apparently word is spreading like wildfire. I just learned that the stadium is already starting to fill up."

"Sheriff's office? State troopers?"

"I'm told there are only a handful of them at the school now. Seems there was a little resistance at first, but eventually the crowd got so big there wasn't much the authorities could do without taking drastic action. I'm thinking they don't have too many men to spare at the moment, what with the Jackrabbits still at large. Not to mention *us*."

"That's good. Hopefully they'll have only a bare-bones staff at the sheriff's office when I get there. Any Badgers fans driving over from Elmwood yet?"

"I just got off the phone with Tallie Mayhew. You know her?"

"Sophomore, brunette, high tits . . ."

"And not a brain in her skull. Yeah, Logan, that's the one. Tallie's already at the stadium. She just told me there's a line of traffic backing up on Jenkins Avenue, coming in off the interstate. The Elmwood folks are definitely on their way."

"Well, keep making those calls. The bigger the crowd, the better."

"Enough about me. How are you going to handle this jail-break?"

"I thought I'd rely on my brute strength and cunning."

"I figured you'd say that, which is why I took action myself."

"What kind of *action*?"

"Thought maybe you could use a little diversion to help you get into the station. It's already in the works."

"Savannah, what are you talking about?"

"Let's just say I recruited a few volunteers to help us in our cause. You'll see when you get there."

"Wait . . . *recruited* them how?"

"I challenged their school spirit and promised them a cover story in the paper. I'll text them now, tell them you're on your way and to be ready. Just be careful, keep my dad's phone handy, and don't screw this up."

"You're really starting to enjoy this, aren't you?"

"Good-bye, Logan."

CHAPTER 45

C OLE had to hand it to Savannah. Her diversion tactic was inspired, if not genius.

After ditching the stolen car in a nearby neighborhood, he made it the rest of the way to the Killington Sheriff's Office on foot. He'd had to jump fences and duck behind hedges to avoid the continuous stream of squad cars running hot all over town.

Crouched behind a Dumpster across the street from the KSO, he saw Savannah's "recruits" successfully executing her plan with intended effect. The recruits were members of the Jackrabbits cheer squad. They were washing down the four remaining squad cars in the parking lot while six uniformed deputies looked on with wide eyes and lagging tongues.

The cheerleaders' effort was admirable. The rain had let up some, but the conditions were still bleak. Clouds hovered low over town, and the gusting wind bit hard. The girls wore only their game uniforms—short skirts, haltertops, and ankle socks. Their bare legs and midriffs remained exposed to the harsh elements.

Two girls stood at the edge of the lot beside the road. A large banner was stretched between them that read *Give a Cheer for the*

KSO! They hooted and hollered at every car that passed and got honks and cheers in return. The rest of the girls worked on the squad cars, keeping the deputies engrossed with their flirtatious employment of bucket, sponge, and foam.

Cole waited on anxious knees for his chance to move. Soon, three of the cheerleaders bent to scrub a low fender. The deputies circled in behind them, and Cole saw his opportunity. Keeping low, he sprinted onto the lot and dove unseen behind the last patrol car in the row. Out of breath and buzzing with adrenaline, he checked the rear door, found it unlocked, and climbed into the floor of the backseat. Tucking his knees under his chin, he pulled the door closed behind him.

A few minutes passed before Maxine Wiley stepped into view above him, pressing a soapy sponge to the window. The head cheerleader had once been Cole's lab partner in biology. Sophomore year, she'd also been his backseat partner in the stadium parking lot following the loss to Gurney. Ancient history.

He cracked open the door and whispered her name.

Maxine jumped back, startled. She started to speak, but Cole shushed her.

"Keep working!" he hissed.

She glanced down. "That you, Cole Logan?"

"Don't look at me. Just keep washing."

She smiled and whispered, "God . . . you totally scared the hell out of me. We've been expecting you, you know."

"Can't tell you how much I appreciate y'all doing this, Maxine."

"Yeah?" A shiny set of porcelain veneers parted her candy-apple lips. "So you gonna make it up to me, or what?"

The deputies burst into laughter nearby. Cole tensed. "Are they coming this way?"

Maxine shook her head. "No, it's all right. They're watching Mindy Lynn do a backward walkover. So is this game really on, or what?"

"Not without your help. Listen, see the fat deputy over there, got a stupid look on his face?"

"Can you be more specific?"

"The one with the keys on his belt."

"Yeah, I see him."

"I need those keys."

She glanced at him, then looked out over the roof of the car. "No problem. Be right back." She gave her hair a flip and her breasts a lift and moved away.

Cole waited, listening to chuckles from the deputies mixed with giggles from the girls. He came up just enough to see out the window. Maxine had her back to him. She sat in a full split across the hood of a squad car, wearing the appointed deputy's uniform cap. She was waving a pair of foamy sponges overhead like pom-poms and getting spirited applause for her effort.

Cole lay back down. Minutes later the keys fell into his lap. Maxine went back to scrubbing the window above him.

"I thought this was supposed to be hard," she whispered.

"You're a champ, Maxine."

"So how come you never took me out again, anyway?"

"After this, Maxine, I'm ready to take you to Paris."

She winked. "Wait sixty seconds, then go for it. I'll make sure they don't see a thing."

"I owe you one."

With another wink, she moved away.

Cole clutched the keys in his fist. He sweated through the next sixty seconds, then bolted. Giggling and play fighting, Maxine and the girls lured the deputies away from the building as Cole dashed into the station.

He stepped through the double doors unseen. The recent bustle had left the main room in disarray, but for the moment it was empty. A male voice droned at the dispatch desk off the connecting hallway. Cole heard curses, questions, commands, and patrol units being ordered in various directions. It sounded like all hell had broken loose across town. *Good.*

He moved farther into the room and got a narrow view into Curtis's office. The room was dark, Curtis nowhere in sight. He weaved through the grid of cluttered desks, file cabinets, and water coolers until he reached the cast-iron door that led down to the cell blocks—a door through which he had passed more than once over the years.

He tried six different keys before finally hearing the desired click. The door opened without a creak. He was halfway inside when a ringing phone suddenly broke the silence.

Cole's heart stopped. His eyes darted around the room until he realized the phone was on his person. He cursed his carelessness, having forgotten to switch off Hickham's cell phone. The phone rang again. He reached frantically into his pocket, pulled it out, and switched it off.

There was a pause in the dispatcher's chatter.

"That you, Smitty?" The dispatcher called.

Cole looked toward the hall and grunted.

"Say 'gain?"

Another grunt.

"Christ, Smitty, it's about time. You said two minutes. Come on, it's my turn. Take over the lines so I can go see those pom-pom girls."

"Lemme piss," Cole mumbled through a cough.

"Well, hurry it up, will ya? I got the numb-ass. Been sittin' here all damn night. I'm five hours into overtime as it is."

Cole shut the door behind him and started down the darkened stairs.

The smell of the cell block hit him instantly—a rancid mixture of sweat and body odor. Grunts, groans, and curses echoed off the sterile walls. There was also the unmistakable sound of skin slapping skin and heavy bodies slamming into concrete and steel.

It sounded like . . . football.

He moved into the dim corridor at the bottom of the stairs. A numbing sight greeted him. It seemed the Jackrabbits weren't the only football team that had transformed into something less than human over the last twenty-four hours.

The improvised scrimmage ceased the instant Cole stepped in front of the bars. The cell block fell quiet. Heavy breathing was the only sound as the forty Elmwood Badgers turned and fixed predatory eyes on Cole.

Their fury was evident.

If the Jackrabbits were merely lost souls in search of heaven, then the Badgers had unquestionably become something destined for hell.

That was the thought passing through Cole's head as he heard the slow, wet click of a revolver behind him.

CHAPTER 46

S TEP away from those bars."
        Cole recognized the voice even before the sheriff moved around to face him. Curtis's face remained a shadow under the brim of his Stetson.

"Perhaps you didn't hear me. I said step away."

"I can't do that, Curtis. You know what I'm here to do, and I'm not leaving until it's done."

"We're gonna fuck you up, Logan!" said a voice from the cell. "Let's get this shit started."

Cole turned, expecting to see Booker Flamont. A quick scan of the cell revealed no sign of him. "Where is he, Curtis? Where's Booker?"

Another Badger answered when Curtis didn't. "They separated us. Booker's through that door over there."

The boy who had spoken was a vision of puberty gone awry—wild hair and acne covering overdeveloped muscles. His sloping forehead bulged over a distended brow. Much of his hair had fallen out in irregular patches. Slick, ruddy skin stretched tightly over his bare chest and arms.

Cole gave him a nod. "You're Larkin, right? Tommy Larkin? Three-time All-State? Defensive cocaptain?"

If the man was flattered by the recognition, he didn't show it. "What's it to you, fuckwad?"

Cole held up the ring of keys, close enough for Tommy to grab them through the bars. "Go next door, get your teammates, and bring them back here."

Tommy's dilated pupils shifted to the sheriff for either permission or denial. Receiving neither, he took the keys, and went to work on the lock.

Curtis turned his aim on the cell. "Stop now, Larkin, or I'll shoot."

"No, he won't," Cole said evenly. "Keep going."

But Tommy did stop.

"You can't kill us all, Curtis," Cole said.

"I don't have to kill you all."

"I found the Jackrabbits. They're suiting up in the Killington locker room as we speak . . . under Coach Hickham's authority. The stadium is already filling up. Half the town of Elmwood has driven over, and the rest are on their way. And you know as well as I do that you don't have the manpower to prevent this game. You can't fight it, Curtis. It's over."

"It's far from over, C-Cole." He coughed. "I'll be the one who . . . who says it's . . . over."

He sounded short-winded. There was resignation in his tone, but his grip held firm on the pistol. His aim left Tommy Larkin and returned to Cole's chest.

"I won't quit now," Cole said. "I *can't* quit. So if you wanna stop me . . . you're gonna have to shoot me dead."

"Dead?" A phlegmy laugh trickled from Curtis's lips. "You know a lot about death now, don't you?"

"What do you mean by that?"

"You've been up to your neck in d-d-death these past few days . . . haven't you, C-Cole?"

Cole wasn't sure where this was going, nor did he know what had brought on Curtis's stutter. "What the hell are you talking about?"

"Enough of this shit!" spat one of the Badgers. "Are we gettin' outta here, or what?"

"It all f-f-finally began to make s-sense when I went into Mona's house." Curtis's words fell on Cole like prickling needles. "You see, Cole, I had to borrow a phone on account of my radio being so c-cleverly d-disabled. So I broke into the home of Ms. Monasa Beechum . . . your nearest n-neighbor." More hacking coughs seized him. "You and B-Black Mona have become quite close, haven't you?"

The sheriff's head twitched. His speech sounded slurred by pain. Every word was labored. The man standing before Cole now was not the same one who had been at his house that morning.

In a measured tone fit for a child, Cole said, "Curtis, I need you to tell me what happened at Mona's. You have to tell me what you saw."

"I never t-took much stock in what they said about that crazy old w-w-woman. I m-mean, I'd heard all the stories about her hexes and s-s-such, but—"

"What did you see in there? Curtis, I need you to tell me!"

"Books," he wheezed. "Stacks of b-books. Dusty . . . handwritten volumes on m-magic and spells, and . . ." He exhaled a slow, lingering hiss. "And r-r-raising the dead." He twitched again. His knees buckled. Cole moved to him but stopped when the gun came back up. "Stay b-back!"

Cole raised his hands. "Calm down, Curtis. Take it easy."

"How did she do it, C-Cole! How did she b-b-bring those boys back? It's not p-possib—"

"Tell me what else you saw. I have to know!"

Seconds passed. "I saw some kind of . . . *thing*. An animal."

Cole stepped forward. Inches separated him from the gun now. "Was it a *cat* that you saw? Curtis, did it bite you?"

Curtis answered the question with one of his own. "Cole . . . what's . . . h-happening . . . to me?" He removed his hat with a palsied hand, ridding his face of shadow.

A collective gasp came from the cell. In his periphery, Cole saw the Badgers retreat a step.

Curtis's face was a rictus of mutilated flesh. Claw tracks had turned his cheeks into sagging flaps over bare bone. His flesh was drained of color to the point of translucence. His upper lip was peeled back like the lid of a sardine can, forming a wicked grin of long, coffee-stained teeth and lacerated gums. A half-dollar-size hole gaped at his jugular, exposing severed veins that bubbled red.

His milky, listless eyes looked intently back at Cole.

Cole told Tommy to open the door.

Tommy glanced alternately between Cole and the sheriff. "What . . . what the fuck's the matter with that dude?"

"Just do it. Now!"

Tommy did as instructed, but neither he nor any of the other Badgers emerged from the cell.

"Co . . . Col . . ." Curtis choked again on his own breath.

"What is it?"

"The b-bite . . . I have to know about the bite. Will it turn me into . . . into one of . . ."

"You're gonna be fine, Curtis. I'm gonna get you out of here. I just need you to—"

The sheriff collapsed. The pistol came free of his grasp and skidded past Cole's feet. Cole moved to him and dug two fingers into the clotted wound at his neck. There was no pulse.

He stood and extended a hand toward Tommy Larkin. "Keys."

Tommy met his gaze, then tossed him the ring.

Cole rushed to the door at the end of the corridor, employed the appropriate key, and stepped inside the adjacent block.

"Well, well, well! Lookie what we have here, boys!" Booker turned to his friends, who were sleeping on the cell floor behind him. "Hey, Manny, Elray . . . wake the fuck up! Our chariot's arrived. I was beginning to think you'd pussied out, Logan."

Cole fumbled with the keys and turned the lock on the cell. Before opening the door, he fixed his eyes on Booker. "This ends today, asshole."

Booker smiled. "Fine with me. How 'bout we do it right here."

Cole reached through the bars, took Booker by the back of the neck, and yanked.

"Get the fugg uff me!" Booker barked around a mouthful of steel.

His friends had awoken and come to their feet, but kept their distance.

Cole warned them to stay back.

Manny held up his hands. "You don't have to worry about us, Logan. Do as you will. Me and Elray have had it with Booker and all this 'roid shit. In fact, we're done with the whole damn team. Every one of them's gone Mexi-fuckin'-loco, and I'm washin' my hands of all of it."

"Shud the fuggup, Manny!"

Cole tightened his grip on Booker's neck. Through gnashed teeth he said, "We'll settle the rest of this on the field. If you got the balls, you'll get your team to Killington High as fast as you can. I think you'll find quite a crowd there awaiting your slaughter."

Booker pressed his fists against Cole's chest and broke free. He raked his tongue over a bloody lip and spat red at Cole's feet. "Do you even know what kind of team you're about to face, Logan?"

"Yeah, I do," Cole said. "Do you?"

"Let's just go, Booker." Tommy Larkin stood at the dividing door, the rest of the Badgers crowded behind him. "We're in the clear, man. Let's just get the fuck outta here, get to the field."

Booker turned back to Cole. "All right, then. Guess the next time I see you, you'll be picking your teeth out of my facemask. It's gonna hurt, you goddamn son of a whore. I can promise you . . . it's gonna hurt."

He moved past Cole and joined his teammates.

Cole waited until they were gone, then crossed back into the other block. He knelt at Curtis's side, rolled him onto his back, and closed the sheriff's copper eyes.

"I would never have wished for this, Curtis." His words echoed off the dank concrete. "Hard as you were on me, I always knew it was for my own good. You certainly gave me more chances than I deserved . . . and I'll never forget it." Drying moisture from his eyes, he stood and started back up the stairs.

He made it halfway up, then stopped, descended the steps again, and removed the handcuffs from Curtis's utility belt. He dragged the sheriff nearer to the cell, then closed one cuff around Curtis's wrist and the other around one of the bars. He dropped the key into his sock.

It wasn't until he made it to the top of the stairs that he heard the cuffs rattle behind him.

CHAPTER 47

HICKHAM'S whistle reverberated off the tile. "All right, men, circle up!"

Cole's stomach coiled. Ten minutes ago he'd been on his knees, hovering over the toilet, trying unsuccessfully to purge his nerves. Now, fully dressed in helmet and pads and about to take the field, it was all he could do to hold his sickness down.

He moved away from his locker and fell into step with his teammates as they moved toward the exit that led to the field.

The coach waited by the door. He ordered the gathered team to take a knee in front of him. The players complied. Cole and Hickham shared a look, relieved by the show of obedience.

An hour had passed since Cole had rejoined the team in the locker room. His conversation with Hickham upon arrival from the sheriff's office had been brief. Cole recounted the scene in the cell block. Hickham took the news of the sheriff's fate with the same mix of shock and regret that Cole had felt upon witnessing it. Both men resolved to put the issue out of mind, at least until after the final whistle.

When Cole asked after Savannah, Hickham had told him he'd insisted she view the game from the press box above the stands. Cole had learned that the order was met with vehement protestation. Savannah had pleaded to be allowed on the sidelines, but the coach had refused, and Cole was glad for it.

Hickham crushed his ball cap between his hands. "All right, gentlemen. The time is now, so let's get to it. I expect you all to remember what we talked about. Straight football . . . regulation rules . . . no exceptions. And I have one more thing: helmets stay on at all times. Even on the sidelines. Anyone in those stands gets a good look at you, and this whole deal might be off in a hurry . . . no offense. Now let's go claim our title."

The Jackrabbits' entry onto the field brought instant mayhem to the home-side stands.

The first thing Cole saw when he stepped onto the muddy grass was the brawl transpiring at the fifty-yard line between the opposing mascots. Spurred on by the capacity crowd, the zipper-spined Jackrabbit and his cross-town counterpart were already off their paws and locked in a vicious tangle at midfield.

The Jackrabbits moved to their sideline without so much as a wave to the adoring crowd. Cole looked across the field. The Badgers had, in fact, made it to the stadium and were suited up in full dress. They were huddled at their own bench, jumping and waving and working the visiting crowd into a frenzy that matched that of the host school. Cole spotted Booker immediately. The linebacker stood apart from his team, ten yards inside the playing field. He was facing the Killington stands, grabbing his crotch with one hand and waving a middle finger with the other.

Cole felt a tug on his arm. He turned to find Maxine Wiley before him, out of breath and grinning porcelain, a pom-pom tucked under each arm. She shouted into the ear hole of his helmet. "I was told to give you this!" She slipped a sheet of folded notebook paper into his hand. "Guess I'm not gonna get Paris after all, huh, Logan?"

He peered through his facemask bars. "Why's that?"

"'Cause if I didn't know any better, I'd say the coach's daughter has already staked her claim." She teased him with fluttering eyelids. "Now get out there and kick ass, will ya?"

Cole waited until she moved away before he unfolded the sheet and read what Savannah had written. He looked up to the press box. Savannah was a silhouette among many others jammed into the smoke-filled room, but he had no trouble spotting her. She raised her hand and pressed it against the glass.

Before he could return the gesture, a fist yanked his face mask around. Hickham slapped his helmet hard enough to ring his ears. "Unless you're otherwise indisposed, Logan, I think we're being summoned."

They walked shoulder-to-shoulder to midfield. Ted Wafford, the Elmwood head coach, waited alongside Booker and four other team captains. The Badger coach looked like a redneck version of Nikita Khrushchev—balding crew cut of white hair, eyes too close together, teeth too far apart, and bowed legs a kid could ride a tricycle through. A chewed cigar butt ran a continuous circuit from one side of his mouth to the other.

Neither coach offered a handshake.

"Hey, shithead!" Booker called to Cole across the mingling officiating crew that separated them. "You ready for a skull fucking?"

Cole had been too preoccupied at the jail to truly note what had become of Booker's appearance over the past two days. Whatever poison coursed through his system had turned him into something no more human than the men he was about to meet across the line of scrimmage. His eyes watered with rage, pink and alert. His infected cheek was a puss-filled tumor ready to pop. His breath came in blue clouds, shooting from a seething grin.

The stare down between the sides was silent and taut. It was Coach Wafford who finally spoke, yelling to be heard over the crowd and the opposing bands competing for decibels.

"All right, Hickham, here it is! I don't know what rock you crawled out from under, but around here it's goddamn kill or be killed. So don't think that just because your boys took a little plunge into that river that my boys are gonna go soft on 'em. You asked for this, so now you're gonna get it. You understanding me clear?"

"We gonna talk or we gonna toss the coin?" Hickham's cold eyes shifted to the head referee.

The heavyset official blinked to attention, then dug into his pocket for a coin. Before he could present one, Coach Wafford stopped him with his laughter. "You know what, Hickham? Fuck the toss." He pulled a football from Tommy Larkin's hands. "It's your field. Let's just say you won the sumbitch." He flipped the ball into Hickham's hands with more zip than was necessary. "I figure you ought to at least win *something* tonight."

Booker and his fellow captains laughed at their coach's gesture.

Hickham turned to Cole.

Cole told the referee they would kick.

He and Hickham had already decided that in addition to his duties as quarterback, Cole would be playing defense as well. They thought it best to keep at least one fully functioning brain on the field at all times. Cole's decision to open on defense was twofold. First, there was the fact that he had yet to take a snap with only eight fingers, much less tried to throw on target or hand off. The jury was still out on his ability to do either. Second, he preferred the idea of getting in a few good licks on defense—and hopefully shaking out some nerves in the process—before having to produce something on offense.

The referee clapped his hands and paced between the two lines. "All right, gentlemen, the Jackrabbits have chosen to kick. The Badgers will receive from the north end. Now, I'm expecting a clean game out there. If I see even a hint of foul play, I won't hesita—"

"Cut the shit. Let's play." Coach Wafford turned and headed for the sideline.

"Don't make yourself scarce out there, you hear?" Booker winked at Cole, then spun away and fell into step with his coach.

The drill teams and color guards from both sides fled to their respective end zones as Cole and Hickham moved to their own sideline.

When the field was clear, the Killington band struck up the national anthem. The opening notes coincided with a metallic bang that rocked the stadium. The light towers fluttered to life. The purple shades of dusk faded, replaced by white-hot electricity.

Cole rechecked the security of his chinstrap for the fifth time and asked Hickham for any final words of advise.

"Just hit your targets and stay away from the big guys."

Cole looked at him, his teeth grinding a nervous trench into his mouthpiece.

Hickham held Cole's helmet between his hands. "You're gonna be fine. You're not alone out here. Remember that. You've got me, and you've got your team. Just do what you've been doing all season, and we'll all get through this together."

A whistle blew. Players marched onto the field. Stalling was no longer an option.

Cole took a ball from the trainer's table and marched over to Belfry Ingram. The kicker had suffered a significant skull fracture in the bus crash. His helmet now sat low and crooked on his head. As a football player, Belfry was an embarrassment. As a three-year letterman on the soccer team, he had made a habit out of kicking balls into the next time zone, which is why he had been moonlighting as the Jackrabbits' place kicker since sophomore year.

Cole found him staring reverently at the lights like a baby watching the spin of a crib mobile. Cole slammed the ball into the kicker's stomach and told him to get his ass on the field and boot the goddamn laces off the thing.

•   •   •

As it happened, the Jackrabbits played offense first after all.

Belfry Ingram did as he was told. The opening kick sailed like a comet into the far corner of the field, a yard and a half short of the goal line. But the ball happened to land in the hands of a nimble Walter Payton type who managed to shuck, jive, spin, high step, and stiff-arm his way through the Jackrabbits kick defense as though their feet had taken root. By the time the returner made it to the end zone, he was twenty yards clear of the nearest defensemen—more than enough cushion for him to moonwalk the final eight yards to the goal line.

Eleven seconds had ticked off the clock—time enough for Cole to conclude that he was fucked. His teammates had been pummeled like crash-test dummies in every corner of the field. Blood had sprayed. Limbs had cracked. Cole had been a nonfactor on the play but had still taken an illegal spear in the back that left his teeth humming. No flag was thrown.

He hadn't even touched the ball and already he was less concerned with winning the game than merely *surviving* it.

The Badgers converted on the extra point.

Eleven seconds gone . . . 7–0, Elmwood Heights.

O'Dell Lamar managed to shake off his dislocated hip and shattered ribcage to return the subsequent kickoff all the way to the Jackrabbits' thirty-seven. Cole stepped back onto the field, his first time making the long jog to the offensive huddle. The crowd exploded. Cheerleaders soared in his periphery. The band broke into "Born to be Wild." It was the kind of moment Cole had once lived for. Now he was certain it was the moment he would die for.

He knelt in the center of the huddle. A ring of empty eyes peered down at him through face mask bars. "All right, men. You showed me yesterday what you're capable of. Now it's time to show it to those shitheads who did this to us. Let's not fuck it up."

He opened his mouth to continue, but drew a blank. Hickham had just sent him in with a play, but for the life of him he couldn't remember what it was. They hadn't had time to confer on an offensive strategy, much less decide upon an opening sequence, but Hickham *had* given him an opening play. Cole shut his eyes, thought hard. Nothing came. With nothing to lose, he decided to go for broke. He called a play that left Shane Butler, the primary receiver, running the left sideline until he either caught the ball or hit the parking lot.

He searched Shane's eyes for a glimmer of understanding. The eyes were empty, but the receiver did manage a throaty belch.

The huddle broke, and the teams met across the line of scrimmage. Threats and slurs poured from the Badgers' side. The linebackers showed blitz, hovering on the heels of the front seven.

Cole crouched under center and went into the count as Booker cried a wolf's howl, then told him to prepare for a dick stomping. Heeding the threat, Cole retreated into shotgun formation. Kirby Kirkpatrick snapped the ball with jackhammer force and the sides collided like battering rams.

The blitz came quick. Cole struggled to set slick fingers on the laces. The world blurred. To his left he saw Shane Butler sprint free of his coverage. Cole set his arm to throw, but hesitated. A figure approached on his blind side, pulling his focus. He heaved a wobbling ball into the rainy sky.

The hit was ferocious.

Booker's helmet slammed like a wrecking ball into the small of Cole's back. A crack, like the turn of a ratchet handle, rippled the length of his spine. He was facedown in the mud before the whistle blew.

Even in his haze Cole knew the cheers he heard were coming from the wrong side of the field. Racked with pain and on the edge of consciousness, he raised his head. Cleats pressed into his neck, pushing him back into the mud. When he came up the second time, Booker was standing over him.

"Nice completion, dickhead. Went right into his arms." He pressed his face mask against Cole's. "I hope that didn't hurt, asshole . . . because you don't even know hurt yet." The dick stomping came next—a swinging heel between Cole's legs.

The pain was blinding.

Cole came up off the grass to learn that his interception had been run back for a touchdown. Some recessed part of his mind waited for his teammates to rush over, slap his rump, tell him it was okay, to put it behind him, they would get 'em next time.

But he stood alone as the Elmwood Badgers sent out their extra-point team.

"What the hell was that?" Hickham asked when Cole made it back to the bench, still hunched at the waist. Anger boiled in the coach's eyes.

Cole didn't have the breath to answer him. His lungs burned, and the pain at his groin was creeping around to his kidneys.

The Badgers' extra-point kick split the uprights and sailed into the Arby's parking lot.

"I asked you a question, Cole: why'd you hesitate?"

"I didn't hesitate!"

"Well, then, what the hell do you call that? You had Butler in the clear, and Toony wide open at midfield! And that wasn't even the play I called in the first place! What's going on out there?"

"Hell, Coach, you tell me! In case you hadn't noticed, your wise little gem about hitting my targets and avoiding the big guys isn't exactly panning out."

Hickham squared up to him. "What is this? Are you angry? Is that what this is?"

Cole flicked mud from his face mask. "Damn straight, I'm angry!"

"Good!"

"What?"

"I said *good!*"

Cole wondered if Booker had rung his bell even harder than he'd previously thought. "Coach, all due respect, but just say what you're trying to say, because clearly I'm too fucked up at the moment to figure it out."

"I'm telling you to get fired up! 'Cause I can guarantee you those boys across that field are already in flames." He planted a finger on Cole's numbers. "Logan, we aren't just playing a game here, so stop thinking that way. You and I both know this has gone far beyond that. Our time is now, Cole. Right now! Show me . . . show your *teammates,* and show all these people watchin' the man who came into my office with two missing fingers on Friday, begging to play. Show us the man who jumped into that river to save his friends from a sinking bus. 'Cause if that man ain't here, then we both best throw in the towel right now."

Cole let the coach's words sink in. He slapped a hard palm on his helmet to clear his head, then turned his gaze to the field.

"They're gonna blitz heavy, Coach. Every play. They can kill us at the line and they know it."

"I know they can. Which means you're gonna have to keep the ball in the air. But throw short and throw quick. No hesitation." Hickham shifted the bill of his cap, then brought it back low. "Now let's open up with an I-right, twenty-three Big-D slant. That blitz should open things up across the middle. I'd bet my truck you can hit Toony at midfield."

Hickham's play was a good call, but Cole negated it.

"Coach, I wanna open with a run. Option right, TB round." On Hickham's look, he said, "Trust me."

Cole rejected Hickham's pass play in favor of a quarterback keeper that would give him the option of pitching out to O'Dell Lamar.

More specifically, it gave Cole the opportunity to put the stick on Booker Flamont, which is exactly what he did.

Cole's bulldozing block sent the linebacker tumbling into a

pyramid of Badgers cheerleaders, stacked four-high just off the sideline.

While Booker dug through pom-poms for missing teeth, O'Dell Lamar picked up thirty-seven on the carry. Cole had found his rhythm. On the next play, he swung right on a bootleg and hit Sam Toony on the numbers. With the help of a crucial block from Steely McFadden, Sam found the end zone to put the Jackrabbits on the board.

Bedlam reigned in the Killington stands.

On his way to join his team in the end zone, Cole moved past Booker Flamont still at the fifteen-yard line where he had gone down. "You're dead, Logan! Fuckin' dead!" His loss of teeth made it sound more like "Yer ned, Rogan! Vuggin' ned!"

The Jackrabbits converted on the extra point.

The score was 14–7 in the Badgers' favor.

Four minutes to go in the first quarter.

The teams exchanged possession in a stalemate well into the second quarter. Each hard-fought series reaped a quick three and out for the offensive side.

It wasn't until Ollie Vanhoover forced a Badgers turnover that the Jackrabbits leveled the score. Leaping off his fractured left leg, Ollie struck the Badgers tailback with a textbook tackle that stripped the ball loose. Slick Gilpen, defensive guard, retrieved the fumble and lumbered on cracked shins into the end zone untouched.

The sudden turn sent Booker into a rage. Cole couldn't determine whether the Badger was more furious with his opponents or his own teammates. Booker's fury did rekindle some spark in his team, however. The Badgers soon answered with a lengthy drive up the field, which melted eight minutes off the clock and ended with another Badgers touchdown. They'd scored on a flea-flicker fake that left Cole and the rest of the Jackrabbits defense stunned.

The score at the half was 21–14. Badgers on top.

• • •

A dead buck lay near the shower stalls when the Jackrabbits entered the locker room. The congealed mark of a 30–30 slug glistened at the base of its neck.

A napkin stamped with the logo of the Buttered Bean Diner hung on one of the antler tips. Below the logo a handwritten message read: *Courtesy of Kip Sampson and Don Paul Klevin . . . GO RABBITS!* It seemed that Savannah had employed the services of her trusted friends. Cole was grateful for the gesture. Although his teammates were still playing with reckless abandon, Cole had noticed that both their focus and their coloring had faded some in the waning minutes of the half. Probably meant they should eat.

As his teammates feasted on deer, Cole went horizontal on the bench in front of his locker, hoping some feeling would return to his extremities. Hickham paced the floor nearby, wringing his cap in his fists.

The Jackrabbits were down, but Cole took hope from the fact that his teammates' understanding and execution of the plays had improved over the course of the first thirty minutes. He was not only proud but grateful. He already owed his life to them many times over, having been spared great harm with some crucial blocks and heroic pass protection.

Hickham appeared above him. "How you feelin'?" He spoke over the sounds of bones crunching between teeth, innards being slurped.

"Like them," Cole answered, jabbing a thumb across the room. "Dead and numb."

Hickham nodded. "Well, it ain't great, but we'll take it, right?" He handed Cole a squirt bottle of Gatorade. Cole sucked it dry in seconds.

His knees creaked like bags of loose gravel when he sat up. He reached down to rub them and another pain stabbed his left elbow, the result of a hit in the final play of the half that had undoubtedly torn cartilage.

"Tell me again why I didn't just take up golf as a kid."

Hickham patted his shoulder. "You're doing fine."

"They're getting a little crazy out there, Coach."

"Well, they're walking dead, what'd you expect?"

"I'm not talking about the Jackrabbits."

"Oh." Hickham sighed knowingly. "Yeah, I've noticed. Whatever junk those Badgers are on, it's got no place on a football field."

"They're like animals, Coach. Hell, they're much worse than our guys."

"Yeah. And getting worse every minute. It's like the damn *Lord of the Flies* without spears."

"You notice that Elmwood did us the courtesy of supplying their own officiating crew?"

"It occurred to me, yeah. Listen, you just keep doing what you're doing. I'm gonna stack your left side as much as possible, try and keep Flamont off your blind side. That middle is still opening up off the blitz, so I want to keep going shallow." He glanced at his watch. "It's almost time. Take another minute to catch your breath, and I'll see you out there. I'll take care of the rest of the guys."

"Wait. Shouldn't I be there? I mean, what are you gonna say to them?"

"Nothing. I've just gotta turn the shower heads on, hose 'em off."

Cole took Hickham's advice and threw shallow across the middle. It wasn't glamorous, but it was efficient. On the opening play of the second half, he hit Shane Butler on a slant for a gain of nineteen. He followed it up with a dump to Zack Moody for a pick up of twelve—an admirable grab for a man playing without a liver. On the following play, he hit Butler again on a hook. Butler spun from his coverage after the catch, broke two loose tackles, and made it to the end zone on a thirty-eight-yard play.

Booker waited until after the referee signaled the touchdown, then went in for the sack, driving a shoulder into Cole's kneecaps.

"That's it!" Ned Balooka, the *Killington Daily* sports editor beamed at the others in the press box. "You see that pass? Perfect!"

"Oh, hell, what happened? I was scribbling a note."

Ned wagged a finger at Savannah. "Ah, you just learned the first rule of sports reporting, young lady—hands stay on the pad and pen, but the eyes never leave the field."

"Cole's pass just tied the game is what happened!" Don Paul gave Kip a hard slap on the back. "Hot damn, Savannah, looks like you were right. That buck we bagged must have really done the trick! Say, tell us again what that little special delivery was all about."

Savannah shifted uncomfortably. "Uh . . . *luck*. Everyone knows that a dead buck in the locker room brings good luck on the field."

Ned Balooka turned from his laptop. "What's that you say . . . *a dead buck?*"

"Never mind. Not important." Savannah pressed her forehead to the glass. "Is Cole okay? He looks a little shaken."

Bernice bit into a nacho. "That bastard Flamont got him a good one in the kneecaps, long after the play." She sucked melted cheese off her fingertips. "But he's fine. Look, he's getting right up. Don't worry, honey, he's a tough kid."

Midway through the third quarter, Booker broke Philip Meekin's already broken neck.

Phil had just brick-walled a Badger tight end after a six-yard gain. Both players landed on the sideline in front of the Elmwood bench. Cole had filled in at deep safety on the play, and watched from a few yards away as Booker came off the Badgers bench, took hold of Phil's helmet, and twisted like he was working the stubborn lid of a pickle jar. No flag was thrown.

Gasps swept the crowd as Phil returned to the huddle, his head turned 180 degrees. His wobbly gait betrayed some loss of balance, but there was no noticeable sign of discomfort.

Cole returned Phil's head to its rightful position with a swift yank, and both boys went back to work.

The Badgers came gunning again on the next play, a third and short. Their quarterback found daylight on a keeper, then pitched to the fullback a split second before Kevin O'Flannery drove the QB into an ice chest. With the benefit of a crucial block, the fullback made it down to the Jackrabbits' nine. Fortunately, the Badgers' advance crumbled after that. The drive ended with two blown snaps and a fumbled pitch that rolled out of bounds. They settled for a chip-shot field goal, but had regained a three-point lead at the end of three.

The clock seemed to go into overdrive then. The sides exchanged possession twice with little gain by either team. As the clock ticked below seven minutes, Belfry Ingram had a look at a field goal from the forty-three. It had the distance but caught the wind and sailed an arm's length wide of the upright.

Cole compiled a mini–highlight reel on the next possession but couldn't quite convert it into points on the board. The pain in his back and elbow had returned with a vengeance. Given that his teammates felt no pain and required no oxygen, they seemed to be faring much better than he was.

The clock ticked on. Six minutes. Four minutes. Three.

The Badgers had possession on their own fourteen at the two-minute warning. First and second downs reaped no gain. On third and long, a spry Mexican halfback with tree-stump legs churned his way through the grappling arms of Cody Bender, Marvin Bumbgardner, and Slick Gilpen before Cole got him down by a belt loop on the Jackrabbits' thirty-eight.

Cole came up seeing double. Hickham threw his cap to the mud and cursed a blue streak over the halfhearted arm tackles his team had displayed. Back in the huddle, Cole told his defense to pull their heads out of their dead asses and make their tackles stick.

The Jackrabbits complied.

On the next play the Badgers got cute, and paid handsomely for it. Stacking the right side of the line, the Elmwood quarterback juked left as the ball was hiked. The tailback received the snap and hurled the ball toward three open receivers running the right sideline. Only one man stood in their way. Tucker Jolson, the Jackrabbits cornerback, stuck an arm up, bobbled the ball, then caught it for an interception. Tucker's momentum carried him out of bounds, stopping the clock.

The Jackrabbits had regained possession on their own eighteen, fourteen seconds remaining on the clock, down by three, no time-outs.

Cole looked to Hickham for a signal, then relayed the play in the huddle, adding: "For all of you not going long on this fucker, you damn well better be putting the stick on someone. It's heaven or hell time, boys. The choice is yours, on three."

Cole stepped under center.

Booker angled straight toward him. The linebacker's face was a mask of mud through which washed-out eyes glowed white-hot.

Cole shut his own eyes to erase his nemesis from sight and mind.

His head went silent.

The bands muted.

The crowd vanished.

His pain—physical and otherwise—faded away.

Suddenly, Mona's dying words fell on him in a whisper: *"Only victory can save their souls now . . ."*

Eternal victory—for his teammates, Mona, Curtis, even for himself—would be gained or lost in this moment. This play.

His eyes opened.

He went into the count.

"Hut one . . . hut two . . ."

He took the snap on three, a blistering crack of leather slapping skin.

A wall of jerseys rose before him.

He dropped back. Sam Toony, tight end, cut a quick slant across midfield into heavy coverage. The pass rush closed in immediately. Cole was left with no choice but to risk a desperation pass. He went into his motion, then stopped. Booker had broken through the protection, too close now for Cole to get the pass off.

Cole tucked the ball and rolled right. Booker cut left to angle him off. In the corner of his eye, Cole saw O'Dell Lamar swing around behind him. He pitched the ball to the tailback, then ducked his head and drove a shoulder into Booker's chest. The linebacker's ribs cracked like dry twigs. He turned a full somersault over Cole's body before hitting the mud.

Cole's block kept O'Dell on his feet, but the blitzing defenders closed in fast, forcing the tailback toward the sideline. The pass coverage left no option to throw.

Cole somehow maintained his footing and started downfield at a full sprint. He found open grass within ten yards and began to wave his arm. O'Dell spotted him and fired a tight, lobbing spiral toward the end zone. Cole went airborne at the five. The ball found his hands just as he crossed the goal line.

The final second ticked off the clock.

Instant pandemonium.

The Killington students had begun their charge across the field before the play even ended. The rest of the crowd rushed from the bleachers in a mad stampede. In less than a minute the north goalpost tipped under the weight of clambering bodies.

A mixed rush of exhilaration and panic gripped Cole as the sea of people descended on him. Screams stung his ears. Flailing arms fell on him from all sides, pulling, grabbing, and squeezing. Wild faces melded into a dizzying blur. Cole accepted the fanfare with controlled grace as he fought to push his way through the crowd. When he finally reached the edge of the pressing mob, he turned a circle in place, scanning the field until he found who he was looking for.

Booker stood where he had landed. The linebacker's eyes found Cole. He spat a gnawed mouthpiece to the dirt. A toothless grin of blood and grit spread his lips.

Cole removed his helmet and approached until they were nose to nose. The sight of the face-off halted the fans' pursuit. The crowd fanned out, allowing the confrontation a wide berth. Screams faded to dull murmurs. The band music wilted midtune.

Not a word passed between the two boys. Seconds ticked by. Then Booker's eyes moved to Cole's throat. He attacked before Cole could even move to defend himself. They toppled to the grass in a tangle of grappling arms. Booker landed on top, pinning Cole beneath him. As Cole squirmed to break free, his head rolled back, exposing his jugular. Booker's jaws clamped on with the speed of a striking snake. But before his teeth sank in, O'Dell Lamar stepped in behind Booker. With lightning quickness, the tailback hooked gloved fingers into Booker's eye sockets and yanked. Booker tumbled backward over the grass before rolling to a stop fifteen feet away.

The crowd held their silence.

O'Dell offered a hand and pulled Cole into a sitting position. Cole coughed breath into his burning lungs and ran his fingers over the indentations in his neck. Beyond O'Dell, he saw the rest of the Jackrabbits pressing toward the front of the crowd. Their expression was uniform—childlike and aimless.

"Logan, you fuck!"

Cole turned.

O'Dell's assault had clearly left Booker disoriented. He blinked through watery eyes. But there was still fight in those eyes. He was a bull, ready to charge.

Spittle flew from his lips as he said, "This shit ain't over, Logan. You think that hatchet job on your hand was the end? I'm gonna hack you to goddamn pieces!" He turned to the rest of the Jackrabbits. "And I'm gonna kill every one of you fuckers, too . . . like I should have done the first time!"

Five sheriff's deputies emerged from the crowd, batons clutched in their hands. As they closed in on Booker, a wall of Jackrabbits jerseys wiped away Cole's view. His teammates had begun to move on Booker as well. Their steps were predatory. There was hunger in their groans.

Cole wanted to let them proceed. It was an ending that a part of him had hoped for all along.

But it was another part of Cole that shouted for them to stop.

The Jackrabbits did as instructed. All heads turned back toward their captain.

Cole came to his feet and for the first time realized the change in his teammates' appearance. The deterioration was striking, even since halftime, when he'd last seen them without their helmets. Looking beyond their face masks, he saw recessed eyes, like lumps of coal sunken into the head of a melting snowman. Skin had lost what little color it still had. Postures had begun to slump. Muscles had atrophied.

It occurred to Cole that Mona's work was finally complete. Her last wish had been granted, and now her beloved team was dying its second death.

Cole couldn't let it happen here. Not in front of the fans, the parents . . . anyone who didn't know the truth of what was about to transpire.

But there was one thing left to say before he took them away.

His teammates parted way as he stepped forward. Booker rose to meet him, bringing them face-to-face again.

"Take your last look at the district champs, Booker. In spite of everything you did to prevent it, the title is ours."

Booker's lips compressed with fury. "Damn you, Logan. Damn all you Jackrabbits straight to hell."

Cole shook his head. "You already did that. You did it to us, and you did it to yourself. The difference is that *we're* gonna be saved. You're not. I hope it was worth it."

Booker cocked a fist, but the deputy standing behind him moved quicker. The taser gun hit the Badger in the left kidney. It took a deputy at each limb and another strangling with a baton to restrain Booker. There was a series of violent convulsions before Booker's strength had been sufficiently depleted for the deputies to drag him through the parting crowd, foam bubbling from his slack jaw.

The honk of a familiar horn turned Cole around. The Jackrabbits' bus was wobbling onto the corner of the end zone. Coach Hickham was driving, with Savannah standing beside him in the open door.

The wheels creaked to a stop. Hickham ground the bus out of gear but left the engine running as he came out of the seat and stepped down onto the grass. The coach's eyes found Cole, and he extended an arm toward the bus door. "It's all yours, Cole. You better hurry."

Cole nodded, then turned to his team.

"Load up, Jackrabbits. You're going home."

CHAPTER 48

Y ou missed the turn!" Savannah yelled. "I thought we were taking them to the river."

"We have to make a stop first."

"Cole, we're losing them fast. Where are you going?"

"Sheriff's office." He floored the accelerator.

"Now? Why?"

"It'll just take a second."

"But why the hell would we go *there*?"

"You'll see." He swerved hard to the right, pitching the bus onto two wheels. They hopped a curb and skidded over a grassy median. "I know a shortcut. We gotta get there before the cops arrive with Booker. Nobody can see us."

They pulled up to the KSO minutes later. The bus squealed to a stop over slick pavement. Cole brushed past Savannah. "Stay here, I'll be right back."

"But—"

"Don't worry, you're okay with them."

She looked over her shoulder. "They aren't looking good, Cole."

"They won't hurt you." He bent at the waist and squirmed out of his shoulder pads, dropping them at his feet. "They don't have the strength for it anyway. Everything they had went into that game."

He leaped the front steps three at a time and raced inside the building.

Curtis sat where Cole had left him, the handcuff still secure around his wrist. The sheriff had risen to a sitting position with his back against the bars. The physical deterioration had begun, just as it had with the Jackrabbits. Curtis's uniform was draped loosely over his slumped body. His skin hung flaccid on brittle bones.

Cole heard vertebrae creak as the sheriff turned to him.

"Don't be afraid, Curtis. It's me, Cole. Everything's gonna be okay. It's time to go now."

Cole took the key from his sock and unlocked the cuff. He lifted Curtis off the floor, folded his wasted body over one shoulder, and headed back up the stairs.

Three patrol cars were approaching up Goliad Avenue as Cole exited the building. They were less than a quarter mile away, lights and sirens screaming.

Savannah stepped aside as Cole hustled onto the bus and placed Curtis on the floor behind the driver's seat. He sat back behind the wheel and noted the shock on Savannah's face.

He answered her unspoken inquiry with one word. *"Coodles."*

Cole had to maneuver the bus around police barricades and streams of yellow crime-scene tape to get to the center of what remained of Leightner Bridge.

He shut off the engine. Silence stretched out for a few seconds before Savannah whispered Cole's name.

He pivoted toward her. Tears welled in her eyes, even as her mouth formed a fragile smile.

"I think we've done it right, Logan. I think this is where they're supposed to be." She motioned for him to look back.

He came slowly out of the seat and turned.

A chill raked his spine.

His teammates were glowing a brilliant cerulean blue. And they were whole again.

Strong. Healthy.

Healed.

The wounds had disappeared. Life shone in their eyes. Their expressions were serene, almost euphoric.

They were the boys Cole had known before.

He made a visual connection with each boy in turn. There was peace in every pair of eyes, understanding on every face. Even forgiveness.

Seconds later a blinding light from above washed away Cole's vision. A swift, warming wind whistled through the open windows, and the bus began to tremble on its busted axles.

Savannah reached for Cole's hand. There was grief on her face, but no fear.

Their eyes met, and he told her it was time to go.

As they moved to leave, Cole felt a squeeze on his leg. The grip was strong, the skin warm. He looked down to find Curtis peering back at him from beneath his hat brim. The sheriff's arm came up, his hand holding his badge as an offering.

Cole accepted the tarnished star with a nod. The men shook hands. Curtis offered something close to a smile, then motioned Cole away with a shift of his eyes. It was a gesture Cole had seen countless times before—a gesture that said, *Now get the hell out of here before you really get in trouble with me.*

Cole followed the directive, pulling Savannah behind him as they stepped off the bus and moved away.

The clouds overhead parted in a slowly expanding circle, like a giant whirlpool of vapor in the sky.

There was a shutter of metal and glass, and the bus began to rise. The ascent was slow, steady. Ten feet. Twenty. Fifty.

Cole's arm fell on Savannah's shoulder as the wrecked heap of rubber and steel continued its slow creep upward. When it rose above the cloud level, the opening in the sky began to close. The aperture of swirling fog narrowed underneath the vehicle, enveloping it.

When the bus was out of sight, an explosion, like a sunburst, sent vibrant blue streaks of lightning across the sky. The image was as awesome as it was beautiful. Thunder quaked the ground before rumbling into the distance. The sound faded slowly, along with the hiss of the wind, until the world at last fell silent. Still.

Cole held Savannah close. They stood motionless, unspeaking, for some time. He stepped away, only far enough to wipe tear tracks from her face.

"Are you okay?"

"I'm unhurt if that's what you mean." Her speech was fractured. She pulled a Kleenex from her jeans pocket and wiped her eyes. "Some fireworks, huh? As victory celebrations go, I found that to be as bitter as it was sweet."

"Yeah. Me too."

Victory. The game had ended only a half hour before, but it already felt so distant, even inconsequential. Cole looked back toward town. The glow of the stadium lights were still reflecting off the low-hovering clouds.

Savannah followed his gaze. "They still don't know, do they? All those people. The fans. The parents. They still don't know the boys are gone."

He shook his head. "No. They still don't know. No one does, but us."

"That's what hurts the most, you know? What just happened, beautiful as it was, it was still the end of a lot of lives. Young lives."

"But it was a *better* end. Like you said before, what's done is done. All we can focus on is what happens next, right? So I guess the question is, how much do we tell?"

"All of it," she answered without hesitation. "We tell the whole story, from beginning to end. And we tell it truthfully. The people of this town deserve that."

Cole didn't have to consider it. He knew she was right. "Yes, they deserve the truth. But the truth isn't easy to believe, and we're the only two people who can verify it. How do we convice them?"

"It's my job to convince them." Her determined eyes came up to meet his. "I'll write it exactly as it happened. From the very beginning I was in this for the story, remember? Guess I should be more careful what I wish for."

"I know what you mean. I always wanted a team that played like their lives depended on it." He squeezed her hands. "You write it. I promise to back up every word. And if people still find it hard to swallow, we've still got Coodles to—"

Her eyes widened. "My God! Coodles. I'd forgotten." She brought a hand up to her open mouth. "God, Cole . . . seeing what became of Curtis, I'm guessing Coodles's bite is contagious, right?"

He nodded soberly. "I can't say it for sure, but I have to find out."

"That badge Curtis gave you . . . I don't think he would have left it with just anyone, Cole. You think he was trying to tell you something?"

"Like what?"

She shrugged. "Maybe he thought your future holds a career in law enforcement."

Cole shook his head. "God, can you imagine?" He took the badge out of his pocket and turned it slowly in his hand. "Hell, who knows? Maybe Curtis did think I'd broken enough laws to know a thing or two about how to enforce them. In any case, shooting that damn cat is gonna be my first act of public service. That is, soon as I find us a ride back to town."

"To be honest, I'm happy just to walk." She took his hand. "With *you*."

She started away, but he pulled her back, brought her into his arms, and kissed her. Their bodies melded together as the kiss drew out, long and slow.

When they finally broke apart, she asked, somewhat off-balance, "So just what am I supposed to read from that, Logan?"

"Consider it my response to the note you sent down to the side-lines. At the time I wasn't sure whether or not to believe what you'd written. I thought you might have just written the words to wring a victory out of me."

"I see. So tell me, Logan, do you believe me now?"

"Yeah. I think I do." He laughed. "After all that I've seen in this town, I'm prepared to believe anything."